The Sacrifice

Bounty Hunter/ Early Years 1

By A. M. Helmuth

In memory of my husband;

Daniel J. Helmuth 6-19-1963 – 11-12-2018

Missing you Fuzz.

Prologue

High General Lynia looked up from her daily reports just in time to see a tall, broad-shouldered figure step through her balcony doors. She cursed, leapt to her feet, drawing her long-sword from her harness slung on the chair back.

The big male, for the figure was definitely male and that was about all she could tell about him, showed her his empty hands.

"You sent for me, General," the voice was deep, quiet, with no discernible accent. He was garbed head to toe in black and gray. Eastern style sword hilts jutted above both shoulders. Even the metal of his harness was wrapped with cloth or leather to quell any sound. The only visible skin was a stripe across his eyes. He'd even disguised that much with soot from the fire so she couldn't tell where he was from. His eyes were cold... frozen... the color of the deepest purest glacial ice. All they told her was that he was probably arede022 or a mix.

"And you are?" better to be sure.

"The best bounty hunter in the northern provinces." He made it sound like a statement of fact rather than a boast.

"Tymiran," she breathed.

He gave her the slightest inclination of his head in acknowledgment then gestured to the naked sword trailing forgotten in her hand.

"Of course," she sheathed the blade, recovering her composure. The bastard wasn't supposed to sneak into her private chambers. "Be seated," she invited, "wine, ale?" Might as well be courteous, it couldn't hurt.

"Thank you, no," The bounty hunter moved a few paces into the room as Lynia resumed her chair. "You want me to find your first born?" It was more statement than question.

The general strove to keep the shock off her face, very few knew he was missing. "What do you know of the situation?"

"I know Flaxon is missing, he left in the night about a week ago. He's seventeen, over seven feet tall with long golden hair and blue Ororri eyes. There was some talk of an arrangement between you and Lady Demiria to have him sworn to her first born. Did I miss anything of importance?"

She swallowed hard, "How do you come by such information?"

A cool laugh, "That's my business. The horse he took was found in a small town to the south east. He even left the tack behind. I don't think he wants to be found."

"You can find him, bring him back?"

"I could."

Arrogant bastard... "Are you quite sure? I don't want him harmed in any way. He's skilled, very strong."

"I could take him, unharmed. What are you offering?"

"Two hundred gold pentas." The bounty hunter nodded. Lynia went on, "I have two other provisions."

The bounty hunter made a slight beckoning gesture.

She stifled the urge to snarl at him but he was so infuriating. "You may not make use of him..." she trailed off. Something blazed behind the frozen gaze. *By Werdeka, I've managed to offend the heartless bastard...* "It's rumored you've taken certain liberties... with the males... to start breaking them to the collar... It would be better if he remains untouched. The criminals, I can see that..." *Stop, just stop...* "My son is hetro."

"I do not violate my prisoners. The second?"

The high general wrestled with the urge to squirm in her seat under that glacial gaze. Officers did not squirm. "He needs to be back before the spring equinox so he can be sworn."

The bounty hunter seemed to consider.

"I'm aware you don't hunt with a deadline under normal circumstances but... it's a generous sum. And these circumstances are unique."

He nodded once, then turned and left the way he'd come so quickly she didn't have time to add anything. With a sharp exhale, she went to her wine stand, poured herself a healthy drought and tossed it

back. Then she poured another. Now that Tymiran was
hunting Flaxon for her, she had no doubt he would be
returned with all possible speed.

One

Flax sat back, leaning against the wall, stretching out long powerful legs and holding out his mug for the coppery skinned rojoi slave to fill. The tall... relatively tall, Kylonian lady was seated across the small round table from him. His blue feline eyes met hers; a mischievous half smile tilted his mustache. She waved the slave away when both mugs were full, considered him over the rim of hers.

"Thank you, lady, for the ale and the meal." He raised the mug, downed a healthy draught.

Slender fingers slid along his bare forearm above his bracer. "You are welcome and..." Her tongue ran along upper teeth, lip, lust lit her hazel eyes. "It was part of the bargain, along with three gold tres for the night."

"Of course," he agreed. Flax was half Byrynthian, first born of High General Lynia. He was also half ororri. Long blond hair fell to his hips. Flax was fair skinned as most Byrynthians though he was lightly tanned from being outside much of the time.

It was summer and he'd forgone a shirt of any kind. The dark brown straps of his harness hugged his powerful torso tightly. His assassin's blade angled across both shoulder straps. Pairs of throwing knives rode the left primary and right secondary straps. All the rings and centerpieces were brass, brushed finish. There was an overabundance of rings, basically because Flax had a hell of a time finding a harness that would fit him without some personal alteration. He was seventeen, not really of age to be in here or making any kind of bargain for the night, but no one noticed. Most folks put him at twenty-five or so simply because of his size.

At seven foot and one inch, he was definitely the largest male, the largest person, in the Rykor's Claw Inn. Whenever he inquired about having a harness made for him the cost was well beyond his means. His weapons were the largest and heaviest he could find and yet the supposedly double fisted sword hilt wouldn't accommodate both his fists. Snug leather breeches dyed in streaks of brown, black and gray sheathed strong thighs and calves to be tucked into flared brown boots. A boot knife jutted from the right and he had two slender blades hidden in the left.

He'd been on his own for the last four months traveling, experiencing life. He'd worked as a constable in a town near the boarder of Byrynthia and Kylonia until two weeks back. A heated argument with his commanding officer got him dismissed. Personally, breaking a prisoner's fingers and toes merely for the hell of it just went against his grain. He didn't look young and innocent and he wasn't, innocent at least and he'd been called pretty, even beautiful. That's why he'd grown the beard. Handsome was a better word. He had no problem getting paid for a night in the furs. He enjoyed it and he always made sure the ladies, ladies only for that matter, treated him with respect.

Dextera, the Kylonian lady purchasing his favors for the evening, was over six feet tall, about six-five and strongly built. Her close-cropped golden blond hair accentuated strong attractive features, high cheekbones and a full, kissable mouth. She was garbed all in deep blue leathers from the tight-laced halter cupping her breasts to her low-slung breeches and her harness. Both thigh high boots sported boot knives in plain view. The leather wrapped hilts jutted from the boot tops along her outer thighs. She was very attractive and he was looking forward to being alone with her.

"You sure are a beauty, all this luxurious hair, too," her eyes drank him in, fingers lifted into his mane, gripped and gently drew him to sit up, lean across the small round table. "Gimme a taste."

He grinned, obliged, meeting her mouth with his. The kiss was long and lingering, slightly, but only slightly, possessive. As they parted he heard, sensed someone approaching and looked.

A tall, relatively speaking at some six foot four inches, Byrynthian male garbed all in shades of red strode towards them. He, too, had forgone a shirt and reddish hair caught the light on his broad muscular chest and rippled stomach. His red-gold hair curled and spiraled in a foamy curtain nearly to his waist. A deep reddish-brown north Byrynthian style baldric and sword-belt held his weapons instead of a harness. His tong, what there was of it, was low slung, barely cradling what no one could help but notice was a considerable stash of maleness. Flax had taken note of this red-haired northern Byrynthian when he walked in and he knew the tong had but a slender Y shaped set of straps for the back. Two burnished copper rings fastened just inside the hipbones. The northern Byrynthian's riding-leggins were as low cut as he'd ever seen on anyone. The belt fastened low about the hips, under what there was of the hanging front of the tong. The straps at the flanks were only an inch and a half wide and ran down the outside leg almost to mid-thigh. There, the leather scooped in, wrapped around the thigh and sheathed strong legs like a second skin. They were tucked into soft red boots that came just over the ankle in a cuff. A knife was strapped to the right calf. Red-brown bracers that covered only the hand, not the fingers or thumb, rode the forearms. The left bracer sported five wickedly sharp extending blades while the right held three knives ranging in length from five inches to seven arrayed across it. The northern Byrynthian's beard was redder than his hair and trimmed in a neat mustache and goatee. A narrow band of beard running below the cheekbone connected the goatee to sideburns.

Flax supposed he was handsome, even beautiful in a savage, feral way. The most striking feature was the eyes. The color of the darkest, purest, coldest glacial ice; they were frozen. Any other would have been intimidated meeting that cold gaze. Flax wasn't, he didn't want a fight but he'd finish it, if it came to that

Dextera released him; resting both elbows on the table, she watched the redhead saunter towards them. He moved with a dangerous, feral grace that was also somehow suggestive.

Fur-warmer for hire, he has to be, no one else dresses like that... He might as well be naked...

The redhead took a mug of ale from a passing slave. With a sharp swat on the bare rump, he sent the slave on his way, strode to the table.

"Evening, lady." A broad suggestive grin flashed strong white teeth, "Mind if I join you?" One brow was set with a ring near the outer corner of the eye. Two gold earrings were set in the left lobe and a broad band rode the upper outer curve of the ear. There was even a ring set in the redhead's navel.

His jaw tightened as Dextera's eyes roved over the redhead. She wet her lips, looked at him a moment then back at the redhead. "Not at all."

"I mind," Flax rumbled. He didn't mean it to be menacing but he didn't make any effort to make it non-threatening. He couldn't help it that his deep voice rumbled low like an approaching storm.

The glacial eyes met his unperturbed, "No one asked you, lad." The northern Byrynthian pulled up a stool, sat down equidistant between them.

"Jealous, Flax?" Dextera asked, eyes dancing.

He shook his head, cracked his crooked smile, "Just don't like interruptions."

"Flax, huh?" The redhead looked him over and didn't appear intimidated by his size in the least. That was a first. "It fits, lad, good choice." The redhead sipped from his mug, referring to his choice of an alias. Most fur-warmers for hire used an alias.

"It happens to be my name." *And I am no mere fur-warmer for hire...*

A single brow lifted, the redhead nodded. "I'm Rufus." The glacial eyes turned to Dextera, "And you, lady? Whom do I have the honor of addressing?"

She laughed, "Rufus ay? By Senshalla, I've heard of you."

The redhead, Rufus, grinned, it was loaded with sex, "I'm flattered."

The bastard practically radiates it, but then again he is nearly naked... Wonder how many other piercings he's got... Wait, I don't wanna know...

Dextera's fingers lightly touched the redhead's shoulder, the hair spilling down his back. "I'm Dextera and I'm very pleased to meet you."

Flax gripped his mug, settled back in his chair, stretching out his legs again. "Yeah, me too."

Those frosty eyes shifted to him, "Does she know how old you are, lad? Or perhaps I should say how young."

His brows knit, he'd never actually had to lie about his age, normally he just let people think what they wanted. "I'm twenty-two, what of it?"

When Rufus laughed it almost gave him a chill. "If you're over twenty then I'm a negosi."

He just grinned. *The bastard is right, what can I say, after all?* "So, Rufus, to what do we owe the honor?"

Rufus studied him, searched his features and he held the piercing gaze. "You're not yet eighteen are you, lad? I don't think... No, she won't be the first. Still, I hope she's paying you well. Big, beautiful bastard with ororri blood no less, you should go for gold."

"Like it's your business," he growled, started to lift his mug.

The redhead caught his mug opposite his hand; "I'll pay you in gold."

For a moment all he could do was stare incredulous into the frosty eyes.

Dextera broke the silence, "Oh, no, you're not hiring him away from me, Rufus. In fact I'd like to hire you as well."

Flax gathered his composure. "Now just hold on..."

At the same time Rufus turned to Dextera, "I think that can be arranged."

The strong hand wrapped around his mug moved deftly to his wrist, up his forearm. He put his mug down as the grip became a caress. "Just wait..." Sitting up, he subtly moved out of Rufus' touch, took up his mug again. All to no avail, Rufus' hand dropped to his knee. "Hey, none a that..."

"Three tres gold for the night," Dextera offered.

Rufus's gaze turned to him. A feral grin leaden with raw sexuality spread across the redhead's features, lit the glacial gaze. "I usually go for gold pentas but for you, lad, done."

"Done," Dextera agreed.

Damn, that was way too fast... "No." At that moment Rufus leaned towards him. He caught the redhead's wrist as the caress slid up his thigh. "Look," he met Dextera's gaze then Rufus' pointedly. The redhead easily escaped his grip only to catch his hand, Rufus' thumb stroked along his skin. He freed his hand; "I don't roll in the furs with other males."

Dextera smiled slyly, "You promised to do as I asked..."

"That was before you brought him into this and you didn't mention another male when we made our arrangement."

Rufus' hand dropped to his thigh again, caressed, drawing his undivided attention. "I'll be as gentle or as rough as you like, lad. You can take me or I'll take you or things can be as equal as you want them. It'll be completely up to you."

For a heartbeat, he looked into that frosty gaze and had the feeling that there was something more going on here than met the eye. There was intensity to Rufus' gaze, not heat, not need or desire, an urgency more sensed than seen. Still, the hand on his thigh was getting too high. He caught the redhead's wrist, "Stop it, okay," it was a demand, not a request. He tried to keep his voice even but a growl leaked into it.

Flashing a grin, Rufus leisurely lifted the hand from his thigh only to brush the backs of strong fingers along his jaw, "Ah, lad, you're so touchable."

"That may be, but I'm not interested in bein' touched by you." His own grin flashed but it was hard, dangerous.

Rufus wrapped both hands around the mug in front of him. That gesture was leisurely too and he didn't look the least bit intimidated or nervous. "Sorry, lad, didn't mean to make you uncomfortable."

Dextera sighed with disappointment, "C'mon, Flax, don't knock it before you try it. Look at him; he's beautiful and strong. His hair is gorgeous..."

Shaking his head, he rested forearm and fist on the table, "I'm not interested."

"I've already purchased your meal..." Dextera started.

"I'll cover the meal, lady, no problem. I'm not going to bed with another male. Doesn't matter the circumstances. I won't do it. You want me, fine. I'll be happy to go to a room with you and light the furs on fire. Ya want him," he gestured to Rufus, met the glacial eyes and the redhead drank from his mug. "That's fine too. I'll just pay for my meal and rent my own room. No trouble."

"You're going to make me choose." Dextera sighed heavily. "Do you realize how hard this is?"

Rufus looked into his ale, "I am more experienced, lady. Flax is very young, seventeen. I am of age and then some but not too much more and I can go all night long." The mug was drained, "And I did agree to three gold tres tonight. I'll stick by that, for tonight only."

His jaw clenched but he sat back, folded his arms and waited for Dextera's decision. *Damn, what a pain in the ass... And here I was just after a good time...*

"Flax?" Dextera reached across the table to lightly touch his arm, "Warm my furs?"

At least she asked... "If it's your wish, lady." He couldn't help meeting Rufus's gaze and thought he saw that serious intensity again. Then the redhead shrugged.

"No hard feelings, lad. I've just one thing to say to you."

"Oh yeah?"

Rufus nodded, "You're not property, remember that, always."

"C'mon, Flax." Dextera rose. She called to a slave for a skin of ale and a room.

He rose too, finished off his ale. Casually, Rufus glanced after Dextera. She was paying for their accommodations and the ale at the bar half the room away.

"Later," he started past the redhead toward Dextera. When Rufus caught his arm he cursed.

"Quiet, lad and listen." The redhead growled and there was no sexy suggestion to it at all. In fact the redhead didn't seem so much like the fur-warmer for hire any longer.

His brows knit and he met the glacial eyes.

"Don't drink any more, not even water if she pours it." The frosty gaze held his a moment then watched Dextera warily.

"What?" He wasn't sure he heard that right. Everything blurred then straightened out.

"Watch your back and remember, I'm not your enemy."

His crooked smile tilted his mustache, "I never thought ya were."

"Later, lad." Abruptly the redhead's entire manner shifted back to sexy suggestion, fur-warmer for hire. *Like he's a different person, or like it's a cloak he puts on... Damn, ale's strong...* Rufus smiled at Dextera, lifted his mug in salute, releasing him.

The room was in the back on the second floor. As they entered, Dextera turned. He shut the door behind them as she gripped the shoulder straps of his harness pulling him down to a long devouring kiss. Warmth and need rekindled in his loins, burning pleasantly through his blood as she devoured him, drank him in. He met her mouth, caressing, moaning quietly, melting inside, into her kiss.

"Kneel," she breathed against his lips when they parted.

He chuckled, dropped to his knees opening the rings on his harness. Meeting her gaze, he shrugged out if it, let it slip to one hand, running his other up her body, ribs.

"Give it to me, I'll hang it up."

He set the shoulder strap in her palm, dropped his hands to his thighs as she moved to the door. Watching her, he felt heat thudding in his loins, growing with each passing breath. Then the room tilted, blurred... He blinked, shaking his head to clear it.

"Something wrong?"

Her voice was above, before him again and he opened his eyes, looked up, flashing a crooked grin, "Buzzed, ale was strong." Rising off his heels, he put his hands around her waist, slid them up to cup her breasts.

She grinned, sort of growled in her throat running her hands into his hair. His mouth was guided to hers, taken long and thoroughly. Her hands delved into his mane, slid caressing along his scalp. He moaned, heat spread though his limbs, skin tingled with warmth.

Her fingers tightened in his hair as she parted from him. He gasped, obliged when she tilted her head back. Flax licked, kissed her neck, throat. His hands caressed her breasts, feeling rigid nipples beneath the leather.

"You did have five mugs full."

He moaned an affirmative, intoxicated by her scent, taste... the feel of hard nipples under his hands, under leather. He found the laces, tugged and worked at them wanting to explore, lick and suck at the warm globes in his hands.

"You're drunk, Flax."

I am... Damn... The room tilted and he dropped back to his heels reeling a little. Putting one hand down to the floor, he braced himself. "Goddess... I'm drunk." Shaking his head, he looked up and everything blurred, slid.

She smiled coyly, moved back to sit on the low pallet that served as a bed. "Come here, my lovely, crawl to me." Dextera beckoned.

Damn, he was drowsy too and his eyes really wanted to close. Flax shook his head, forced his eyes open. His eyes met hers... *I didn't have but a mug and a half of ale, I'm not drunk, I can't be... I ate and... even if I had five mugs I shouldn't feel like this...*

She leaned back, braced on both arms, extended a leg, waved her foot at him. "Come, take my boots off."

Without even thinking about it, he obeyed. Flax crawled to her on hands and knees, knelt at her feet. Sitting back on his heels, he met her gaze and everything slid again.

Her foot pushed lightly against his shoulder, "C'mon, Flax, my boots."

"Sure, lady," he obliged. But he never had such a hard time with laces before... His fingers felt... clumsy, unsure but he managed.

"Now yours, you won't be needing them."

The world had narrowed down to her voice, the two of them, the limits of the room; the walls seemed to fade off into the distance. It was damn hard to keep his eyes open and they just about refused to focus. Shifting to sit on the floor, he took his boots off, pushed them to the wall. It took a supreme effort but he met her gaze. She blurred, slid and it made his stomach churn. He'd never gotten sick from ale in his life, not even five mugs full... *No, wait; I only had a mug and a half... I shouldn't feel like this...*

She beckoned, "C'mere, my lovely."

He complied, shifting to his knees. She caught handfuls of his hair, drew him to her kiss. His blood thrummed, seared in his veins. The heat rose from his loins again, and he met her mouth eagerly. Her hands slid down his back, caressed, then slid up to his neck, his hair. His hands found her breasts, caressed, then moved to the laces of her halter. Again his fingers were almost numb, unresponsive and clumsy and he briefly considered getting a knife. Finally, he managed to open her halter, parted it to push it off her shoulders. His big hands slid over the curve, the valley, stroked the outside of her breasts to her ribs. Caressing neck, shoulder, with his lips, tongue he worked his way down, over the top of one creamy mound to the cleft between. Then his tongue traced the bone over the heart, slid to one hardened nipple. He sucked, swirled his tongue around the crinkly flesh while one hand stroked and rolled and tugged at the other. His free hand cupped and lifted the one in his mouth then slowly slid to her waist, the rings on her breeches. Her body arched, pushed her flesh into his mouth but her hands in his hair tugged him off.

Somehow, though his lids were so heavy he could hardly keep his eyes open, he met her gaze.

"Yours first," she kissed his mouth then her lips moved to his neck, her hands pulling his head back. Large hands sliding slowly down her thighs, Flax moaned as he felt her teeth in his neck, shoulder. Her hands caressed his back, shoulders biceps while her mouth nibbled and tasted his neck, throat. He fumbled at the single ring on his breeches, fingers growing clumsier and more unresponsive.

Goddess, I shouldn't be this drunk... What the Hell's wrong with me?..

The ring on his breeches finally opened and he parted them. His long thick shaft throbbing with need was free. Dextera drew back, looked down between them and cursed.

"By Senshalla, who could take all a that?" Both her hands curled around him and his hips bucked, thrust. Flax groaned, rocked as she stroked him. "You are literally hung like a horse. And these," one hand stroked him slowly from base to head while the other cupped his nuts, tucked up close. She rolled them, explored and stroked between his legs. "These are magnificent."

He moaned, tilted his head back, shuddering. She pulled his breeches open more, slid her hands around his flanks shoving the leather down. She pressed against his powerful body. Pushing bare breasts against his chest, her mouth explored him ardently. His brows knit with the effort it took to lift his arms, caress her thighs, now flanking him. Caressing, tasting him she let out soft sounds of pleasure only slightly muffled against his skin. He caressed, tasted with lips and tongue, moaned against her quietly. His heat pulsed, thudded in his temples, cock, seared in his veins.

Teeth bit his ear, tugged his earrings, "I'm going to bind you."

He moaned an affirmative before it registered in his brain.

"Put your hands behind your back, cross them. You want to, Flax. You want to do whatever I tell you to do." She whispered gently pushing on his shoulders.

Slowly, he settled to his heels and she rose.

Where's she going?.. Long blond hair fell around his face as his head dropped forward. Pushing back his mane with one hand, he braced the other against the pallet. The room wanted to tilt.

"Come now, my lovely, cross your wrists behind your back." She was behind him, standing...

Why?... So she can bind me... BIND ME!?

Flax shook his head, "No." It barely came out so he could hear it, she certainly hadn't. Shaking his head again, Flax pushed to one knee, "None a that..." A hand gripped his wrist, pulled his arm back.

"Flax, you promised you'd do exactly what I ask." Leather wrapped around his wrist.

When did I lose my bracer?.. I shouldn't feel like this, damn it... What'd that redhead say?.. Don't drink any more, not even water if she pours it... Damn strange thing to say... Unless... Something in the ale?..

He felt her drawing his other arm back. "NO!" Flax grunted shaking his head hard. He didn't think; it was all instinctual. He pulled both arms from her grip, pivoted on his knees and looked up, damn if his eyes didn't focus.

Dextera cursed. Light glinted off the strange blade in her fist.

The room blurred, slid but he could see the blade. It glinted wickedly, slashed and he blocked it with a forearm. Flax snarled when the blade sliced his flesh, blood ran up his arm, elbow.

"What the fuck?" Flax shoved with both legs, pushed up onto the pallet.

"Be quiet, damn you," Dextera hissed, reversing the blade in her hand, she slashed. He blocked again with the opposite forearm and found he had one bracer. Sparks struck from the mail on his arm. He thrust back, kicked at her belly but missed. The knife flashed and he rolled upright... and collapsed in a heap, his breeches around his thighs, knees. The whole room rocked, his stomach rocked, clenched on the meal and the ale he'd ingested. Then he heard the strangest thing; the lock clicked. Trying desperately to see, get his damned breeches pulled up and protect himself all at the same time he pushed himself into a corner, got to his knees. Holding his arm with the bracer up before his face defensively, he made a supreme effort, forced his eyes to open, focus and looked up... And saw Dextera turn toward the door.

"Who's there," she growled impatiently. "I paid to be left alone."

Using her distraction to his advantage, he gripped his breeches firmly in tingling fingers and jerked them up. Hot blood ran down his arm, hand and he paid it no mind. If he got out of this needing no more than a few stitches in his forearm he'd count himself lucky.

Dextera moved toward the door stealthily. While her back was turned, he gained his feet, shoving himself up the walls at his back. She was between him and his harness... *To Hell with my harness...* The room slid, blurred and he shook his head fighting it, whatever it was. She gripped the latch, lifted it and the door opened abruptly hitting her hard in the face. Flax blinked, shoved back his mane and the redhead was in the room. Dextera recovered and the redhead hit her square in the chest so hard the knife went flying and she met the wall, sprawled in a heap at its foot. Cold eyes met his for a moment then the redhead stood over her as she reached toward the knife, struggled to gain her feet.

"I should kill you, bitch. If I didn't need you alive I would," the redhead growled. It was low, rumbling and loaded with menace, the promise of violence. Without hesitation, he gave her a sharp blow to the base of her head and she crumbled. Crouching, the redhead took up the leather strap she was going to use to bind him and bound her wrists behind her back, looping the strap around her stomach, knotting it securely. Drawing his assassin's blade, the redhead then cut two pieces from the disheveled linen. He wadded up one piece, forced it between Dextera's teeth then tied it in place with the other. Another strip of linen bound her ankles then the redhead rose, turned to him. Flax met his gaze though he was blurry and kind of smeary around the edges.

"How you feeling, lad?"

He blinked at the unexpected question and had a Hell of a time getting his eyes open again. Flax staggered, almost fell. A hand on his shoulder steadied him, braced him against the wall. He jerked away and ended up sitting in the corner again. "Fuck... The hell's goin' on?" He stared at the floor, strove to get his eyes to focus. When he heard tearing linen, he looked up through the curtain of his golden blond mane, growled.

The redhead crouched before him, "Listen, Flax. The arm is cut deep. You're really bleeding and I want to get it stopped, or at least slow it down. Remember what I told you?"

"Don't drink?" *What the hell does that have to do with anything right now?..* He squinted through golden strands into frosty blue eyes.

A wry smile cocked the red mustache, "I'm not your enemy. I want to bind the wound, that's all. On Sheposha's Bow, lad, I swear."

And what's Sheposha's Bow to you fur-warmer for hire?.. Should be swearing on Estashe's Stamina... It was difficult but he searched the redhead's features, "You're not..."

The redhead put a finger to his lips, "Name's Rufus, remember?"

You're named Rufus like I'm twenty-two... He offered his bleeding arm to "Rufus".

The redhead wrapped linen around the wound, tied it snugly. "I can give you a few stitches later. Right now I have to get you and me and my prisoner out of here. I need you conscious and functioning. I can wait for a little while but not long. We have to be well away by first light. Now, tell me, how are you feeling?"

"Like shit." He managed, met frosty eyes when the redhead looked at his face.

"I gathered that. Can't see too straight can you?" The redhead finished tying up the linen then shifted to one knee before him.

Why should I trust you?.. Cause you can tie a good dressing?.. Flax wasn't sure he wanted to answer; he didn't know this damn redhead any better than he knew Dextera and she'd tried to... well, only the Goddess knew what she was trying to do. There was a handful of shit going on that he knew absolutely nothing about, the whole situation sucked royally.

"Flax, I need your help to get you out of here. You're too damn big for me to carry." The redhead sighed, "If I wanted to harm you, lad, I'd've done it by now. I'm capable and you know it. If you talk to me, trust me a little, I can help you. If you don't, we're both going to be in deep shit."

Briefly, he considered, then, "Can't see worth a shit. Everything's blurry and wants to slide." He closed and opened his hands, gripped his breeches with tingling fingers, struggled to stand. The redhead gripped his biceps and helped him, bracing him against the wall. "Hands are," his brows knit.

"Numb?" The redhead supplied.

"Not exactly, more like, getting there, tingly and... clumsy."

"Let me get your breeches up and fastened, okay?"

He swallowed hard, embarrassed and humiliated. "Rufus..."

"I'm not your enemy, Flax. And I'm not after you, I'm not a rapist." A strong hand pushed his hair from his face and he met the glacial gaze. It was honest, sympathetic, no longer icy.

"Yeah, sure." His breeches were tugged up and fastened in place.

"How's your stomach?" Rufus gently braced him against the wall, turned and scanned the room.

"Kinda sick when the room slides, otherwise okay."

"It might help if you threw up but personally I'd rather wait until we're outside." The redhead met his gaze, flashed him a wry smile.

He nodded, "Yeah, me too."

"If you sit on the pallet we can get your boots and harness on. It'll be easier than me carrying everything and supporting you too. Understand?"

Again, he nodded, "I got it."

"I'm going to put my arm around you, lean on me, I'll support you. I don't want to have to get you up off the floor again, okay?"

He chuckled, "Yeah, right."

Rufus moved into his side, put an arm around his waist and he draped his arm around the broad shoulders. The redhead felt like steel, hard and almost impossibly strong. "Not getting intoxicated, are you?"

"Uh-uh." He leaned on Rufus and was guided to the bed. His legs felt heavy, like he was mired in mud to his waist. "Shit," he groaned.

"Easy, lad, it'll pass." Carefully, Rufus lowered him to sit on the pallet, released him.

His eyes shut and he leaned heavily on both arms. His body wanted rest, desperately, but he didn't lie down. He opened his eyes when he felt his lower leg lifted.

Rufus was on one knee before him, slipping his boots on. "Okay, if you're not intoxicated then what was so damn funny?" The glacial eyes searched his.

"Got a picture a you tryin' to pick me up off the floor." He watched Rufus stand; retrieve his harness. If he concentrated the room didn't slide so much. Still, concentration was elusive.

A broad grin flashed, "I'll wager I could do it, but I wouldn't get far carrying you. I don't carry bears around for fun and profit and you weigh about as much as a good size bear."

Flax managed a crooked grin, then it faded. The redhead had his harness and crouched again before him. "My legs feel leaden... This really sucks. She put somethin' in my ale..."

Rufus nodded, "She did, when she drew you across the table to kiss her. She just didn't give you enough to really put you under. It'll pass, I swear."

"You... want me to talk, to keep me... Thinkin'."

"Smart, lad. Yeah, I do, at least until I can get you someplace safe where you can pass out and sleep it off." Rufus maneuvered between his knees, slid the harness onto the pallet next to him. "You trust me?"

He considered that a moment, "Like I got a choice?"

The redhead sighed quietly, "I tried to get you out of it, lad. It didn't work. Put your arms around my shoulders, I'll get your harness on."

He searched Rufus' features for a moment then struggled to sit up, lean forward toward the redhead. His arms felt leaden too. It was getting worse, whatever it was. Rufus maneuvered closer, drew him against the powerful body, guided his arms around strong shoulders. "Rufus..."

"It'll be okay, lad. Don't panic but fight it." The redhead took most of his weight, supported him and put his harness on. "Can't find one quite big enough, huh?"

"Naw, costs too much to have one made." His eyes closed and he laid his head on the redhead's shoulder. "Swords are too light, grips aren't large enough. Wish I could get an axe made for me."

"That's it, talk to me."

"I really want an axe. Double bladed northern one and made for me... My size, strength. Every one I try is too damn light, too slender a shaft... Feels like a toy in my hand."

Gently, Rufus pulled back only enough to fasten the rings and centerpieces of his harness. While he did that he talked. "Now listen close. I'm going to take Dextera first. You're safer in the locked room then outside alone. Understand?"

"Yeah," he grunted, tried to lift his head and meet the glacial eyes.

"What'd I just say?" Rufus gently pressed him back. His jaw was caught in a strong hand and lifted. His eyes met the redhead's.

He pulled back, shook his head trying to clear it, "You're takin' Dextera first. I'm safer here than outside alone." A feeling of helplessness made him sick to his stomach, Dextera drugging made him angry.

"Good, hang on just a little longer, Flax." Rufus rose, went to Dextera then crouched to check her breathing and pulse.

He watched, concentrated. "Rufus?"

The redhead was slinging Dextera across his shoulders. Rufus rose effortlessly and turned to meet his gaze sidelong. "What?"

"What the Hell's goin' on?" Flax strove to concentrate on the redhead's features, frosty eyes.

Red brows knit, "I'd rather explain later. When we're safe and you've... slept off the drug."

He nodded, "Okay. Don't take too long, huh?"

"I won't, lad. I'll be right back. Count by threes, keep your mind awake."

To his surprise Rufus left by the window. The room was a mess, there was blood, torn linen, Dextera's boots. *Three, six, nine, twelve, fifteen, eighteen... Her boots, should mention that. My pack's with my horse in the stable down the street... Count by threes. Twenty-one, twenty-four, twenty-seven... What'd the hell she drug me for?.. He said he'd explain... And give me a few stitches?.. I think he said he was going to... Hate to leave my horse and pack behind. Maybe I can come back for them once... I sleep this off... Oh, Goddess, this sucks... I hate feeling like this, almost helpless... Although, I did manage to defend myself... Like that would've lasted...* He dropped down to his forearms before he realized it. "Shit..." Flax cursed quietly under his breath, shoving laboriously up on both arms again. Then he pushed himself up almost straight, bracing his hands on his knees. *Where is he?.. Damn... Count... Where was I?.. Thirty, thirty-three, thirty-six, thirty-nine, forty-two, forty-five, forty-eight...* He sensed... something and forced himself to look toward the window. Rufus entered, met his gaze and flashed him a grin. "My pack..."

"I know. The big sorrel draft horse is yours, right?" He nodded as the redhead came to stand before him. "I'll get her, and your pack. Coming back in this tavern may not be good for your health after tonight but I'll see what I can do. Ready to stand?"

"Sure, no problem." He offered the redhead his uninjured arm, hand. Rufus crouched, drawing Flax's arm across his broad shoulders again. He pushed with his legs, forced them to straighten. They obeyed but trembled. "Goddess, damn her to Morditha's Hell..." he growled under his breath.

"I'll wager she's already damned, lad." Rufus told him as he leaned on the redhead. "Now listen. Whatever I say, go along with it. I can't take you out on the roof so we're going right out the front door. Dextera attacked you; she cut you then fled through the window. She was crazy, like a demon took her over. I heard and came looking." He felt linen wrapped around his waist and looked. Rufus was tying a dressing around his ribs and stomach. "Hold your arm close to your side like that's real. Anybody asks, I'm taking you to a healer I know. Repeat it back to me."

He did and he had it straight, thank the Goddess. Leaning heavily on the redhead they moved toward the door. They reached it and Rufus gripped the latch. "Rufus, her boots... an' mount, an' pack."

"She was crazy, remember. She left everything and made off through the window."

He nodded, "Makes sense in a backwards kinda way."

"Ready to go?"

"Oh yeah, by all means."

Rufus laughed quietly, "You're going to be all right, lad."

They made it through the tavern without any trouble. Rufus acted pissed, cursing the proprietress for allowing such things to go on. For the cut she wanted the working environment should be secure. The redhead drew his sword when she approached, offering to send for the healer herself. Rufus was taking him to a healer that could be trusted and they all just better stay out of his way. They were out in the dimly lit street quicker than Flax thought possible. Rufus retained his long-sword, took them down the street into an area even more poorly illuminated. Then they were traversing dark and dank alleyways, crossing dimly lit streets only occasionally. It didn't seem long before they were on the edge of town, then in a brushy gully. Rufus went slowly through the gully, mindful of his footing. Flax wasn't sure but he figured they were almost a mile out of town before Rufus paused, eased him to kneel on the ground.

"Want me to do it or do you want to do it yourself?" the redhead asked.

Kneeling back on his heels, head hanging, hands braced on his knees, he had to think about that for a moment. "Throw up?"

"Yeah, get what's left of it out of you." The redhead was on one knee at his side.

He swallowed hard, "I'll do it." Raking a hand through his disheveled mane, he took two fingers and shoved them down his throat, along the back of his tongue till he gagged. Then he dropped to all fours, stomach heaving. His blond mane fell around him and he heaved again, tried to shift to just one hand so he could hold it back to no avail. Then his hair was gathered back, even his braids. Just in time too, everything came up. He heaved, vomited from what felt like his toes for far too long. When he could breathe, gasp for air, he realized Rufus was holding him, keeping his hair back and keeping him steady on all fours. Squeezing his eyes shut, he eased back to his knees.

"Come with me, lad." Gently, Rufus got him to move over a few feet and he heard water trickling. The redhead released him. He heard water splash. "Here, Flax, drink."

Shaking his head slightly, he opened his eyes and saw the redhead's cupped hands brimming with water. He cradled Rufus' hands in his own and drank deeply, thirstily. Vaguely, he realized the redhead's bracers had been removed. When the water was gone, he released Rufus and managed to lift his head, meet the glacial gaze.

"There's a spring," Rufus gripped his shoulder, pointed to it. Trickling from between a couple boulders it filled a rocky pool. "Get another drink if you want. Don't lie down, not yet. I'll be right back." With that the redhead was gone. He heard Rufus move away, shifted to more easily reach the spring. He drank, splashed the cool water on his face. Fumbling at the rings on his bracer, he removed it, bathed the forearm not wrapped in linen. Splashing more on his face, he got another drink then knelt back. Shaking his head, he tilted it back, felt a light breeze on his face, chest. He could swear he smelled a horse. "Any better?" Rufus crouched at his side again.

"Some, but I'm not trying to stand either." He managed to meet the frosty eyes again and the redhead wasn't quite as blurry, nothing seemed to slide, at least for the moment. The redhead caught his right hand, turned it palm up and put his bracer on, fastened the rings deftly, quickly.

"Well, you're gonna try now. Just like last time, put your arm around me."

He complied and made it slowly to his feet. This time his legs, though heavy, leaden, didn't tremble and he could see a little better. There was a horse, Dextera was draped over the saddle and Rufus took up the reins. Flax shook his head, "Wait." He wavered and Rufus waited patiently. "I can... Take the rein... Ya might need your sword and I can at least lead the horse."

"All right. Hang on." Rufus released him, passed the reins from one hand to the other around his back. Then he felt them pressed into his left hand.

He gripped them, wrapped them around his hand. "Okay, I got 'em."

"We'll go slow, the footing is treacherous along this gully even if you've got all your faculties. Hate to have to set a bone for you."

He chuckled quietly. With Rufus supporting him and him leading the horse they traversed the gully, crossed relatively open grassland to another rocky, brush-choked gully. He wasn't sure how far they went. It seemed like quite a ways, maybe a couple miles but his body ached for rest, practically screamed for it. Fighting whatever she slipped him was almost as exhausting as the drug itself. Still, he was feeling a bit better, his limbs were leaden but keeping his eyes open, focused wasn't such a strain any more. Finally they stopped. Rufus pulled the brush from an opening between two boulders. "Tug the reins and drop 'em. Copper'll ground tie." He did it then Rufus turned him, sort of crouched, drawing him down a bit. "That's it, the passage is kind of small for both of us but we'll make it." It was narrow. Even alone he'd have to traverse it sideways. He raised his left hand, touched rough stone right in front of him as they sidled between the boulders. A few feet in and it widened and stone above blotted out the sky. "Just a few more feet and you can rest, lad." Abruptly the passage opened up into a room. Rufus guided him to a skin spread on the floor. Gratefully, he eased down to recline on it. Flax rolled to his back, let his eyes shut. He listened to Rufus leave, drifted off. The redhead returning roused him, but only a little. He thought he felt the fake dressing around his waist being cut from him. The knife sliding along so near his skin should have brought him fully awake. The fact that it didn't was a testament to how strong the drug was, how tired he was from fighting it. His brows knit and he grunted with the effort it took to force his eyes open.

"Easy, lad. You're safe, rest."

Even if I wasn't I don't think there's a damn thing I could do about it... gotta trust you, "Rufus", I don't have any choice... hope you're worthy...

Darkness claimed him.

Two

Flax stirred, heard chain clink. *What the Hell?...* He moved his left arm and heard it again, felt steel encircling it. A surge of anger burned through his veins. Cursing, he pushed up to one forearm, looked at his left wrist. Sure enough a manacle encircled it. *That bastard... just what the Hell is going on...* A shining length of thick, serpentine chain went from his wrist to a ring in the wall. Flax clenched his jaw, fists, squeezed his eyes shut and drew a long slow breath, let it out, *Stay clam and think...* Hearing a quiet sound, he looked between his boots and across the room, toward the entrance. Dextera was lying on her stomach, trussed up like a prize hog at the butcher's on a single ratty looking fur. She was gagged, blindfolded. The linen bindings had been replaced by leather cuffs, straps. The gag was a wide leather strap and he'd wager it had a ball of cloth sewn to it that fit in the mouth. The blindfold was thick dark cloth tied securely around her head. Her ankles and thighs were bound with leather as well. To his surprise he noticed a leather collar fastened around her neck and a leash tethered to a ring set in the floor. On closer inspection her ankles were bound to a second ring. He lay back down, considered. *"Rufus" shackled me. Why? Well, I'll just ask the bastard when he shows up.* His brows knit and he rose up to lean on his shackled arm. To his immediate right, definitely within reach, were his harness and all his weapons including his missing bracer. His pack lay across the room to his right by a low pallet or bunk. On the bunk lay a brown pack. The red-brown baldric and sword belt hung on a hook above it. He rolled to his side, looked around the room. It appeared to be a natural cave that had been widened here and there. A little hearth was constructed at the rear beneath a makeshift chimney. On a natural stone shelf that served as a mantle there was an iron pot, an oil lamp. It was unlit though and, as far as he could tell, it was most likely morning.

Flax reclined to his back again, closed his eyes. *So, "Rufus", why the shackle? My harness is within easy reach. Only my left hand is tethered... I'm dressed... Breeches and boots complete with boot knife and my right bracer... So, why? Maybe so I don't take off. Or kill Dextera. He said... I think I heard him say he needed her alive. Why would he need her alive? Well, Hell, why'd she drug me? Maybe she's a slaver. But she had a knife not a collar... Strange looking knife too. Single edged, curved the wrong way if you ask me. Why did Rufus intervene? Why help me? Wish I knew what's going on...* He sensed... Something and opened his eyes, met the glacial gaze.

"Hey, Flax," the redhead greeted him. He was dressed in leather beeches dyed in shades of sand and green that closely matched the rocks and brush of the gully. They were tucked into soft padded leather boots of mottled brown. Knives jutted from both boots. The red-brown bracers were in place. The harness was gray and black, gently curved eastern style swords rode crossed on the back. Pairs of throwing knives rode every strap. The brow ring and earrings were gone, even the navel ring had disappeared. The red-gold hair was bound in a braid rather than a topknot. The redhead didn't look much like the fur-warmer for hire who'd sat down at his table last night.

"Rufus," Flax growled, lifted his left wrist. "Free me."

The redhead considered a moment. "I think we should talk a little first."

He sat up cross-legged, "I want this shackle off, now." He jerked on it, raked his free hand through his hair.

A cool smile flashed, "Remember what I told you?"

"If you're not my enemy, prove it. Release me."

Rufus studied him, "In a few minutes, lad. We do need to talk and I'd rather talk with you than fight you."

"Damn right..."

"Don't," Rufus warned.

His blond brows knit and he glared at the redhead.

"Don't threaten me." The eyes were glacial, features frosty. "Yeah you're big and strong and you may have skills to go with all that size but I'm better, faster and meaner, so don't fuck with me. We're allies for the moment, don't go out of your way to make it otherwise." Rufus paused; some of the ice thawed and a smile, a real one crossed the redhead's features. "I didn't help you last night to kill you today."

Flax exhaled, pushing some of his anger away. "All right, then why did you help me?"

Rufus approached, "Because you don't deserve what she had planned for you. No one does."

"Why the shackle?" He raised his left fist and moved to put his back to the wall.

"Rufus" crouched, moved his harness next to him and sat cross-legged. "I didn't want you to kill her before I could talk to you. And I didn't want you taking off either."

Makes sense, maybe I'd trust it more if I hadn't thought of it myself... On the other hand, maybe that's a good reason to trust it.   "What'd she have planned for me?"

The redhead straightened his goatee, mustache. "Dextera fashions herself a priestess but not to any Goddess we know. Her so called goddess requires a sacrifice every year."

For a moment he was speechless then wrath burned in his veins, "Human sacrifice?"

"Rufus" nodded,"You and four other fair-haired, blue-eyed males. The hair is important. I was supposed to be her target last night but she set her sights on you first. At that point I hoped to get you out of it any way I could. Unfortunately I couldn't. I guess I'm just not blond enough." Fingers combed the red beard. It looked like "Rufus" hadn't shaved this morning either, or he was letting his beard grow in.

Flax raked a hand through his hair, "You're not a fur-warmer for hire are you?"

The glacial eyes studied him, delved into him, reading, analyzing and he looked away from the scrutiny. "No, I'm not."

It was his turn to search the redhead's features; he was damn near unreadable. All Flax could see was a measure of wry amusement. "So, who are you, what are you?"

That cool grin flashed, "Who I am isn't important. I'm a bounty hunter, have been since I was about your age. And let's just keep that between you and me, ay lad?" It was almost a request, more a subtle demand.

And if I refused? Does it really matter? No, not after last night, not if he takes this damn shackle off my wrist. "Sure," Flax agreed for now, he didn't give his word; he wasn't bound.

The redhead rose smoothly to his feet, "Rather take those stitches before or after breakfast?" He asked, moving to the brown pack on the bunk.

Flax considered his bandaged forearm, cuffed wrist. He'd much rather have the shackle taken care of before breakfast. He'd feel more comfortable eating with the redhead if he wasn't shackled. "Before." He looked to "Rufus" who was crouched by the bunk. Flax blinked, squinted, whip scars crisscrossed the powerful upper back under the plaited mane. There was a scar from what he'd wager was a knife in one shoulder, a few other scars from blade or arrow but... The whip scars captured his attention. They were old, years old. *Must have been a Kylonian long whip. A slave whip doesn't leave scars and a long whip cuts the skin rather than tears... Damn...*

The redhead rose, turned to him with a cylindrical box in his hand. The glacial eyes met his, "Are you a warrior of your word, Flax?"

His brows knit and he was unsure if he should be insulted at the question or amused. "I am."

"And would you consider your word to a stranger, a passing acquaintance as binding as your word to your sword-mate?" The redhead approached until he was standing where he'd been sitting. The features, frosty eyes were unreadable, cold.

"If I give my word I keep it, doesn't matter to whom I give it." He cocked his head, met the glacial gaze, "What the Hell kinda question is that?"

"I consider it an important one." The redhead sat down cross-legged again. "There are people who consider giving their word to a stranger less binding than giving it to a close friend. I need to know if I can trust your word to me because I'm about to ask for it." Working a clasp on the side of the cylinder, "Rufus" opened it, splitting it in half long ways. Inside was the special thread, curved needle of a surgeon, a small jar, a tiny flask, and a few cut pieces of soft cotton cloth.

"Ask," he prompted watching the redhead clean and thread the needle.

Frosty eyes met his pointedly, "Your word you won't attack or attempt to harm or kill my prisoner."

Thorough, wants to make sure there's no loopholes in it. Yet he didn't ask me to swear I'll stay out of whatever's going on and he didn't ask me to swear allegiance, not yet anyways. "You have it. She's yours."

A single nod, "Wrist," two fingers beckoned curtly to his shackled limb. Then "Rufus" held out a hand in which to place his wrist. Glacial eyes locked with his.

Holding the piercing gaze, he complied, laid his wrist in the calloused palm. "Rufus" smiled slightly, produced a key from somewhere and unlocked the shackle. The key disappeared; the shackle was removed.

"Thanks." He mentally breathed a sigh of relief, stifled the urge to rub his wrist. The shackle hadn't chafed at all; he didn't really need to.

"No problem." Drawing a slender throwing knife "Rufus" deftly cut the bandage from his forearm. The blade captured his attention, then, as it was returned to its place, the rest of the harness hugging "Rufus's" chest. All the centerpieces and rings, all the hilts and cross-guards were painstakingly wrapped in dark cloth or leather. There were no tertiary straps because the swords were mounted on the back rather than at the hips. Before he thought about it, he reached to grasp one wrapped centerpiece. His wrist was seized in a manacle strong grip and he met the redhead's cold eyes. Something passed behind the frosty gaze and he was released, "Go ahead, lad."

Tentatively, he touched the centerpiece, then gripped the rings experimentally, "This... is to keep it silent. No sound at all, by Werdeka. And your swords?"

A quiet laugh, and "Rufus" reached over his shoulder, drew his short-sword. Reversing the blade, the redhead offered the hilt to him.

He accepted, adjusted his grip on the weapon. It came closer to fitting him than any other he'd tried. The hilt was long, closer to being long enough for both his fists than any other as well. The blade curved gently and looked razor sharp. The small round guard was wrapped in leather as was the hilt and pommel. The weight was better than that of the short-sword he carried and the balance was perfect. "This is a fine weapon."

"Thank you, I like it." The redhead grinned. "You can look at my long-sword outside if you wish. Can I get that arm sewn up now?"

He ran his free hand through his hair self-consciously, "Sure, sorry... Weapons..." Flax passed the blade back.

Deftly it was returned to its sheath, "Are the bread and wine of life to a true warrior." "Rufus" finished his thought more poetically than he would have.

"Yeah," he agreed. *It's true, they are.* "Combat runs in my blood."

"I know; it's in my blood too." The redhead unstopped the flask, dampened a swatch of cloth and he smelled strong spirits. "And it was no trouble." Gently, "Rufus" gripped his left wrist, turned it to easily get at the wound, "This is going to sting."

No kidding... Shit! It did. The dampened cloth was swabbed along the wound. Flax clenched his jaw tightly, breathed through it. Nevertheless his brows knit. When "Rufus" set the cloth aside he exhaled then cursed as another was dampened. "Ya couldn't a done this while I was out?" He asked tightly as the second cloth soaked with spirits slid along the wound.

"I didn't want to wake you, Flax."

"Fuck," he growled.

"Rufus" cleaned the needle with the cloth then set it aside. The red head didn't even ask him if he could be still, if he could take getting stitches like this. In a way he took it as a compliment but it might have been a test as well.

"What do I call you?" he asked as the needle pierced his hide for the first time.

"What do you think you should call me?" Very neatly the redhead tied a knot, then pierced his flesh with another stitch.

"Son of a bitch?" he offered through his teeth. "Bastard maybe?"

"Probably shouldn't make me laugh, lad." The second knot was just as neat as the first.

"Yeah," he agreed. "The Goddess only knows what I'll end up with embroidered on my arm if I do."

"That's right."

He studied the cool features, then his gaze drifted to the harness and then the scars wrapping around the ribs, shoulders. He sensed... Met the glacial gaze.

"If I tell you that story, lad, you might put a name to me. It might be better for both of us if you didn't."

"I'll keep it to myself, I swear, on Werdeka's Axe, bounty hunter," he volunteered.

A single brow lifted then the redhead went back to stitching up his arm.

He clenched his jaw tightly as the needle slid through his flesh again. "Ya know, when you swore to Sheposha that you only wanted to bind my wound..."

"Yeah?" The knot was tied.

"It kind of made me think," the needle slid through his flesh, thank the Goddess it was nice and sharp. "That you weren't exactly what you appeared."

"As it was meant to, lad."

He exhaled, drew a deep breath as another knot was tied. "May I call you Hunter?"

"That's fine." Another stitch, another breath. He was kind of getting a rhythm.

"Well, you want me to trust you, right? And I trusted you last night."

"As you pointed out," another knot and the glacial eyes met his for a moment. It was brief, the bounty hunter went back to sliding the needle through his flesh but he read a measure of amusement there. "You didn't really have a choice."

"If I didn't trust you," his freehand gripped the redhead's heavy bicep, drew his gaze, "I could've broken your neck when you came within reach."

A hard grin flashed, "You could've tried, lad." The redhead returned his attention to the knot he was about to tie. "I wasn't really concerned about it, you're far too honorable to just jump someone and cold-bloodedly kill them merely because you don't fully trust them."

"How do you know that?" He exhaled with the tightening of the knot then drew a deep breath as the needle pierced his skin.

"It's written on you. Like your age or the fact that weapons and combat run in your blood. Like the fact that you're hetero as the day is long is written on you."

"You telling me that you're not?" He asked, not that he really cared. It turned his stomach if he thought about it too much but if... Hunter knew he wasn't interested at all then the chance of attempted seduction was nil.

"I'm bi, though I figure you gathered that last night. At first I thought to hire you away but it was all too obvious that you wouldn't be interested the moment I sat down at your table. So, scaring you away became an option or being hired to join you. She'd already given you the drug. It leaves one open to suggestion, very open to suggestion, so she might have been able to kind of suggest you into it, though I doubted it. That left "Rufus" being hired to take your place and that failed because I'm not quite blond." Three more stitches were done, knotted and the glacial gaze met his, "I disrespected you in the hope that it would scare you off, I'm sorry for that but I wanted you out of it. Sorry about the cuff too, but I wasn't sure what you'd do when you came around and I need her alive and able to speak. I apologize."

He was rather taken off guard; he hadn't expected this hard, cold bounty hunter to apologize at all. Flax shook his head, "Accepted. You were just doin' what you thought you had to do." Another stitch, another breath. "So, how many do ya think?"

"How many left or how many all together?" Hunter tied the knot.

"Oh, what the Hell, let's go for how many left, huh? I can add. I'll figure out how many all together all by myself." The needle pierced his skin again, that made thirteen.

The redhead grunted quietly, "What'd I tell you about making me laugh?"

"Just answer the question. And I prefer ivy to stars, thanks."

Sitting back, the redhead met his gaze, amusement lighting the glacial eyes, "Do you need me to stop, Flax?"

"No, by all means, go on." His crooked smile cocked his mustache, "I think I'm beginning to like it, really." He laughed, he couldn't help it.

So did Hunter. "Ivy. See what I can do." Shaking his head, Hunter went back to his stitches. "I figure you need another twelve or fourteen."

"Can't wait." Another stitch, another breath. "My point was I trusted you and I had no idea what was going on; you can trust me. You already have in a way, bringing me here. This camp is secret, right?"

"Right." The knot was tied. Hunter was doing a very nice job, neat, clean, even professional.

How many of your own wounds have you sewn up, bounty hunter? Who are you? Can I keep it to myself for the rest of my life if I do figure it out, if I figure it out because he tells me about the scars? Yeah, I can, I swore I would and I will. It's enough for me to know, I don't have to talk about it... Lightly, he touched the powerful shoulder, traced the scar wrapping around the muscle.

The glacial eyes, cold, frozen, met his gaze.

"You can tell me, unless it's too hard."

A single brow lifted but the eyes didn't thaw. Hunter went back to the stitches. "Why do you care?" The needle pierced his skin.

"Huh," he thought about it for a moment, "I don't know."

"Sure you do, lad," Hunter tied another knot. "You want to know who I am, who I really am. Some part of you thinks if I can trust you with that I'll trust you implicitly. Well, I don't trust anyone implicitly, for good reason. And you shouldn't either."

Flax swallowed hard, *He's right, about all of it...* "You're right. Forget it." Another stitch, another breath and another knot. "So, about Dextera, you said me and four others?"

"That's right." Another stitch and another breath. "Five young, blond haired, blue eyed males die tomorrow night on the blood moon. Unless I can get her to tell me where so I can stop it." The knot was tied.

"Why's the hair important?" Flax clenched his jaw, brows knit. "There a water skin handy?"

"Hold this." The needle was placed in his left hand. Hunter rose, retrieved a skin from the bunk near the brown pack. The redhead resumed his seat, unstopped the skin and handed it to him. "The sacrifices are... Flax, are you sure you want to hear this?" Soaking another swatch of cotton with spirits the Hunter wiped the needle.

He was taking a few swallows. The water was cool, probably from the spring he drank at last night. "Ah-huh," he grunted affirmatively, lowering the skin. He wiped his mustache with his uninjured forearm. "I'm not as innocent as you seem to think I am and she was gonna show me first hand. I think I have a right to know."

Gently, Hunter caught his injured forearm, "I don't think you're innocent, Flax." Another stitch. "And at your age that's a shame, though I've no room to judge anyone." Hunter drew a deep breath, sighed quietly. "The scalp is taken while the sacrifice still lives. Then he's bled. The blood is collected. The scalp and blood are offered up on an altar."

"Damn," Flax cursed. "How'd you come to know of this?"

"I've noticed the last couple years around the blood moon there are rumors of some three to five fur-warmers for hire disappearing. Occasionally a couple youths disappear in the outlying areas as well. No doubt their mothers think they've run off. Three weeks ago I was in a tavern hunting a thief when I noticed Dextera and a young blond male. The next morning neither of them was around. After I caught the thief I did a little investigating. Seems these priestesses have been operating in Kylonia for three years. I decided that it was time to put a stop to it. The disappearances are all over Byrynthia, Thalusia and Kylonia but they're all centered on this area. The altar has to be close. She couldn't have taken you far no matter how she secured you and she was supposed to take you alive. I think your resistance to the drug and her suggestions that you wanted to be bound made her decide to murder you and take some other youth."

"Are you... Hunting them or... I dunno what to call it." There was only about eight or ten stitches left to go.

"You're asking me if I have a client, or I'm getting paid for this hunt?"

The needle slid through his skin and he decided it was getting easier, as long as he didn't think about it. "Yeah, I guess." The knot was tied.

"I'm not getting paid. I might if I turn them all in to Byrynthian authorities. I might get my ass into shit if I try Kylonian authorities though. They aren't overly concerned with the kidnapping and murder of their male citizens. Especially males as lowly as fur-warmers for hire." Hunter gave him another stitch, tied another knot. "This hunt is mine. I doubt there will be much left of them to turn in when I'm through."

"You're gonna stop them alone?" Flax was rather surprised, it sounded like something that required ten or twenty swords to handle.

Hunter shrugged, "The Byrynthian garrisons aren't enthusiastic about sending their own Hunters into Kylonia to stop it, not right now at any rate. My word alone isn't enough, if I could produce bodies, evidence... Of course that would mean I'd have to wait until the sacrifices they have lined up are dead. I'd rather prevent it than punish it after the fact." Another stitch and another neat knot, "Besides, I prefer to work alone. It's easier than having a garrison Hunter looking over my shoulder and telling me what I can and can't do. My main concern is saving the victims. I've no real worry for how I do it as long as they come out of it whole."

"Need another sword? I can guard your back." Flax offered. "I worked as a constable in Bysinisa a few weeks back, I'm not untried."

A slight cool smile, "Have you killed, lad?" The needle slid through his flesh.

Hunter didn't mean animals, deer, hogs, foul. He meant another warrior, other people. "No," Flax admitted. "I've been training since I was old enough to hold a tojo..."

"It's not the same thing, and you know it."

Another knot. *That makes twenty-two, almost done... Thank the Goddess...* "I won't balk and get you killed." Another stitch, another breath and another knot.

"Open your fist, Flax." Hunter urged him to open his hand. He hadn't even realized he'd clenched it. Strong fingers wrapped around his, rubbed into his palm, ran along the bones in his hand. "I'm almost done."

"I know, I been countin'." He strove to relax his hand, arm. "I'm not a coward."

"Getting stitches isn't easy and I never said you were." Hunter's strong right hand rubbed, massaged and he did manage to relax the arm.

"I didn't mean the stitches." Flax took a slow deep breath, pushed it out just as slow. "If it's my life or theirs, it's mine."

"Easy words to say, lad." The needle glided through his flesh again.

Twenty-four... "They're my enemies too. She planned to sacrifice me to her goddess. I have a blood debt to them. And they're not just words. I wouldn't say it if I didn't believe I could do it when it needed to be done." The knot was tied.

"I'll consider your request." Hunter's voice was cool, collected as the needle ran through his arm again. "You've no blood debt except to Dextera, she cut you."

Shit, that's true... So what's he want from me?.. "I want to help you, help them... or save them or if necessary avenge them."

"Like I said, I'll consider your request." The glacial eyes met his gaze; Hunter winked. "I don't plan on any of the priestesses surviving." He went back to the stitches. "Not even her." A slight nod indicated the prisoner who groaned behind the gag, struggled weakly. "The only remaining question about her death is; how fast? That's it."

His crooked smile cocked his mustache then he did his damnedest to sound serious, shocked, "You could do that? In cold blood?" The needle pierced his hide yet again. *Twenty-six...* It looked pretty good, neat, straight, well closed.

An icy grin flashed and the frosty eyes went positively glacial, "My blood is never cold when I kill. It runs so hot in my veins I sometimes think I must burn from the inside out."

Goddess, that's true, real, he meant that and not just to scare her... He clenched his jaw as the needle pierced his hide. "If she doesn't tell you?"

The glacial eyes met his gaze, thawed some. There was amusement in them now. "She dies slow, very slow. I've flayed uncooperative prisoners before, it's rather amazing how long one can live."

Another knot. It looked closed to him. *That was to frighten her... He's not easy to read and yet I can tell the difference, maybe because he means for me to...* "Nice, job, thanks."

Hunter shook his head, "You're welcome, lad, but I'm not quite done. One more turn and a knot. It'll keep it from pulling open again. Nothing pisses me off like having my hard work pull out at the wrong moment."

"Yeah, that sucks." He flashed a crooked grin when Hunter met his gaze.

The redhead smiled, finished. "Flex your hand and arm now, see how it feels. If it's too tight I can pull it out and do it over."

Oh yeah, let's do that again... "Hey, there's no ivy." He did as Hunter suggested. It was okay, he could feel them in his flesh and it sort of stung but he could handle it.

"Ivy costs extra, I didn't mention that?" Hunter cleaned the needle, put it away. He soaked another swatch of cotton with spirits, held out his hand for Flax's arm.

"You've got to be kidding."

"If it gets infected do you really want me to tear all that out, cut it, drain it and stitch it up again? Or worse, leave it open and clean it three or four times a day with this stuff?"

Resignedly Flax placed his hand in the bounty hunter's grip, sighed.

"Reasonable, lad." Hunter swabbed the stitches and he wanted to jump out of his skin.

"Oh shit," he hissed through his teeth when it was over. The redhead held onto his arm though and he met the glacial eyes questioningly. Retrieving the little jar, Hunter opened it. "Can I persuade you to let me in on just how that ought to feel?"

"I think it feels good. It's healer's salve and it's got white willow bark in it to ease the pain." Two fingers dipped into the jar, "Ready?"

"By all means." Hunter applied it gently, more gently than he thought possible. It did feel cool, and the pain, burning, stinging, did ease.

Releasing him, Hunter closed up the jar, replaced it in the cylinder. Closing it up the redhead put it in his hand. "You'll need to clean it with spirits every day, at least twice, then use the salve. You can wash it; just clean it after. Hungry?"

"Starved." His gaze dropped to the kit in his hand as Hunter rose. He watched the redhead go to the bunk, open the pack. Clothing dyed in shades of browns, greens, and combinations of both were laid neatly on the bunk. Then a pair of leather cuffs and a leather hood emerged. Picking up a bundle lying near the pack, Hunter gathered it all up and approached.

The bundle happened to be quite a meal. Inside was a pouch of dried meat, another of fruit, a nice hunk of cheese and a few pieces of fresh flat bread. Feeling mildly guilty, he looked at the bounty of provisions the redhead gave him. "Hey, ya don't... I don't need all your provisions and there's some in my pack." He met the glacial gaze as Hunter took up the water skin, moved toward his prisoner.

"I picked all that up when I got your horse and pack, lad. Figured you'd be hungry." The redhead crouched next to his prisoner and she stiffened. The bounty hunter freed her ankles only to cuff them securely together.

"Thanks," he dug in, watched as Hunter released the leash from the ring and dragged his prisoner to her knees.

He heard her groan behind the gag and wondered if Hunter had broken some ribs last night. Then Flax wondered why he was worried about it. The lady had been planning on scalping him and bleeding him dry for some strange goddess. He almost didn't give a damn what Hunter did to her. Almost, there were things he wasn't sure he could stand by and allow. On the other hand four, maybe five lives rode on getting Dextera to tell them where the altar was hidden. He started on his meal, watched.

The redhead removed the blindfold. Dextera blinked, glared at her captor then the dark eyes flicked to him.

"Listen, bitch. You holler and the gag goes right back on, understand." It wasn't a question. From the frost lacing the deep voice Flax figured the bounty hunter looked frozen.

She glared at the redhead, searched then nodded. The moment the gag was removed she spoke, "I want food and water, now, bounty hunter."

"Really?" Hunter glanced at him, cold amusement in his glacial eyes. "Well, by all means, drink." He held the water skin for her, allowed her a taste then took it away.

"I'm still thirsty." Dextera informed Hunter haughtily, "Release me, and give me that skin…"

"No." The bounty hunter refused flatly.

Dextera drew a deep breath; let it out like she was striving to maintain her composure and her patience. Which wasn't easy considering she was still trussed up. "The Kylonian authorities don't tolerate…"

"I won't be turning you over to a Kylonian garrison," Hunter informed her coolly.

Her jaw tightened, she shifted her shoulders, "I'm hungry and thirsty. Even the Byrynthian authorities…"

"I'm not wasting any of my provisions on a corpse."

Dextera swallowed hard, "You think for one moment Dehegra will allow you to treat her priestess in such a manner? Release me."

Hunter laughed quietly and it almost gave Flax a chill. Dextera shivered. "Your goddess is all ready allowing me to treat you however I choose. You're in no position to threaten me. I'm not feeding you, get used to the idea. I won't waste the provisions. Besides, I don't want you throwing up all over later on."

She opened her mouth to speak then changed her mind, eyes widening. A touch of real fear stole into her features.

"It's sinking in, isn't it, Dextera. You're in deep shit, here. You think about what you do to your sacrifices. Now, think about this, I'm willing to do the same to you, only I'll pour your blood out on the ground."

"I won't tell you anything..." she snarled.

"You'll tell me everything I want to know. But not right now." Hunter laid the skin aside, gripped the leash and rose, jerking her to her feet. She wavered but he steadied her, turned her around and pushed her against the rough stone wall. Flax heard her suck air in through her teeth and guessed that it hurt. "Don't fight me. If you do, I'll make you regret it for every second of what remains of your life." He put the hood over her head, tightened the laces. "Don't move. I'll be right back."

"Damn you..." Dextera snarled.

"Don't piss me off, Dextera. Get me angry enough and I might just get out my favorite skinning knife," Hunter growled in return.

Turning, the redhead went to the bunk, dropped to one knee and reached underneath. He pulled out a long low box, opened it. Flax looked on curiously, working his way through the hearty meal he'd been given. After a moment Hunter closed the box, pushed it back in its place, rose. Glacial eyes met his as the redhead turned and a smile crossed the cold features. Hunter saw his curiosity and showed him what he held, put a finger to his lips for silence.

He nodded, swallowing the mouthful he had, eyes widening slightly. It was some kind of shackle but Flax didn't think he'd ever seen its like. It seemed to be two metal rods, one sliding inside the other. It also appeared that it could be fixed at a just about any length between three to six feet by means of a pin through the rods. At each end there was a two pronged, curved fork that resembled the two outside prongs of a trident. A thick leather cuff was riveted inside the fork and appeared to adjust to fit almost anyone. His brows knit; *I'd wager it'd even accommodate my wrists... Or ankles... shit... but... he's not my enemy... If he wanted to, he'd've bound me up tight last night while I was out...* Flax popped a piece of dried apple in his mouth, chewed, watched thoughtfully as the bounty hunter returned to Dextera. Leaning the rod against the stone next to her, Hunter removed the binding from her upper arms, then her thighs. "Fight me and I'll beat you and gag you. Got it," Hunter demanded.

"Yeah," Dextera grunted as best she could hooded and leaning with her face pressed against the rock.

Slowly, smoothly, Hunter crouched, watching his prisoner closely. Flax watched her too, if she was going to try anything, now was the time. Deftly, the redhead released the clasp between her ankles without looking at what he was doing. With equal dexterity he removed the cuffs, watching her warily, almost expectantly.

There's a tenseness to her shoulders, back...

The moment the cuffs were off she kicked blindly at the redhead. Hunter caught her ankle, rose so fast Flax was sure he must have missed something. Holding her ankle, he lifted her leg high, foot near her rump. A strong hand grasped one cuffed wrist and Hunter slammed her into the wall. She grunted, cursed under her breath, what there was of it. Flax could tell she was struggling but the Hunter had her pinned and was holding her with unsettling ease.

"Ah, Dextera, didn't we already have this conversation?" the bounty hunter growled near her ear.

"By Dehegra, I swear…"

"You're goddess isn't listening." For good measure he pulled her off the wall and shoved her back against it. Flax heard the air pushed out of her. He heard a feral snarl, akin to an angry wolf and realized it was Hunter. "Ware, bitch. You're makin' me angry. I'm thinkin' of that skinnin' knife. Careful you don't make me forget why I want you alive and relatively undamaged."

Her ankle was released. Before she could put a foot down, Hunter released the locking clasp between her wrists. She started to struggle again and Flax rose. Dextera was strong lady, a formidable warrior and she was taller than the redhead. Her strength, size didn't matter. Hunter gripped her wrists and forced her arms over her head. Her arms shook with the strain of resisting him to no avail. Without looking, Hunter found the ring in the stone ceiling above her head. He threaded the clasp through it and fastened her wrists together again. The whole operation seemed effortless on the bounty hunter's part.

Abruptly, Hunter stepped back. Dextera twisted, kicked, cursed and fought but she was secured. There was no way she could pull the bolts from the stone ceiling. Crouching, the redhead came up with a long leather binding strap. Coolly, he wrapped it around his hand. A loud crack and a sharp intake of breath split the silence in the stone chamber. The redhead cast him a glance, searching, delving into his eyes, reading his features. Are you going to interfere, lad? He could almost hear the question. *Hell, no,* he thought and Hunter read it on him.   Flax dropped to one knee, went back to devouring his meal. The slight hint of a frosty smile and Hunter turned back to his prisoner. She cursed when he struck her again, then again. She twisted, fought, cursed. Despite it all, the bounty hunter striped her back and shoulders, breasts and belly with chilling efficiency. Finally she subsided, stood shaking with strain and indignation.

"You bastard, Dehegra will punish you..."

"Shut up," the bounty hunter growled frostily. "When I want you to talk I'll tell you. Got it," it was a demand not a question.

Muscles tightened in Dextera's back, shoulders shifted slightly.

"Nod if you understand."

Goddess, she's a stubborn one... Can't believe how stubborn... Flax looked down at his meal, tried not to laugh. It wasn't really funny. She must have nodded.

"Good. Now we're getting somewhere."

Dextera nodded hesitantly keeping her chin up, trying to appear collected. Still no easy task, she didn't even have a shirt, just her breeches and he'd wager Hunter wouldn't let her keep them much longer. In fact he'd wager she had to piss at the very least.

Wonder how he'll handle that... Wager however he does it will be damn humiliating for her... Do I care? Not really... I want to stop the sacrifice too, probably as badly as he does...

"Now, I'm going to secure your ankles and you're not going to fight me. Do it and I'll whip you. Understand."

Dextera nodded. Her body was streaked with sweat, striped by the strap, and trembling with indignation. He could read it.

She should be scared but she isn't... She's furious and maybe a little crazy if ya ask me... Aren't all fanatics a little crazy, anyways?

Retrieving the rod that Dextera had knocked over in her struggles, Hunter grasped one ankle and she kicked him with the other foot. A low growl reached him and then he heard her gasp in pain. Her ankle was locked in the cuff while she struggled to kick Hunter. He stayed so close to her that it was nearly impossible for her to get a good shot in but a couple sounded rather solid. It didn't matter. Hunter caught her other ankle, forced it into the cuff and locked it. Then he roughly slid the rods out to their longest point and pinned them in place. Dextera groaned, twisted. Her legs were spread wide, arms stretched taunt above her head. She looked really uncomfortable. And still she tried to struggle. Hunter held the rod easily and pushed back the single fur she'd been laying on. There was a ring in the floor and Hunter bound the rod to it. Rising, the redhead drew a knife, cast a glance his way again. Flax rose, eyes narrowing. Hunter offered him that slight, frosty smile then held up a hand, a gesture for him to wait.

Flax shrugged.

Turning back to his prisoner, Hunter cut the breeches from her and tossed them toward the cleft in the rocks that served as a door.

"Oh, you bastard..."

"I told you to shut up," the bounty hunter growled. Wrapping his arm and the hand that gripped the knife around her, he held her tightly to him. "Go ahead,

Dextera keep fightin' me. Really piss me off. Come on, don't ya wanna fight me? C'mon, squirm against me, get me all fired up."

Oh shit… If he… Flax shifted almost took a step towards them. Hunter heard him, held up his free hand, another gesture for him to wait.

Meanwhile the bounty hunter continued to snarl in her ear. "Then I'll fuck your ass like you're some pretty little slave in a tavern. Flax'll take his turn too." The redhead turned, met his gaze over one powerful shoulder. *Just wait, lad.* He could read the request… or order, in the glacial gaze. "He's getting' hot just watchin' us right now. Wonder what he's thinkin'. Goddess, he's big, but so am I, we'll sunder you in half, bitch, really ream you out."

Flax heard a whimper. Dextera, it had to be. "Please?" she gasped and her voice shook.

"Don't you wanna fight me anymore, Dextera?" The bounty hunter growled, moved against her. "C'mon fight."

"No… I won't… just please…"

A low laugh rose from the redhead's chest and Flax took that step. The glacial gaze met his again and the bounty hunter slowly drew away from her. He did it as if it was what he'd been meaning to do, like it was time. Definitely not like he was doing it because he thought Flax might interfere if he didn't.

The strap cracked, struck her across the thighs, back, rump just that fast. She flinched, tensed, gasped but otherwise didn't move. Of course, she really couldn't anymore. Coolly, efficiently, he striped her from her shoulders all the way down her legs to her calves. Abruptly, the bounty hunter stopped. Dextera was trembling, slicked with sweat, striped with welts. Watching her closely, the hunter crouched; found the gag without looking. "Fetch me a cup, lad. There's a couple tin ones inside the pot on the mantle."

For just a moment, he considered then shrugged and complied. When he arrived at Hunter's side he offered the redhead the cup. A slight smile touched the hard features.

"Fill it with water for me." The glacial eyes met his gaze for a heartbeat. "I'll wager my prisoner is thirsty."

"Okay," Flax crouched, complied then stopped the skin and rose. He was about to loosen the hood to give Dextera a drink when the bounty hunter produced a metal tube from somewhere. Deftly removing the lid, the hunter tapped some silently into the water. The lid was replaced and the vile disappeared while he swirled the water around until the powder dissolved.

The bounty hunter caught his wrist lightly, met his gaze and took the cup, trading it for the strap that had served as a whip. "Watch her, lad. She makes one move, feel free to remind her to behave."

"No problem," he agreed. Flax moved so Hunter could pass between him and Dextera and so he'd have a cleaner shot at her back if the need arose. She stiffened. Now she was afraid. Not necessarily of him and his makeshift whip though. She was afraid of what the bounty hunter told her he'd do if she wanted to fight some more. Correction, what he threatened we'd do. Well, I know what I won't stand aside for now.

Standing between Dextera and the wall, the bounty hunter loosened the laces on the hood, pushed it up just far enough that he could give Dextera the cup of water. She drank it thirstily, downed every drop. Flax wondered what she'd just been given, besides water.

Hunter dropped the empty cup, caught her jaw. With a deft squeeze he forced her jaws open whether she was resisting him or not. The redhead pushed the gag in place and fastened it. The hood was tugged down, the laces tightened. "No more trouble with you, Dextera, my patience isn't limitless."

She grunted, nodded.

"One more thing," Hunter moved to her side, near her shoulder, "You piss or shit on my floor and you'll be sorry. Think I'm nasty now, try it, and I'll show you nasty."

She shook her head like that would be last thing she'd even think of trying.

The glacial eyes met his, totally unreadable. "Don't be disappointed, lad. Maybe she'll decide to fight us later."

He blinked with shock until Hunter winked. Then he couldn't come up with a reply so he just grunted. Gathering up the cup, ankle cuffs, binding straps, Hunter even took the one he was still holding. Flax watched as the bounty hunter returned them all to their places. Then the clothing was replaced on top of the restraints. A shirt with long sleeves that matched Hunter's breeches, a scarf like strip of cloth and a slave-whip were left on the bunk. The red-head scooped up the clothes and whip. The slave-whip was laid on the floor near Dextera and Hunter moved toward the passage outside, beckoned. With a glance to Dextera he followed.

Three

The passage was narrow but he navigated through it easily... well, easier than he and the bounty hunter had together the night before. He blinked at the brightness of the sun in the rocky gully. It was almost directly overhead; he figured it to be around the eleventh hour. His eyes adjusted quickly, coming to rest on Hunter, leaning casually against a boulder across the gully some fifteen yards away. The redhead was in the act of removing his harness. Glacial eyes met his, serious now, rather than frozen, like he'd been inside with Dextera.

So, was he playing a part again? Maybe... or is he playing one now for me?

He was just about to say something when Hunter overrode him. "Keep your voice down, lad, she's not deaf." It was cool, even and low enough Dextera probably hadn't heard.

Drawing a deep breath, he crossed the grotto to the bounty hunter, "What the Hell... I mean... shit..." Raking a hand through his hair, he looked away, tried to gather his thoughts. The bounty hunter took off his bracers. *Could be he was just trying to scare her. She wasn't really afraid, not till he said... all that. So maybe... hopefully it was all part of the act. Or just maybe... he did say he's bi... means he likes it with ladies and males... but rape? That's something totally different... Goddess, gimme strength...*

"Flax," Hunter's quiet address brought his gaze back to the redhead. "Do you believe I'm a warrior of my word?"

Raking his hand through his unbound mane again, he looked across the grotto to the narrow cave entrance. *Do I? Would someone who wasn't, who didn't take their own word seriously... ask about how I take mine? If he were that unscrupulous he probably wouldn't have released me... Hell, if he was like that he wouldn't have tried to help me last night... and he wouldn't be on this hunt... Nor would he ask this of me now...* He nodded, met the glacial eyes, "Yeah, I believe you are."

A slight smile, "I swear to you, on Sheposha's Bow, I have **never** raped anyone, nor will I ever."

For a moment he studied the redhead's features, "Okay. Then all that was... to scare her?"

The bounty hunter nodded, laying his bracers aside. "I don't have much time and I had to get to her as fast as possible. I don't care what kind of tales she tells. That's inconsequential." Sighing quietly, he slipped the shirt on, "Look, lad, if you want no hand in this you can walk away." The plaited mane was left inside the shirt for the moment.

Flax cracked a half smile, "I don't recall ya tellin' me I'm in."

The glacial eyes met his, mildly amused. The left bracer went on, catching the sleeve; Hunter fastened it. "I haven't really decided yet."

He shrugged, looked down the grotto. The horses were hobbled and nibbling on some leafy bushes. "Knowing what you know... or what you told me, would you?"

The right bracer slipped into place to be fastened around forearm, sleeve. Hunter shrugged, "No, but you're not me." The glacial eyes met his again, searched. "You really want to help?"

"Yeah," he answered simply, folding brawny arms across his powerful chest.

The bounty hunter slung the scarf-like thing around his shoulders. "I'm not planning to harm her, not as long as there's no escape attempts or..."

"Kicking?" he provided with a crooked smile.

Hunter grinned, "Kicking, punching, elbowing, you get the idea and absolutely no spitting. Goddess, I hate that."

Flax wrinkled up his nose, "Yuk, I would too."

"Wager you would, it's disgusting." The black and gray harness was on and fastened faster than Flax had ever seen anyone manage. "At any rate I won't have to harm her. I gave her the same drug she slipped you last night minus the sedative. She won't be able to hide anything from us in a few hours." He produced the vial, rolled it between callused thumb and fingers. "If you really want to help me stop these murders will you do as I say for the next... oh, say forty-eight to seventy-two hours?"

He watched the bounty hunter deftly roll the vial in his hand for a heartbeat, "Like you're my captain?" Flax met the glacial gaze.

The bounty hunter shrugged, "Never been a soldier or a constable but... yeah, Flax, I guess, like I'm your supreme commander. I can use the assistance but I don't have time to fight with you. Understand?" This time, for him, it was a question.

"Answer a few questions before I agree?"

"Sure," the redhead leaned back comfortably on the rock, resting one foot on it. "Wouldn't want you to go into anything blindfolded."

His crooked smile flashed at the jest. "Will you explain things to me, when you get the chance, or when it's over?"

Red brows knit, "When I get the chance, sure." There was a seriousness to Hunter's expression that made Flax wonder what the bounty hunter was thinking. For the moment he let it go.

"You think you might be asking me to do things that conflict with my... honor?" A half smile played at his lips, tilted his mustache a little.

"Yeah, maybe. You're going to have to trust me. I know; you don't even know who I am." For a moment Hunter looked at the vial in his hands, brows knit like he was thinking then the glacial eyes lifted to his. "You'll have to take my word for it that I'm a bounty hunter, a damn good one. I know the laws in the northern provinces and for what I want to do, right now, there's no other way. For the most part, everything I'll do is justified and won't land either of us in a lock-up in Byrynthia or Thalusia but Kylonian authorities are a different matter. This'll definitely get you in trouble with them, no doubt, unless somehow we keep your identity secret and it's too late for that, Dextera knows your name. Of course there are ways around that, if I work it right. Still, she'll believe what she wants to believe no matter what we tell her. As to what she overhears... That'll depend. So far, you're a damn good actor for someone so blatantly honest."

He grinned crookedly, smoothed his beard, "Thanks, I think."

"Oh, that was definitely a compliment, lad." A broad grin lit the redhead's features. It was friendly, amused, not sexual and for that he was thankful. Hunter offered him the vial, "You with me?"

He accepted hesitantly, "I got a couple more yet."

"Okay." Hunter tied the Cyrcanian style shirt; it covered his broad chest concealing the red hair that spread from the center completely.

"What would I be doin' with this?" he held up the vial.

"Giving Dextera a capful in a cup of water every hour or so while I'm gone," Hunter answered like it made perfect sense.

Flax nodded, "Gone where?"

A cool rueful smile crossed the bounty hunter's features. "Into town. I'm going to see if I can find my own answers. I won't be gone long. Three hours at the most."

Three hours, alone here... No, not alone, with Dextera. He drew a deep breath, sighed, raked his hand through his hair. "So what do I do with your prisoner while you're gone? Besides give her this, I mean."

"You know you play with your hair when you're nervous? You might want to learn to control that." The redhead grinned when Flax looked at him. "As for

Dextera, don't talk to her or touch her with your hands. I don't want her to know who's watching her. I know you can walk lightly, be as quiet as you can, at least inside with her. Prod her with the whip handle; give her a few swats if she makes a sound. Don't let her sleep. Give her water with a dose of that drug every hour. And don't let her know you're doing it." The glacial eyes studied him, mild amusement in them, "Feel free to search my pack and my other things, just don't leave a mess."

His eyes widened and he felt a spark of indignation, "I wouldn't..."

"Why not? I would. Hell, I already did. Don't worry; your pack and saddlebags are in order. And I'm not a thief."

His arms and shoulders tightened, jaw clenched and he stared down the grotto after the horses, "What else did ya do while I was out?"

"I re-shod your horse. Brushed her and fed her. Obviously, I hobbled her and let her loose with mine." The bounty hunter offered him a slight smile when he met the glacial eyes. "Let's see, I cleaned and sharpened your weapons. Except for what you've got on you now. They didn't need much attention though; you take good care of them. That's about it."

He sort of grunted unsure how to take all of it. It seemed an invasion of his privacy yet... Then something occurred to him, "Did you search me?"

"Yeah. I swear on Sheposha's Bow I did not take liberties."

"Goddess," he growled under his breath.

"Flax," a strong hand gripped his crossed forearms. "I had to know that you're what you appear to be. I don't trust anyone implicitly; remember that. I trust you at my back, I trust you as far as I can but not implicitly, understand?"

Searching the hard features, glacial eyes, he considered a moment. *I could just walk away, yet... four maybe five young male's lives hang in the balance... If I can help, I want to... And he is being honest with me, as honest as he can be... And I am so curious. If I don't stick around I'll wonder about this for the rest of my days...* "Oh Hell, I agree, commander. I might even learn somethin'."

"That you might."

"There is just one more thing?"

A red brow lifted inquisitively, "Yeah?"

"What do I do? She's gonna have to..."

Laughing quietly, the bounty hunter straightened, "I'll handle it right now."

It didn't take long. The bounty hunter let her arms down only to fasten the cuffs behind her back. A strap was looped around her stomach, tied tightly to the clasp between the cuffs. The ankle restraint was exchanged for conventional leather cuffs with a chain of about eight inches between them. Using the leash Hunter led her through the narrow entrance with him following. It wouldn't do to have her crack her skull inadvertently. Once outside the bounty hunter slung her over his shoulder and took her some distance down the ravine. Then he let her do her business and washed her off. Bringing her back to the cave, Hunter secured her like before, rod like shackle and all. Through the entire proceedings she was tractable, co-operative. The only words the bounty hunter spoke to her were short, concise commands.

Once she was secured again Hunter beckoned him outside. Emerging from the cave entrance the redhead lifted the scarf-like thing over his head like a hood then wrapped it around to conceal his features to the eyes. He led Flax away from the entrance. "Need anything in town? Provisions, anything?" They strode leisurely in the direction of the horses.

"Won't it look funny if you buy another load of provisions?" His brows knit curiously.

"I didn't buy provisions last night, Rufus did." A single red brow lifted and he'd wager the bounty hunter was grinning.

"Right," he laughed, "probably provisions then. I eat like a horse."

Hunter snorted, "More like a tolak bull, lad, but I understand. You're growing." Smoothly, with dangerous grace, the bounty hunter loosened his swords in their sheaths. Then the hunter stopped, turned to him as he halted too. Glacial eyes moved over him, especially his hair. Callused fingers lightly gripped the beads in two of his slender braids. "These make a lot of noise, can you lose them, for the time being?"

"No problem," he agreed.

"If by chance I'm not back in six hours, get the Hell out of here. Go to Byrynthian authorities. The Garrison Commander in Byruna, Merissa, she'll listen. Tell her... Tymane sent you. Take Dextera with you, she'll be your proof."

He swallowed hard, "I can't..."

"Leave me? I can take care of myself, and you agreed to do as I say, Flax. Repeat it back to me." The glacial eyes were hard, cold now, unreadable.

His jaw clenched, "If you're not back in six hours I take Dextera and go to Byruna garrison, talk to Commander Merissa. I tell her Tymane sent me."

The bounty hunter nodded, "Good, you learn fast. Later." Hunter turned, strode down the grotto. When he passed the horses he just melted out of sight.

Flax swallowed hard, his throat felt tight and his stomach clenched on the meal he'd recently ingested. "Shit." Turning, he made his way back toward the cave entrance to lean against the rock Hunter had vacated. Glancing down the gully, he looked after the bounty hunter. *Well, lad,* he told himself, *what did you expect? They're planning to sacrifice five young males to their goddess, after all... This isn't a game and they're not just a bunch of thieves or a mistress and her unregistered string of fur-warmers for hire... They'll kill him if they catch him, or try to at least... They could get him arrested, imprisoned... They could use him in my place if they catch him... Oh, shit.* Raking a hand through his mane, he touched on a braid. *Okay, gotta get my shit together... I can do this... Even if I have to go to Byruna with Dextera as my prisoner, I can do this... I have to; I took on this responsibility I have to follow it through...*

Sighing heavily, he rose, raked a hand through his hair, then shook his head. *Maybe he's right; I should control that... Not always a good thing to let others know I'm nervous or thinkin' hard...* Flax took a moment to braid his hair Byrynthian style including his beaded braids.   His brows knit and he looked after the bounty hunter. *He left his hair concealed in his shirt... even made sure his chest was concealed. Would I recognize him if I passed him on the street?.. Maybe... He moves... I dunno... Like a hunting predator but then again I might not... I'd notice someone with their features concealed like that but... probably wouldn't know 'em.*

As quietly as he could, he went in the cave, retrieved his harness and slung it on. For a moment, he stared at the pack on the bunk, considered the box underneath. Then he knelt, pulled out the box. Inside he found clothes fit for a noble, trimmed in gold or silver, made of the finest cotton, silk or leather. Carefully feeling the clothing, he found there were weapons hidden in every garment in the box. There were two harnesses; one was trimmed in gold and back mail, the weapon hilts ornamented in gold wire and inlay. The other was reddish brown with well made but unadorned weapons.

He also found the revealing red leathers Hunter had worn as "Rufus" the night before. There was a slightly less revealing set of red leathers probably for "Rufus" as well and the ankle high red boots. There was a heavy pouch full of gold and silver when he peeked into it. There were also more binding straps, shackles, cuffs. He found a couple more hoods, gags, another slave whip. There were a few things he guessed were of a more intimate nature; he really didn't want to know their purpose.

A box with ink, quills, fine paper and more ordinary sheets was stashed in one corner of the storage box. Inside it he found three seals; one the Protectress', one looked like a noble's and a third he didn't recognize at all. It was a wolf's head, the lips peeled back to bare the fangs as if it were growling. For a few moments he studied it but nothing came to him. He'd never seen it before and he'd wager it was a real clue to the bounty hunter's identity. Replacing it and moving on he found another surgeon's kit like the one Hunter gave him, and two jars of fine powder. The sedative and the other drug the bounty hunter mentioned. The one he was to use on Dextera. Closing the box gently he pushed it back in its place.

His eyes lit on the pack and he wrestled his curiosity. It really wasn't right to search Hunter's pack... But, he'd sort of been given permission... and the bounty hunter did search his... Biting his lower lip, Flax quietly opened the pack. The clothes inside were mostly leather, butter soft. They were dyed in streaks or mottled patterns of grays, greens and browns. One green set looked like spring leaves, another like leaves in the fall. There was a set of dead black and gray. The shirt had a hood and veil that would cover the features to the eyes. There was a pair of black boots, padded so softly that they probably made no sound at all.

As with the clothing stashed in the box, everything in the pack felt like they had weapons and other things concealed all through them. *Wonder what he has on him...* He found the bounty hunter's provisions. He was well stocked, or would be alone. *With me around... definitely a good thing he's getting some...* In a discrete pocket inside the pack he found another pouch heavy with coin. He found an ivory pick, for all the curly hair, a razor and the other things most males tend to use on their beards and mustaches. There was a box with a cake of deer tallow soap inside it. More binding straps and cuffs, a hood, leather collar, and three leashes occupied the bottom of the pack.

Then he found a small black pack and after a moment of inspection decided it would attach to a harness at the small of the back. Inside was a coil of woven silk cord tied to a three-pronged grappling hook. The hook was wrapped in strips of leather. If it made any sound at all finding purchase it would be very little. No jewelry at all, nothing truly personal except the pick and maybe the soap. Absolutely nothing that would tell him precisely who the redhead was, only that he was a bounty hunter or a slaver. On the contrary there were no steel collars, no branding irons, things that would make it apparent he was a slaver. Flax replaced everything just as neatly as it had been feeling mildly guilty. When he heard a quiet sound he jumped and looked toward the entrance but Hunter wasn't standing there watching. *Shit... Dextera... almost forgot about her.*

Closing up Hunter's pack, he rose and strode softly over to her. Picking up the whip he prodded her in the side with the handle and she jumped, groaned. It had been about an hour so he gave her a cup of water with a cap full of the drug in it. Flax was very mindful of everything he did, careful not to touch her with his hands or in any way give an indication of precisely who was with her. He even paid attention to where his shadow would fall so she couldn't gauge his height by it. Replacing the gag, lowering the hood into place and tightening the laces, he stifled a sigh

He really shouldn't feel sorry for her. She was going to kill him, after all. His eyes drifted to the restraints, the ring overhead. *Wonder how deep those bolts are sunk in the stone. Wager I couldn't even pull 'em loose...* His gaze dropped to the welted body before him. *There isn't much skin left unmarked... He delivered quite a whipping with a single strap... He's a bastard. Should I help him? But stopping that sacrifice is the right thing to do... Whoa... hold on a moment...   How do I even know there's going to be one?..*

Placing the cup on the mantle, he went back outside. Flax seated himself on the rock across from the cave entrance turning that revelation over in his head. *What do I know? What things do I know to be fact, not what he told me? Well, I know she put something in my ale... Even five mugs of ale won't make me feel like that and I only had one and half at the most... I know she had a knife and she cut me... I'm pretty sure she was going to kill me... Had to be, what else was she planning to do with the knife?.. I know she wanted to bind me and she was telling me to comply... I know he stopped her... and helped me out of there... He sewed up my arm real nice... She didn't deny anything and she did say that Dehegra would punish him. He's got an air about him... like he's done this kind of thing before. He knows how to handle her... Seems honest but that means next to nothing... He's still hiding a lot from me. But is it anything I need to know?.. No, just things I want to know...*

He rose, took off his harness, stretched. *Think I'll train for a while, clear my head. Goddess, this is some serious shit and I really don't know for sure what's going on. Okay, for the most part, I believe Dextera was planning to abduct me and he stopped it. I believe she's my enemy and a criminal in some way. I believe he's a bounty hunter. And I believe he's bi...* Flax laughed to himself. *Guess I'll just wait and see... Perhaps this is what he meant by saying I shouldn't trust him implicitly either...*

Flax practiced the short-sword, long-sword. He moved through the forms smoothly, with grace and speed that belied his size. When around an hour had passed he took a break, stretched thoroughly then went inside to give Dextera a drink laced with the drug. As before he was very careful not to let her know who he was. When she started to ask him a question he simply ignored it, stuffed the gag back in her mouth. She groaned and he clenched his jaw, brows knitting. She was planning to sacrifice him to an unknown goddess on a blood stained altar he would not feel pity for her now.

Taking the skin outside with him, he took a long drink, dumped the rest over his face. He'd backtrack their trail to the spring from last night and fill it up. Scanning the gully, Flax took in the rocks, brush, noted the horses still down by the thick bushes they'd been nibbling. Now they were dozing in the afternoon shadows. Crossing to the handy boulder that served as a bench, he sat down, unbound his hair. With a quiet sigh he loosed his four temple braids, removed the beads from them. Still, the bounty hunter was right, they did make noise... not a lotta like Hunter said but enough to tell an enemy that someone was there. It'd definitely tell Dextera who was looking after her. For a moment he looked at them laying in his broad palm then closed his fist to scatter them across the gully floor. Then he stopped himself almost in mid toss. If they were scattered across the rocks someone like Hunter might notice them... they might even find Hunter's camp... And the bounty hunter probably wouldn't like it if he did it. *Like I care that much... Well, I still want him to take me with him when he frees their sacrifices... I really don't wanna piss him off over such trivial bullshit... So what do I do with them?..* He rose, intending to put them in his saddlebags when he realized he didn't know where his tack was.

After a rather extensive search of the rocky gully he found the cave where the horses had been hidden. His tack was inside with Hunter's setting across a knurled branch shoved in a crevice of the rock. It stuck out like a saddle rack in a tack room and was just right for the saddles to rest over. The bridles and saddlebags were with them and he tucked his beads into a pouch inside his. Hunter must have forked out the cave along with everything else he'd done that morning while Flax slept. He looked over the bounty hunter's tack. There was a crossbow in a scabbard mounted on the saddle.

The tack was well cared for, oiled and clean. For that matter so was his.

After a brief consideration he searched the bounty hunter's saddlebags. All he found was provisions for the horses, leather cleaner, a horse brush, hoof-pick, tools used to trim and shoe and two more sets of shoes. There was another pouch of coin. Copper and sliver glinted at him when he took a look inside. With a quiet sigh he went outside, stretched and went to pick up the water-skin. He wanted to fill it before the bounty hunter returned.

Wandering leisurely down the gully, past the horses he absently scanned the ground, noted traces of their tracks from the night before, the horse's wanderings... traces of the bounty hunter's recent passage then... the faint trail just disappeared. *By Sheposha...* Flax stopped, went back and tried again. He even searched in widening circles for a few minutes and found nothing.   *Wonder if he'd teach me... Could I do what he does? I dunno... maybe... It'd be a far cry from being a palace guard for the rest of my life or worse yet the consort of some high and mighty noble lady... It's definitely something to think about... if he'd even take me as an apprentice...* He settled on the trail the two of them had made the previous evening with Dextera and the horses. Still it was faint, he'd wager few warriors could track it.

He found the spring, crouched on one knee to fill the water-skin. Stopping it up he cupped his hands and drank deeply. Abruptly he sensed... he wasn't sure, maybe... that he was being watched. Splashing a little like he was still drinking, he listened, strained his ears and heard... birds, insects... nothing out of the ordinary. Still, he felt it...*Hell, I'm gonna feel really silly if no one's around but then again no one'll see if no one's there...*

He dove to the side, rolled upright, drawing his long-sword and whirling. Feline eyes narrowed, scanned the rocks, brush, up and down the gully, along the rim. At the same time he strained his ears, listening for any sound... And the feeling that he was being watched intensified. His guts tightened, blood quickened. His crooked smile curled his lip, cocked his mustache yet it was cold, dangerous. Then suddenly there was movement, a flurry of gray, brown... The redhead rose from amongst an outcropping along the rim with a flourish of that scarf-like strip of cloth that had concealed his features.

Flax drew a deep breath; relaxed his stance yet retained his sword. He was about to call to the redhead when Hunter shook his head, put two fingers to his own lips. He chuckled quietly to himself, watched Hunter approach. Then his brows knit when he noticed a bundle of canvas peeking out from behind Hunter's shoulder. It was narrow, long and slung across his chest like a baldric. There was another bundle, slung from his harness but that looked like the provisions. In moments the redhead arrived at his side. "Hey," he greeted Hunter, slid his sword into its sheath.

"Hey, Flax." The redhead offered him a grin, "What'd you hear?"

"Honestly, nothing." He bit his lip, shrugged, "I just felt like I was being watched."

Hunter nodded thoughtfully, "Grab the water-skin. Let's get back to camp."

He complied, slung the skin on his shoulder, met the bounty hunter's gaze and saw a hint of amusement.

"You've been tending our prisoner?" Hunter asked as they strode down the gully.

"Yeah. I was careful not to let her know who I am."

"Good, she ought to be just about ready to talk."

They traversed the open grassland stealthily then dipped into the gully where hunter's camp was located. He didn't ask about the bundle or about what the bounty hunter may have found out. The redhead strode directly to the cave, slipped inside. He followed curiously and observed from the entrance. Hunter laid the bundle of provisions on the little hearth then approached his prisoner.

Standing just behind Dextera's shoulder the bounty hunter spoke low near her ear. "Dextera, you want to tell us where your altar is. You want to tell us everything you know. Even if it's just to spite us, you want to tell us, show us how weak and ineffectual two mere males are against you and your goddess."

Dextera grunted a negative, shook her head like she was trying to clear it.

"Dextera," Hunter spoke to her almost in a whisper, "you want to tell us so your goddess can show us how powerful she is. So we can be sacrificed to her as we were meant to be."

Flax got a chill. Clenching his jaw, he shrugged it off. It was just to get her to talk... But... it could happen...

"She's too powerful to be challenged by two mere males, Dextera. What harm is there in telling us all about it? Your altar, the ceremony, when and where, tell us everything, there's no harm in it. You'll just be delivering us up to her, practically on a silver platter."

She sort of wavered, head falling forward.

"You're thirsty, Dextera, very thirsty," Hunter told her in that near whisper. The bounty hunter glanced at him and he took the hint. Retrieving the tin cup he filled it with water, swirled the powder in.

Hunter accepted it from him, gave it to Dextera. When he lowered the empty cup he caught her jaw. "Anything to say, Dextera?" he growled gruffly in a more normal tone of voice.

She sneered at him even with half her face covered by the hood, "Dehegra is too powerful to be threatened by the likes of you. If you try to stop the ceremony you will be captured and added to the sacrifice. You cannot possibly hope to challenge Her."

"I aim to try." Hunter folded his arms; a slight smile tilted his mustache.

"You and your pretty blond pup will run to Her altar, offer up your blood willingly when you see her power."

"Then by all means, I must know where to go and when. How many priestesses will be there to greet me and how will the ceremony be carried out." Hunter cast him a glance. The blue eyes were ice cold, frozen, features frosty.

"Tomorrow night... two hours before the climax of the blood moon... The sacrifices are delivered to the altar chamber... They are bound upon their sacrificial beds... the priestesses... make use of them... they are taken... for the glory of Dehegra. She will arrive in flames to watch, then to take them each herself. When she is through with them their lips are sewn shut so they can make no more offensive noise. Their lovely hair is taken, offered on the altar... mounted on Dehegra's altar. Then their wrists are cut; the blood drains into crystal goblets for the goddess... their throats follow... When they are empty the goddess receives their blood, she drinks, bathes in it... Fire lights the chamber and she is appeased..."

Hunter's jaw was tight, the muscles worked. Flax could see the bounty hunter's features were frozen. In that moment he'd wager everything he owned that Hunter was furious.

"Where's the altar?" For all the anger read in the frozen features the bounty hunter's voice was cool, detached.

She described a supposedly closed temple to Werdeka in a disreputable section of town.

Hunter nodded slightly, "And the sacrifices, where are they kept, Dextera?"

Dextera laughed.

The bounty hunter gripped the leash near the collar, tugged firmly. "Where are they held, Dextera? Tell us... Tell us so we can be captured all the quicker."

"I am one," she gasped for breath, swallowing her mirth, "of Dehegra's Huntresses. I provide chosen for two of the other priestesses. We all..." She chuckled quietly, "We keep our sacrifices at places known only to us."

"To whom? The priestesses." Hunter growled.

"Of course," she giggled, "we five priestesses. We are honored of Dehegra, we are privileged with the use of our chosen," she sneered haughtily.

Flax saw Hunter's jaw tighten. The powerful arms and shoulders flexed with the desire to strike her. The redhead seemed to think for a moment.

"Give me the names of the other priestesses, tell me where they live. Tell me how many followers of Dehegra will be present to witness the ceremony. Will the sacrifices be drugged? Talk Dextera, tell me everything."

She did. Merlina lived in an estate in a reputable district; she was a respected and wealthy merchantess. Herlia was a captain of the town constabulary. She had quarters at the lock up next to the council hall. Falla appeared to be an acolyte in training to Werdeka. She'd found them the unused temple for their ceremonies three years ago to please Dehegra of course. She resided in the acolyte's hall next to the legitimate temple grounds. Veda was an influential council member with a fine estate two miles northeast of town. According to Dextera her apprentice or acolyte would most likely be called upon to take her place in the ceremony and provide a suitable sacrifice. The young lady was called Lavia and she was from a merchant family who had ties to the Kylonian royal house. Lavia had quarters in a rooming house. Dextera thought that she'd either have her sacrifice in her rooms or at the temple. There would be some fifty followers allowed to witness the ceremony. The sacrifices weren't drugged, that would pollute the blood and displease the goddess. Listening to it confirmed everything Hunter had told him and reaffirmed his conviction to help if he could. If the bounty hunter allowed him to, that was. After going over everything again three times, Hunter gagged her. He replaced the rod like ankle shackle with conventional leather and steel cuffs. They were connected by ten inches of thick serpentine chain threaded through the ring in the floor.

Flax looked on, assisting when Hunter gestured to him. Then he followed the bounty hunter outside. The redhead stalked toward the dozing horses then turned with a snarled curse.

"It's not bad enough they abduct these young males, murder them, they have to rape them as well. By the Goddess Rathitara's Throne, Crown and Scepter, by Sheposha's Bow, I will stop this slaughter. No more youths die for Dehegra's glory." The glacial eyes met his gaze. Behind the frozen surface a volcano raged. The bounty hunter's blue eyes blazed with cold dangerous fires.

Flax almost ran a hand over his braided mane but caught himself, started toward the bounty hunter.

The redhead saw his aborted gesture, smiled slightly but the eyes didn't change.

"You okay?" he asked. It was lame but it was the only thing he could think of to say at the moment.

The redhead snorted, "I'm sick to my stomach with rage, lad. I don't think I've been this furious in four years." Drawing a deep breath, Hunter rolled his shoulders. "Damn her, damn them all," it was a low growl, like a wolf bearing it's fangs.

"Wager they're already damned," Flax grinned when the bounty hunter looked at him. "Sides, there's nothing we can do right now, is there?"

Some of the ice thawed, fires dissipated. "No, not really. It'd take days to find out where every sacrifice is being held and get them out. Freeing one and killing the priestess would alert the others then I wouldn't find anything until it was too late. Even if I had the time I doubt I'd be able to find and free them all. The ceremony will go on, for now it's going to be held at the desecrated temple. I found that out for myself."

"Nice of Dextera to confirm it." Flax put in. He received a slight smile for his trouble.

"There's a couple ways in," the red brows knit. Now the bounty hunter looked thoughtful, collected.

"Fifty's a hell of a number for one sword," Flax shook his head solemnly when the bounty hunter looked at him again.

"Fifty-seven at the ceremony, lad, counting Dehegra and her priestesses. Then there's two acolytes on the entrances, the priestesses have assistants or apprentices, that makes sixty-five all together. I thought you said you could add." That single red brow lifted again, amusement laced the cool features.

"I wanted to see if you could."

"How are you with a crossbow?" Hunter asked unexpectedly.

For a moment, he was speechless, then he gathered his thoughts. "Good enough to take what I'm aiming at."

Hunter nodded thoughtfully, studied the boulders before them, the layers of rock exposed in the gully's walls.

Flax's eyes settled on the baldric style bundle. It was heavy canvas, made like a tube with a flap and ties that wrapped around the top. He was so curious it was driving him to distraction. "All right, I can't stand it any longer."

A red brow lifted, glacial eyes met his, mildly inquisitive.

"What's in the fuckin' bundle?"

"See for yourself," the bounty hunter shed it, held it out.

He accepted giving Hunter a mildly suspicious look. The moment his hands encircled it his lips parted in astonishment. It felt like... a pair of swords maybe... Flax dropped to one knee, opened it, pushed the canvas down around a pair of eastern swords like Hunter's. They were heavy with longer than average hilts. He laid the bundle down, slid the short-sword from its sheath. He could wrap both fists around the hilt, *By the Goddess.* It felt good, closer to fitting him than anything had since he was fifteen and well over six feet tall. The hilt did fit, the diameter as well as the length.

"How's it feel?"

He looked up, met the bounty hunter's frosty gaze. "Great." He shifted his grip, gave it a practice swing, switched hands. The weight was good too, not perfect but better than any sword he'd owned in years.

"Try the long-sword," Hunter suggested.

He slid the short-sword back in its sheath, took the long-sword from the bundle sheath and all. Rising to his feet, Flax drew it. Hunter held out his hand for the sheath and Flax passed it to him. He dropped into a ready crouch, gripping the sword two fisted. *It fits, by the Goddess and Her Consort it fits... Almost, it's a little light but the hilt fits both my hands... and the weight isn't bad at all...* He wove it back and forth before him, moved through the forms almost forgetting he wasn't alone. After a few passes he straightened, slightly embarrassed. Biting his lip, Flax glanced at the bounty hunter. The redhead was watching the blade in his hands then abruptly tossed him the sheath. He caught it, slid the sword home reluctantly. He started to comment but couldn't think of anything to say. *What do you want for it? That's not really polite, neither is I won't roll in the furs with you even for these swords... What the hell do I say, what the hell does he want?*

"I got you a couple fancy ties for those braids of yours." Hunter crouched by the bundle, withdrew the short-sword and its sheath then reached to the bottom. He dug around for a moment then straightened with a pair of wide leather bands. They laced up with black leather stitched in silver and would tighten down to tie slender braids like the one's he'd taken out. Hunter tossed them to him and he caught them left-handed. "Figured it's the least I can do since I made you lose the beads."

Flax's brows knit, he studied them lying in his palm.

"Flax," Hunter's quiet call drew his attention to the bounty hunter. He met the glacial eyes, now calm, honest. "I don't expect you to sleep with me. Thought we settled that, lad."

"I wasn't..." he started, embarrassed for being so suspicious even though Hunter had told him not to trust anyone implicitly.

"Yeah, you were. Look at it this way, you can be friends with a lady, can't you?"

He considered for a moment, "Well, yeah, but..."

"Even a lady who said she finds you attractive? Or do you just not speak to her, or do you avoid her all together?"

"Yeah... I mean... no, I don't avoid her and I can be friends with her even if she thinks I'm..."

Hunter's brow lifted, waiting for him to finish his thought, that mild amusement written on the hard features.

He dropped his gaze to the ties in his hand, "Nice lookin'," he concluded with a shrug.

"Okay." Hunter started back towards the cave entrance, the handy bench like boulder. When he looked after the redhead Hunter removed his harness, lay it across the rock. "I look at it this way, you deserve some recompense for what Dextera put you through." The frosty eyes met his and he sort of nodded his agreement. "You're helping me, following my orders as if I were your commander, as a mercenary you deserve to be paid." The single red brow lifted and he nodded again. "Since I don't know if I can get any bounty at all for Dextera even from Merissa, I thought I'd pay you now." Hunter untied his shirt, slipped it off and tossed it across the boulder. "I do feel I owe you for making you take the beads out of your hair. Must have taken some serious time to thread them in and braid them like that and there's the original cost... I figure the ties balance that out."

"And the swords? They're... What? My pay?" He met the frosty eyes.

"Sure," Hunter slipped into his harness, fastened it quickly with practiced ease.

"Where'd you find... hilts that fit me?"

"I was lucky," the redhead shrugged. "They'll fasten at your hips if you like or on your back."

"I noticed." He picked up the empty canvas, rolled it up and secured it with the ties. He was confused and touched at the same time. *Like hell, you had those hilts made for me... Goddess, wonder what it cost, and I wonder if I really want to know...* "Thanks," he managed, rising with both swords in one hand, the canvas in the other.

"Welcome, Flax. There's one other thing," the bounty hunter offered him two slender steel... Flax wasn't sure whet they were. "Lock picks." Hunter explained, "You can practice on the shackle I used on you. It's tougher to pick than most any other so if you can open it you can get just about any lock. We'll hide them on you, no-one will get away with restraining you with something that locks. As for any binding leather, I'll wager you could break it."

Flax gave the bounty hunter a skeptical look, "You're not serious?"

"Oh, yes, I am. I'd put gold on it. I'm not sure you realize your own strength."

He nodded, accepted the lock picks thoughtfully, "Thanks again."

"Welcome, again." Hunter rolled his shoulders again, turned his head like he was trying to make his neck crack.

He could see the scars, the whip scars. They wrapped around the ribs, crossed over the upper shoulders... *Like he was tied hanging by his arms, like Dextera is... The knife scar is older, the marks from the whip cross over it... Damn...* He looked at the ground when Hunter glanced at him. "Spar with me?" he asked.

The bounty hunter laughed quietly, "Okay. I can always use the exercise. It'll have to be open hand, lad, we don't have any tojos."

"Fine by me," he shed his harness, brought it to lay with Hunter's carrying the new swords in their sheathes.

The redhead deftly unfastened his old swords from his harness, laid them aside. "You wear your swords right handed," he remarked taking the eastern short-sword and fastening it in place.

"So do you," Flax pointed out.

Hunter nodded, taking the long-sword, fixing it in place. "I'm ambidextrous though. I can wield any weapon with either hand and I can shoot a bow or crossbow just as well left-handed as right." He said it like it was simple truth rather than bragging, like he wasn't out to prove anything.

"Really?" he was impressed.

"You can do it too, lad." The bounty hunter met his gaze then strode to the center of the gully. "It just takes practice and focus."

He turned to face the redhead. Hunter was stretching, warming up. He was already warmed up but he stretched too, following along until the redhead bent from the waist and put his hands on the ground shoulder width apart. He watched as Hunter lifted both legs until his body was straight. The bounty hunter lowered himself slowly, arching his back so his face wouldn't touch the ground. He held it for a moment, then just as slowly straightened to walk over, stand up. A broad somewhat self-conscious grin flashed when the glacial eyes met his gaze.

"Feels good," Hunter shrugged, dropped into a ready crouch.

With a crooked grin he did too. "Looks pretty fancy too," Flax teased. He got only a cool smile for his trouble. When he feinted with a fist to the face, Hunter grasped his wrist, turned and stepped under his arm, a knee lightly banged into his side and then his lower back as the bounty hunter spun around him. He whirled, surprised at the speed and Hunter offered him a grin.

"C'mon, lad, you're quicker than that or you'd be dead."

Without warning, Flax aimed a kick at the bounty hunter's shoulder and he just wasn't there. The redhead landed a kick to his thigh that was hard enough to make every joint in his leg hurt. He grunted, grabbed the bounty hunter by one arm and the throat. Flax twisted the arm up behind the powerful back, let his arm slide around the bounty hunter's throat. Hunter turned with him, submitted to the grip on his arm. He lowered himself to one knee, dragging the redhead to his. A strong calloused hand sought his, pried his smallest finger loose and pulled, bending it back. Flax strove not to yelp but it hurt. Furthermore, it opened his hand, he didn't have a choice and his grip around the bounty hunter's throat slipped.

Instead of trying to pull away the redhead shoved back dumping him on his rump then his back on the stony gully floor. The bounty hunter rolled over, up his chest and belly to stand over him. A foot pinned his braid to the ground when he started to rise. He smiled ruefully, raised his hands as if surrendering then clamped onto Hunter's ankle. He pushed, rolled, kicked with both feet toward Hunter's jaw. He landed a glancing blow to arm and chest because the bounty hunter spun away but he was loose and rolled to his feet to take a kick in the side, the heel of an open hand under his ribs. Flax whirled with it, out of reach and met the glacial eyes.

The bounty hunter grinned, "You're good, Flax. Think fast, too, that's real good."

"Thanks," he grunted turning as the bounty hunter circled him. "You're damn strong for someone so fuckin' short."

Hunter laughed. From then on the sparring session became a lesson and he learned a lot the trainer at his mother's estate never taught him. Towards the end Hunter taught him a slow quiet exercise the lycani used to achieve focus. It was harder than it looked, keeping every muscle tight. Hunter helped him adjust his stance, stretch his flexibility to its limits. He followed and Hunter ran through it until he was no longer following behind. When he was a near perfect reflection of the bounty hunter they ran through it one last time. Slicked with sweat, he was breathing deeply; closer to being winded than he had been since he was twelve.

"Easy, lad, almost through." Hunter straightened slowly, with that predatory grace. He brought his hands before his chest in a rough circle. Drawing a deep breath, Hunter stretched towards the sky. Then he exhaled bringing his hands back to their original position. Flax followed, breathed deeply. He thought about his heart slowing down, his breathing being under his control and it came. Hunter heard him, "Good, Flax, get control." After a few more deep breaths Hunter turned to him, "Very well done. You're a fast learner."

He laughed, "Maybe you're just a good trainer."

Hunter offered him a smile, "Thank you. Now..." The bounty hunter rolled his shoulders, scratched his beard along his jaw, "I need a bath."

"The spring's a little small," Flax commented resting his hands on his hips.

"You went to the wrong spring, lad, but I appreciate the fact that you didn't stray too far from camp." Gesturing for him to wait the redhead disappeared into the cave. Half a heartbeat later he reappeared, "You want a change of clothes?"

"Pair a breeches," Flax shrugged, donning his harness. He wrapped his hands around the hilts just to feel how well they fit.

Hunter nodded, disappeared again. He came out with the box containing the soap, a pair of riding-leggins and a tong, and a pair of his breeches. "Ready?" The redhead took up his harness and slipped into it. It was fastened so quickly it didn't seem possible.

He started to nod then his eyes fell on the cave entrance, "What about... Dextera?"

"I think she'll wait around for us," Hunter grinned.

After stabling the horses back in their cave, feeding and watering them, Hunter led him down the gully in the opposite direction. It deepened, widened and when they'd gone nearly half a mile Flax could hear water babbling over rocks. Within another two hundred yards a creek came into view. It followed the curve of a shear cliff of red sandstone. The bank was all red sand and layers of sandstone. It got deep relatively quickly, dropping off to nearly ten feet at the base of the cliff. The creek seemed to issue from a crevasse further upstream and run along this shear face until it left the gully to fall some twelve feet into another. While he looked around, he shed his harness again, sat down in the sand to remove his boots.

"You're not going to get all Thyrian on me are you, Flax?" Hunter remarked. His harness already lay across a rock near the creek's edge and he was in the act of unbinding his hair.

"No, why?" he asked, trying to look as innocent as possible.

Hunter smiled, "Right. I get the soap first."

"Selfish bastard," Flax chuckled.

"Damn straight." The bounty hunter stepped out of his boots then dropped his breeches. He waded in to his knees then slid into the deeper water submerging. It didn't take them long to get washed. After a while the bounty hunter swam down stream a bit to climb out on a large flat rock. Lifting his mane from his shoulders, Hunter lay down on his back in the slanting sunlight. The long hair was spread across the rock. He splashed the bounty hunter and received only a quiet laugh in response. How the redhead could look comfortable laying on a rock beat the hell out of him. Flax swam up and down the deepest trench in the creek a few times then climbed up on the rock Hunter occupied.

"Not sleepin' are ya?" He wrung out his long hair on the bounty hunter's broad chest.

"You big fucker," Hunter rolled upright and shoved him off the rock.

He fell in causing a tremendous splash, recovered and rose to the surface grinning. Hunter was standing on the rock; arms folded, an amused smile cocking his mustache. A single red brow lifted and he laughed.

"I was dry."

Flax shrugged, "You'll get dry again."

"Yeah." Sighing, the bounty hunter offered him a hand.

His crooked smile cocked his mustache and mischief lit his eyes, "Should I trust you?"

"Generally or at this moment?" Hunter asked looking equally mischievous.

"Right this moment."

"Hell, yes, lad." Hunter grinned, "You can trust me to push your ass right off this rock again."

Four

"Find anything interesting, lad?" Amusement laced the redhead's voice.

Caught in the midst of reaching for another hunk of bread Flax almost jumped at the unexpected question, casting a quick glance to the redhead.

"When you searched my things," a single brow lifted inquisitively.

Swallowing the mouthful of thick venison soup the bounty hunter made, he shook his head, cursed, "Nothing that told me anything I don't already know."

After returning from the swim in the creek, Hunter had let Dextera down. He brought her outside, let her… take care of business then secured her again. This time he cuffed her ankles close together, cuffed her wrists before her then leashed her to the ring in the floor. Hunter told her he'd take the gag off if she'd remain silent. She nodded, then, when he did take it off, she started to complain about the fact he hadn't even given her a tang to wear. Hunter cleaned the gag with spirits warning her that he wouldn't hesitate to use it again. When she didn't stop the redhead strapped the gag back in place. Lighting a fire in the small fireplace, Hunter got the soup cooking. Then, taking a couple furs from his bedroll, he went outside, threw them on the ground, sat down cross-legged to sharpen his weapons. Asking what he could do the bounty hunter suggested he see to the horses, so he did. He cleaned out the makeshift stable again, watered and fed the horses. Then he brushed them down even though they'd already been brushed. When he returned to the bounty hunter's side he seated himself, cross-legged. Just in time too, dinner was done.

"Oh? And what is it you believe you already know?" Hunter tore a piece of bread, wiped out his bowl.

"That you're Byrynthian, from the north, probably the far north. You're older than me, maybe... seven, eight years?"

"Closer to ten," Hunter supplied, setting his bowl aside then taking up a mug of water. "Go on."

"You've got more than a few aliases going on, Rufus is one and whoever you were today when you went into town."

"That one's open to interpretation. For the most part folks figure I'm either a thief, an assassin or a bounty hunter." Hunter took a long drink, filled his mug from the water-skin.

"Huh, guess I did learn more than I thought; you've some identity that requires you to wear fine garments, a rich merchant or perhaps a noble." Glancing up from wiping his bowl clean with a hunk of bread, Flax saw the bounty hunter nod. "You're not a slaver. Dextera is my enemy and she did try to kill me..." He chewed up the bread, swallowed and held his tin mug out to be refilled. Hunter complied. "I did get to wondering how I could be sure that there was going to be a sacrifice. All I knew about that was what you told me." Taking a drink, he watched the bounty hunter, studied the all but unreadable features. "Thinking about what Dextera said... I figured she was what you said she was and that I could probably trust you but I'd just wait and see."

"What'd you decide?" Laying the skin aside Hunter took a sip from his own mug.

"Well, after hearing everything Dextera said I don't doubt you." Flax met the glacial eyes, "I did find a few things I thought were interesting."

"And they were?" Hunter prompted with a mischievous smile.

"Considering everything you travel with and everything you've got stashed here, there isn't a whole lot that really says anything about you. Nothing's really personal or says anything about who you really are."

"Nothing?"

He glanced at the redhead a moment, "The only really personal things were your pick, the deer tallow soap and the wolf seal."

"How do you come to that conclusion?" the bounty hunter asked casually.

He considered that, exactly how to word it so it didn't sound so subjective. "Well, the pick is ivory and it's carved with maple leaves. It almost looks like a gift from a close friend or maybe a lover." The bounty hunter's features told him nothing, Hunter looked mildly curious, attentive. "The soap has almost no scent at all. Better for hunting or remaining unnoticed. If "Rufus" smelled like the anonymous warrior with the veiled features someone might add two and two."

A grin flashed, "Well done, go on."

"As for the seal, I've never seen it's like." He looked at the ground for a moment then met Hunter's gaze. "I'll wager it represents the bounty hunter you really are when you have to sign for your bounty or leave a report with a garrison commander."

Hunter nodded as if he was pleased, "Well done, Flax. The pick was from my sire. He gave it to me the first Solstice I visited after... embarking on this path. I've always preferred deer tallow soap for the simple fact that there's almost no scent at all. As for my wolf seal, you're right about that, most any garrison commander or constable captain would recognize it, if not from personal experience from reputation." The bounty hunter sipped from his mug, then smoothed his red beard. "Now consider this, what if everything in my pack, my box and my saddle bags is personal? What does it all say about me? What about this camp and its location? Or the location of my makeshift stable? Tell me, how long did it take you to find where I'd put our horses and tack for the night?"

He chuckled, thinking about it. It had taken a while. "Probably... two thirds of an hour," he shrugged.

"So what does it all tell you?" The bounty hunter gave him a sly look, lifted that single brow. "C'mon, Flax, tell me what you learned about me."

His brows knit as he turned over his mental inventory of the bounty hunter's belongings. Hunter waited quietly, patiently, drinking water, refilling the mug while he thought. "Well... you're methodical and you think things through, try to be prepared." When he looked up he received an encouraging nod. "The camouflage leathers tell me you've been hunting all your life and you probably started with game. The leathers you wear as Rufus and the rich clothes are camo of another kind. You can gain information better if you fit in and appear to be someone else. You travel alone and work alone." He fell silent for a moment then grinned mischievously, "Taken as a whole it says you're a bounty hunter, a damn good one."

"Exactly." Hunter grinned too, "Well done, lad." Draining the mug, Hunter rose, gathered up the bowls, spoons and took his mug when he drank the last of his water. "I'll be right back." After feeding and watering the prisoner, the bounty hunter washed their dishes, filled the water-skin while Flax watched the sun sink below the gully's jagged rim.

When Hunter returned he seated himself at Flax's side cross-legged. The redhead watched the sun set too, seemingly lost in his own thoughts. Flax was busy trying to appear relaxed while gathering the words to ask some of the many of the questions that had been on his mind. *If you make it through this alive will you tell me who you are? If you live, will you teach me to be what you are? Can you? Can I do it if you agree?..* There were half a dozen other questions he almost didn't dare to think about, things that were really none of his business... but he was curious, so curious and Hunter seemed to answer his questions with endless patience. Before he could get his thoughts ordered and decide how to word his questions darkness fell and the bounty hunter rose.

Hunter stretched, grunted quietly like it felt good. "Sunset was beautiful tonight, wasn't it?"

He looked at the sky, shades of blue and violet where the sun disappeared. Higher it was darker, deep blue turning to velvet black. "Yeah, always is and it's always different."

"Summer's winding down, the days are getting shorter."

He nodded his agreement, "Wish the days would get cooler."

"I don't like the heat either, Flax." The redhead breathed deeply, "Rain tomorrow, by evening. That might be good."

"Think so?" He looked up at the bounty hunter standing next to him.

The glacial gaze swept the gully thoroughly. He looked every inch the predator, feral and dangerous in the growing darkness. "Rain can hide movement, mask sound. Like a gentle breeze though a breeze can turn on you too easily. The rain can too but tomorrow night... it should be an advantage if I use it right." Before he put what he was thinking, what he wanted to ask into words the bounty hunter grasped the furs he was sitting on, "C'mon lad. I need some sleep tonight and so do you."

"Okay," he rose and Hunter gathered up the furs, shook them out. "You want me to keep a watch?"

Hunter offered him a wry smile, "I sleep very lightly and I'll wager you do too."

He shrugged, "Well, yeah but..."

"C'mon, I'm tired." Hunter sighed heavily, "And I'll wager Dextera has to piss again."

Flax laughed, he couldn't help it.

Flax woke, rolled to his back, put both hands behind his head, under his makeshift pillow and stared at the stone ceiling of the cave, Hunter's camp. It was too warm to cover up with any furs at all and he was laying atop his entire bedroll, garbed only in a tong. Hunter had given him a sheet of linen from his own bedroll, the bounty hunter happened to have two. It lay across his legs, loins, belly. He sighed, *It's gotta be around the second, third hour...* Lifting his shoulders, he looked toward the entryway. Moonlight filtered in, casting a silvery glow on their prisoner in the corner. Curled up on the single ratty fur, she was cuffed, collared and tethered to the ring in the floor. She wasn't gagged or hooded now but that was because Hunter had added a sedative to her meal. She was out cold and would be until the ninth or tenth hour according to the bounty hunter. She was still naked as well but she didn't look like she was cold. He lay back, stared at the ceiling again and heard Hunter shift on the bunk. The redhead offered it to him but it wasn't long enough, besides he didn't mind sleeping on the floor. That would be if he could sleep. Hunter was breathing slowly, evenly, he sounded asleep.

Why am I awake? Maybe 'cause there's five young males being held somewhere against their will and raped repeatedly... And tomorrow night... or rather tonight they'll be dragged to an altar to be raped and bled and sacrificed to a false goddess... His crooked smile cocked his mustache but it was bitter. *Naw, couldn't possibly be tha..t. I could have ended up one of them if not for the damned bounty hunter... I'm not sure I'm comfortable with that but he hasn't even mentioned it.*

He sighed quietly. The mild suspicions he'd had melted in the light of all Dextera told them. He wasn't even suspicious of the bounty hunter's motives for getting him the swords and the braid ties, not any longer. The redhead hadn't even looked at him suggestively since he was pretending to be Rufus in the tavern. *I trust him... Hell, I kind of like him even though he can be a damn cold bastard... I respect him... even if I don't know exactly who he is... Maybe I could do this... Hunt criminals for a living... I've always liked hunting game and I'm good at I..t. Maybe he'd teach me... but what would he want in return?*

The possible answer sent a jolt of disgust through him. It was followed immediately by guilt. *I don't even want to think that way. Made sense what he said about being able to be friends with a lady... There's no difference... Besides I'm not Thyrian, self-conscious and afraid of sexuality... So, he's different. So what? I've probably shared a bathhouse or the soldiers' baths or a bunkhouse with more than one male that thought the same... Doesn't matter... So why do I keep thinkin' about it? Said he never raped anyone... I wonder, does that include slaves? Most folks don't even think of slaves as human... Do I? Oh, Hell, I don't know what to think... I know Hunter's treated me with nothing but respect since... I woke up here... Hell, since he broke into Dextera's room... Few ladies treat me with so much respect unless I make 'em...*

Slowly, he pushed to sit up, wrap his arms loosely around drawn up knees and clasp his hands. *Sixty-four fanatical worshipers and one crazy bitch who thinks she's a goddess... He's willing to take them all on. Wonder if he's crazy?..* He glanced to the redhead. Hunter was lying nearly on his stomach with a rolled up fur wrapped in strong arms, pillowing the powerful body. The linen covered hips, rump and one leg while the other wrapped around the fur. The broad back was completely exposed except for a few strands of curling spiraling hair trailing off the shoulders to the side near the wall. His brows knit in puzzlement.

So just how does one male look at another and feel... I dunno, attracted maybe? I don't feel anything. It's nothing at all like lookin' at a lady whose furs I

*wanna warm...   I can see he's built well, real strong...
He fights like no warrior I've ever trained with before.
Amazing how fast he is... He's got nice hair, good-lookin'
I guess... I just don't get it... He's right, I'm as hetro as
the day is long... Or maybe the year is...* he almost
laughed to himself but his gaze fell on the scars and he
managed to stifle it. In the darkened cave, with hardly
any light at all even for his eyes they were pure white
against slightly silver skin.

Without thinking, he shifted to one hip, leaned on
one arm... Then stifled the urge to trace those white
scars. *Outside they're not so white, just lighter against
his suntanned back... It looks like it was bad... and now,
in this lack of light, it looks terrible... must have really
hurt...* Abruptly, he felt like he was being watched and
met the glacial gaze. It wasn't really cold or hard now,
just... neutral, unreadable. Then the bounty hunter
smiled.

"Damn, Flax, those are some eyes."

His half smile flashed and he looked toward the
entrance, ran a hand through his hair. "Thanks, I
guess," he grunted.

A low comfortable sound, "Can you see better
than I in the dark?"

He looked at Hunter, gave him a wry, half smile.

"Right," the bounty hunter grinned, "how the hell
would you know how I see in the dark. So... can you see
colors? Or is everything washed out to monochrome
grays, black and white?"

Brows knit, he thought about it, looked around
the inside of the cave then met the bounty hunter's
gaze, searched his features. "Well, I can see your beard
is red and your hair has red in it but it's washed out

compared to what it looks like during the day. Your eyes are sort of blue gray in this light. The linen looks a warmer white than white if that makes·any sense."

"It makes sense. How 'bout details?" Hunter looked very relaxed, comfortable and he sounded just as relaxed as he appeared. "Like our prisoner for instance."

He looked at Dextera. "I can see her, the bonds, the collar, everything. I can see she's naked." He shrugged.

"Can you see anything else?"

He considered, *What's he asking me?* "Yeah, I can see the stripes you gave her."

"How 'bout..." Hunter pushed to his forearms, casting his own gaze into the darkest corner of the cave. "Back there, by the hearth?"

He turned, "I can see your iron pots and the grate for the fire, your pack and mine in the corner, there."

"That's impressive," Hunter lay down, tightened his arms around the rolled up fur.

"Sorry I woke you," he offered.

"I was awake, lad. And it'd be okay even if you did." The redhead shifted comfortably. "I usually don't sleep all night. Five or six hours tops and I usually go on four or so." The frosty eyes searched his features, "Why are you awake?"

He shrugged, looked toward the entrance, their prisoner. *I'm thinkin' of us as partners... She's his prisoner... but... he just referred to her as our prisoner.* "Just... thinkin' about them." It was vague and ambiguous but Hunter grunted an affirmative.

"Makes me sick too, Flax. Not much turns my stomach any more. Dehegra and her followers do." He heard the linen shift, the bunk creak a little. When he looked Hunter was on his back, the rolled up fur and one hand under his head. The red brows knit, "Someone has to do something. Might as well be me."

Flax looked at the floor, *I'll be your second sword,* he wanted to say, *you don't have to do it alone...* For some reason it stuck in his throat. Then he heard the bunk creak, the linen rustle and he looked up meeting the bounty hunter's gaze.

"They even glow." The redhead was serious now, thoughtful. "The more light the brighter, huh?"

He nodded, looked at the floor again, studied the furs beneath him. "Yeah."

"Don't misunderstand, Flax." Hunter shifted on the bunk, settling to his back. "I don't have anything against ororri or half-bloods or youths sired by slaves. I'm just interested. Those eyes can be an advantage, they could be a liability as well."

"S'okay." He shifted to sit cross-legged. *How'd you know a slave sired me?.. Pretty damn obvious, that... Few arederi females will allow a free ororri to sire their children...* "Sixty some fanatics and one crazy lady who thinks she's a goddess, That's a hell of a force for any warrior..."

Hunter laughed quietly, interrupting. "Flax, I'd like to have a few swords at my back just to keep 'em off me. I've got a few problems with you being there, that's all."

He studied the shadowed features, "Well, name 'em. I'll solve 'em for ya."

Again the redhead laughed then it faded. Hunter rolled to his side, up on a forearm and met his gaze. "The first and the second are linked. Number one, how do I disguise someone your size? Answer, I can't. No matter how you're cloaked and your features hidden, just how many males over seven feet tall with blue ororri eyes are there anyways? I'll wager the number is remarkably few. Then there are those eyes. How do I hide them and let you see? Maybe a veil, but of what? I don't want you practically blindfolded yet those eyes glow like balefire when the light catches them. One glint and we're seen before we mean to be."

Flax listened, considered. "A wagon full of straw or... anything covered with canvas. Find me a veil for my face. I'll hide in the wagon, you can drive it all over town, right to their doorstep, no one'll even see me."

The bounty hunter searched his features, "That could work. It'd hide you from sight completely and provide us a way to get the five sacrifices out of town unseen too." A long pause, a quiet huff then, "I do have a couple ideas about what to use as a veil."

"Two problems solved, go on," he prompted, encouraged that the bounty hunter might actually take him along. Hunter was silent, searching his features. It was intense, uncomfortable and he looked at the floor. "I know I'm untried. I won't balk and get you killed..."

"I know," it was quiet, serious, almost grave.

"Then, I don't get it. What's the problem?" He was truly, downright confused.

The bounty hunter sighed heavily, "There's no plausible way to take Dehegra's followers alive. You are going to have to kill, Flax. There's no way around it. If even one escapes alive she will do her damnedest to hunt us down. If she raises enough hew and cry she could get the Kylonian law after us. I'm distinctive looking but not extraordinary. You are. They will hunt us down and try to exact vengeance. No survivors, I can't afford it and neither can you."

His jaw clenched, "You think I can't..."

"On the contrary, lad, I'm as sure as anyone could be, you can." Hunter's brows knit then the redhead covered his eyes with a forearm. "Don't understand, do you?"

"No." His voice was strained, tight with confusion, frustration, "I don't fuckin' understand at all."

Sighing again, it sounded exasperated. "I wish you were five years older, even three."

"What the Hell's that got to do with anything?" his voice rumbled but he wasn't angry, just confused.

"I don't want to be responsible, Flax." Hunter's jaw clenched tightly, he swallowed hard, "I don't want to sacrifice your innocence and wash you in blood." Strong fingers raked into the red mane then pushed beneath the makeshift cushion. "And I don't want to put you on a pyre."

He sat in silence for long moments strangely touched again and it took some minutes to gather his thoughts, compose a reply. "I don't want to put you on a pyre either."

"I'm very good at killing and even better at staying alive." Squeezing his eyes shut, Hunter clenched his jaw tightly. "Goddess, lad, how did you get mixed up with me?"

"There was this lady in a tavern, some bad ale..." he ventured.

"I don't want to be responsible for this... I won't be..."

"You're not," Flax met the frosty eyes when Hunter turned to look at him. "I am. I've been training since I was old enough to hold a tojo." The bounty hunter was about to say something but he held up a hand, "Hear me out."

"Fine," Hunter pushed up and turned to sit cross-legged on the bunk facing him.

"I've been training to be a soldier or a member of the Protectress' guard all my life; I just didn't know it. My mother had a place all lined up for me. I didn't want that, to have my life charted out for me by my mother... and you don't get to do it either." He bit his lower lip, raked a hand through his hair. Then his fingers found one of his braids bound with the new ties, tugged. "Yeah, you're more experienced and you've seen some serious shit ... and I agreed to do as you tell me... even if you tell me to stay here and wait. I gave my word and I'll stick to it," he drew a deep breath, unable to hold the glacial gaze any longer, looking down. He felt very much like a kid again, self-conscious and unsure and he didn't like it. *How do I convince him I'm not a child when that's exactly how I feel?..* "I didn't ask to be your second sword for... glory or because I think it'll be some damn adventure. I'm not a kid, I know better than that."

"So, why did you ask?" Hunter met his feline gaze when he looked up.

"Because stopping them is the right thing to do."

Hunter laced his fingers in folded legs, leaned back against the stone wall. "I'll see if I can find you a veil, something you can see through that will keep those eyes from giving us away... and a crossbow, something heavy with plenty of range with some heavy broad heads." A single red brow lifted, "You follow me and I'm going to trample your honor all to Hell, lad."

"If I follow your... orders, do we have a real chance to save them?" he asked simply.

"We do."

"Then my honor will survive." Flax flashed his half-smile. He received only the slightest hint of one in return.

"All right," Hunter straightened, shoved both hands into his hair and shook it out. "Provided I can procure a way to hide you, you're in."

Flax nodded. His gut tightened and his blood quickened at the thought of it. *It's gonna be terrible, I shouldn't feel like this... like I want it... I should be scared... but I'm not.* "You got a plan?"

Now he got a smile, "A rough one." Hunter outlined it. Actually it seemed pretty solid for something the bounty hunter referred to as rough. He waited until the redhead finished to ask questions. He only had a few and the bounty hunter did ask.

"Any questions?" Hunter shifted to put both feet on the floor.

"Yeah," his hand wanted to rake though his mane and since some of it fell forward he let it. "You said... you'd clear the doors? I can... do my part."

The redhead nodded, "I'd wager you could. I'd also wager that what conscience I have left wouldn't let me sleep for weeks. Humor me on this, I'll do it."

Flax chewed his lower lip, brows knit, "Okay. Then you said we'd start a count. What'd you mean by that?"

"A slow count, to mark time. That way you wait for me and we go in together even though we're on opposite sides of the building." Hunter explained, rose and stretched. The bounty hunter grabbed his pack, set it on the bunk, "Anything else?"

"Ah-huh, said ya think this Dehegra is sorceri?" He watched as the redhead pulled out the gray and black set of clothes. The small pack with the grapple and cord inside followed.

"I did." Tugging open the rings on his tong, Hunter shed it, pulled on the black breeches.

"How do we... surprise a sorceri?" Again his hand itched to rake into his hair. Instead, he leaned on that arm.

"Easy, lad. I said I think she may have a touch of the gift." Hunter slipped the black and gray shirt on, met his searching gaze. "It doesn't make her immortal or impervious to crossbow bolts."

"Your word on that?" Flax asked with a crooked smile. It was only about half jest despite his attempt to make it sound so.

"You've my word, Flax." Hunter smiled slightly, "She's my target anyways." Laces on the shirtsleeves tightened them against the bounty hunter's forearms. "Don't think about her. Do your damnedest to keep focused and don't think too hard on what you have to do." Hunter took a pair of fingerless gloves from the pack, slipped them on. From the thickness on the backs Flax would wager they were colliette claws. "I've read a lot about sorceri, the gift and how it works. This Dehegra pretends to be a goddess; she may even believe it. Even Morditha's followers don't pretend to that. We can take her."

He nodded, watched curiously as Hunter picked out his hair, then wove it deftly into one thick plait. The braid was secreted down the back of the black shirt. Hunter sat down on the bunk to slip on the pair of very soft black boots. The bounty hunter painstakingly tucked the close fitting breeches inside then laced the boots up snuggly.

"So, where ya goin'?"

That cool smile flashed and the glacial gaze met his, "For another look around inside their temple. I'll wager things will be quieter at this hour of the morning." The shirt was knotted at the bounty hunter's left.

The implications of that statement rolled around in his head for a moment. "Another look?" Flax managed, it still rang with disbelief.

Hunter rose, donned his harness then deftly fastened the black pack at the small of his back. "Yes. How did you think I knew enough to rough out our plans, lad?"

He shrugged, "True. Be careful, huh?"

Raising his hood, Hunter offered him a smile then covered his features with the veil. "I'm always careful, Flax, but thanks for your concern. Try to get some sleep, I'll be back around dawn." Then the bounty hunter slipped silently from the cave.

Flax drew a deep breath; let it out. *Try to get some sleep?.. Oh, yeah, right, like I can sleep now...*

Opening his eyes Flax realized with a small shock that he had managed to fall back to sleep. *Just tired I guess.* He rolled to his back, stretched then slowly pushed to his feet. Running a hand through his hair and his tongue along his teeth, he caught up his pack. It took only a moment for him to find his brush, razor and the salt. Closing up his pack, catching up the water-skin, he headed for the entrance. Pausing briefly, he considered their prisoner. She seemed to be sleeping deeply, peacefully.

He maneuvered outside and scanned the sky, breathing deeply of the morning air. It was too warm for this hour if you asked him, of course, no one asked. Dawn was just a lighter blue hint along the eastern rim of the gully, and he considered waiting but... Hunter would figure out where he'd gone if he happened to come back. Making up his mind, Flax strode down the gully toward the creek where they'd bathed yesterday.

It didn't take long to see to all the morning essentials. After cleaning his teeth, washing and shaving around his beard Flax brushed his long mane then wove it into a Byrynthian style braid. It would get hot later and he might as well do it now. Besides, maybe braiding his hair would help him keep his hands out of it. Running his brush over his freshly trimmed beard and mustache, Flax filled the water-skin then strode leisurely back toward the cave. The sky was lightening all over to deep blue now; he figured it to be near the sixth hour. Flax made a list of chores in his head, things to do while he waited for the bounty hunter to return. *Feed and water the horses, then hobble them and let them out... Then fork out the so-called stable... Oh, yeah, don't forget to clean their hooves. Should I try to start a fire and cook something? Maybe I should just stick to dry rations for breakfast...*

He stopped dead, listened... and heard... the sound of swords clashing. *Damn!* Breaking into a run, he tore down the gully to the campsite. Dropping the water-skin by the cave entrance, he drew his short-sword and slipped inside. Nothing was amiss; the prisoner was sound asleep, dead to the world. Quicker than he figured possible, he sidestepped through the passage and drew his long-sword the moment he cleared it. Flax cursed under his breath, turned his head straining his ears for the slightest hint of the sound. He heard it again; it was out on the rolling grassland between this gully and the one with the little spring. Already running for the trail up and out, he flew along the gully then bounded up the rocky slope. When he was within a few yards of the rim he slowed, dropped to one knee, sliding his long-sword home. Easing down to his belly, he crawled to the rim, still clutching his short-sword.

The moment his eyes cleared the boulders, he saw Hunter amid three ladies on horseback. Before he could get up and join in, the redhead's long-sword flashed, blood sprayed and one rider toppled to the ground. The horse bolted, tearing off across the grassland as fast as it's legs would carry it. Another rider fell headless, another horse reared and bolted.

The bounty hunter stuck his long-sword in the ground, parried a desperate swing from the lady on the horse. In the next instant he seized her calf and shoved her off her mount. The animal took off. The lady rolled, started to clamber to her feet but Hunter was on her so fast she didn't stand a chance. Snatching his long-sword from where he stuck it, Hunter bore her to the torn and blood splattered sod. Blades spun in deft hands, a blur of steel. The bounty hunter's crossed swords pinned her to the ground by the throat. As far as Flax could see, Hunter had a knee planted on her chest.

One arm lifted from the ground and he saw the hand and half the forearm was missing.

I should feel sick... Flax blinked, glanced around them both. No one else was in sight but that didn't necessarily mean no one was there. He scanned again, slower, looking for any movement. The only things that moved were a hare, the panicked horses, Hunter and his enemy. The entire thing had taken only a few heartbeats. Hunter's speed amazed him. *He's devastating. Cut through them like they weren't worth his time, like they were weaponless... Maybe he could take on a force of sixty alone...* Shaking off his surprise, he scanned the horizon, checked down the gully behind him. Flax spared a glance for Hunter and the lady. The redhead stuck his long-sword in the ground again then rose smoothly. Jerking the lady to her feet, he shoved her in the direction the horses had taken. She tripped, went down then scrambled to her feet looking back. The bounty hunter retrieved his long-sword, spun it and she took off again. Hunter stalked to one of the bodies, crouched to wipe his blades on the shirt. The long-sword slid home unerringly.

Flax moved to stand up and the bounty hunter held a hand out to one side, palm toward the ground. *How the Hell's he even know I'm here?..* For a moment, he struggled with indecision then Hunter motioned toward the ground again so he sank back down, waited. Some minutes passed in tense silence while Hunter watched the lady catch one of the horses. She was some five hundred yards away, quite a distance on the rolling grassland. She struggled into the saddle then urged her mount up the slope to disappear over the rock-strewn crest. Hunter glanced his way, signaled to him to stay down and searched the body. Taking a few things, he moved onto the next, searched it. Again Hunter took a couple things then rose.

Just for the hell of it, Flax started a slow count while the bounty hunter stood motionless, watching where the lady disappeared, occasionally scanning the hills. Flax got to one hundred twenty-seven when Hunter turned, sheathing the short-sword and strode toward him. The sun was just topping the horizon when the bounty hunter neared. A nod and slight gesture sent him back down the slope carefully, sheathing his sword. The bounty hunter paused on the rim, scanning all around them. He watched up and down the gully then sensed the redhead's approach.

"Morning, Flax," the bounty hunter lowered the veil, pushed back the hood. The glacial eyes met his and they gave him a chill. They were ice cold, frozen as the glacier they resembled and yet... a volcanic fire blazed beneath the icy surface.

"Hey," he managed, holding that frosty gaze. "What the hell happened?"

A hard grin flashed and Hunter seemed to consider. "They were bounty hunters. There's a price on your hide, Flax. Your mother, High General Lynia, wants you back, safe, unharmed and untouched. Though it's a little late for that."

He snatched his long-sword in blur of steel and took a step back, dropping into a ready crouch. "You're not takin' me anywhere..." he growled. For all his outward composure his mind reeled. *She put a bounty out on me... I thought I couldn't feel any more betrayed... Between my mother treating me like her property and now him... I thought... I dunno... we were friends, at least allies... Damn... this is crazy...*

A red brow lifted and Hunter smiled slightly, "Not my kind of Hunt, lad." The bounty hunter folded his arms casually. "I don't hunt youths who take exception to their mother's rule, not even for two hundred pentas, gold."

His eyes narrowed and he straightened but he didn't sheath his sword. "Oh, yeah?"

"My word on Sheposha's Bow, lad, I'm not hunting you. Never was." Hunter searched his eyes, "I thought we established the fact that I'm not your enemy." The glacial gaze hardened and dropped to his sword for a brief yet significant moment.

The hilt felt good in his hand, comfortable and he really wanted it there. Flax sheathed his sword. "Tell me what happened," it came out hoarse, strained.

Hard frosty features thawed a little, a smile tugged at Hunter's mouth. "I'm sorry, I should have told you sooner but... I allowed myself to get distracted by other matters." The bounty hunter shook his head, "Never mind, that's no excuse." A heavy sigh escaped Hunter, the glacial eyes dropped to the ground and the ice thawed all together. "They tracked you to the tavern, found out about you being injured and leaving with Rufus. They were going to check with a couple healers that many fur-warmers-for-hire frequent, male healers who don't ask questions or demand certain favors. I got onto them this morning and followed them until they were well away from town. I confronted them, told them you were my prisoner and that I'd see you returned safe and sound to your mother, albeit in chains. When I suggested they move on Devia lost her temper and attacked then the others joined in. They thought to take you from me. Devia fell first, Lutina second. As for Mira, I took her right hand. She'll put the word out that the bounty is as good as collected. That should keep them off your back for a while. Although, you are pretty much one of a kind and once word gets around that you're not home or you're wandering around the streets of some boarder garrison or town they'll be after you again."

"But you're not taking me back?" His voice was still strained, tight. *Could he be playing games with me? But he gave me his word... And what does that mean exactly... But I trust him... I think... Goddess... I am so fuckin' confused...*

Hunter was watching him, studying his features and must have read his doubt, suspicions. "Your mother has promised you to Lady Demiria's first born daughter, Mitarha. That wasn't done before you left was it?"

He wet his lips; they were parched. "No, it... she... they were trying to pressure me into it. That's part of the reason I left."

Hunter nodded, "I gathered that when I met with Lynia. I didn't give her any answer to her contract, just decided to let her think what she wanted. I'll carry a letter for you or deliver any message you wish. It just has to wait until I'm through here." The bounty hunter searched his features, drew a deep breath then let it out, "I've got to get the blood out of my shirt, lad." With that he turned and headed toward the cave.

After a moment of hesitation Flax followed. A couple trotting strides and he fell into step at the bounty hunter's side. "If you weren't... aren't hunting me... Why... I mean..."

"Are you really that damned confused, or are you just trying to avoid pissing me off?"

He answered honestly without thinking about it, "I'm that damned confused, Hunter, don't..."

The bounty hunter stopped, caught his arm, turned to look up at him, "Don't what? Drag you back there? If I wanted to do that you'd already be kneeling at her feet in chains. Don't think for a heartbeat I couldn't do it. I could and you know it. Personally, I think your life is your own, not hers to barter for noble house alliances. Besides, I've already offered you my oath that's not my intention. You had best decide if we are allies, lad, because I can't trust you at my back if you're this unsure." The tone was even, cool. He didn't yell or so much as snarl but Flax heard it, saw it in the frosty eyes; the undercurrent of anger.

Flax shook his head, "I was gonna say... Don't be pissed at me." It took every ounce of will he had to hold the bounty hunter's gaze. *I will not look away; I'm not a child and if I want the respect and responsibility of an adult then I have to earn it, prove to him I deserve it... Gotta prove it to myself too...* "I admit, for a few seconds there I was wondering... If maybe you might be... I dunno how to put it..."

"Playing head games with you," Hunter provided.

"Yeah, but... you're right, I know that if you really wanted to... ya could a already put me in chains."

Hunter nodded, "That's better. I prefer honesty to that suspicion in your eyes, Flax." The redhead offered him a smile, a real one, "Now, I really have to get the blood out of my shirt. Do me a favor and fetch me the leather cleaner?"

His crooked smile dawned, relief washed through him, "Sure."

"I'll check on our prisoner. Meet me at the creek, on the flat rock, okay?" Hunter was already heading down the gully, toward the cave.

"Yeah," Flax went to the stable. Just before he went inside Hunter emerged from the cave, strode leisurely in the direction of the creek. Flax shook his head, as if that could shake off his confusion. There were a hundred questions he wanted to ask the bounty hunter not the least of which was one he'd never get an answer to unless he could figure it out for himself. *Why would other bounty hunters back off, merely assume the bounty was as good as collected, just on this particular bounty hunter's word? Who is he?..*

Flax found Hunter right where he said he'd be. The redhead was crouched in the creek down stream from the flat rock, scrubbing his shirt. The black harness was laid across the rock in easy reach right next to the breeches and boots. He strode to the rock, climbed on it quietly.

"You know, for someone your size you move quietly," Hunter remarked glancing at him briefly.

"Still heard me," he pointed out, settling down cross-legged.

The redhead shrugged, "Most folks wouldn't." Rising, he wrung out the shirt. The red-gold hair was still bound in a thick plait that hung nearly to the bounty hunter's waist. "Brought me the leather cleaner, right?"

"Yep." He lifted his gaze to the lightening sky. Wispy clouds were moving in. Breathing deeply he could smell the rain on the breeze. "Did you want me to cook breakfast or anything?"

"Naw," Hunter approached. Climbing on the rock he sat near its edge, one leg hanging in the water, the other folded.

"Brought your tong," Flax remarked.

The redhead looked very much like he was suppressing a grin or maybe some teasing comment. "Thanks." Hunter drew the black breeches across his thigh, held out a hand for the leather cleaner. Flax obliged, putting the tin in the calloused palm. Opening it the bounty hunter placed it before him, went to work on a smear of blood. "I never intended to take Lynia's contract, lad. Didn't follow you either, just crossed each other's paths, that's all."

For a moment he studied the redhead's features, then he shrugged, "Lucky for me we did." Flax leaned over, watched the fish move around in the water at the base of the rock.

"You would have gotten out of it on your own." Hunter methodically cleaned his leathers, working on the blood splatters. They didn't show much at all really as far as Flax could see, just darker blacker streaks against the black leather.

"Nice a you to..." he was interrupted by the bounty hunter's quiet laughter. Meeting the glacial eyes he didn't see any of the frost that was there earlier, nor did he see the fire behind it. He waited patiently while the redhead's mirth passed. "What?" he asked when he thought Hunter was done laughing at him.

"No one's accused me of being nice in a very long time, Flax." Finished with the bloodstains, he cleaned the breeches all over "Found us a wagon. I've got it stashed near the west gate. The only real problem is time. We can't get in until they're all assembled. The blood moon will rise at the eighteenth hour but it won't climax until the twenty-second. They'll assemble before then, about half past the twenty-first. We'll get to the wagon just before dusk; it's easier to get into the city with a wagon before full dark. There are half a dozen alleyways near that temple. I'll get us there then we'll have to watch and wait. You a decent climber?"

"Yeah," Flax listened with interest doing his best to stifle his questions until a more appropriate time. That was, if one ever came.

Hunter nodded, folded up his breeches then slipped into the water. He took up the soap, scrubbed his hands, arms, especially his fingernails. "Then we'll take to the rooftops. We can watch them assemble and go inside. So far they haven't been posting any sentries on the roofs but they might for this ceremony. If they do, I'll take care of it. Once everything outside is settled down we make our way to the back entrance. I take care of the sentries then we start our count." While he talked the bounty hunter approached, climbed on the rock again, took up the tong and donned it. Then he seated himself cross-legged at Flax's side. "I go around front, take care of them then we go in at the count of three hundred. That should be no later than three quarters past the twenty-first hour. Dehegra shouldn't make her entrance until the sacrifices are stretched out on the alters so we'll have about fifteen, maybe twenty minutes to get to the galleries and take up positions to fire. Think you can see me across a fifty yard span?"

"As long as it's not pitch dark." Excitement clenched his gut, quickened his blood. *I can't believe I'm looking forward to tonight; I should be scared to death... I am a little, more wary, cautious than scared. Maybe I'm crazy...*

"It won't be. There are lamps down below and on the gallery walls. There's a pair of fire pits flanking the altar." Hunter retrieved his harness, opened the pack and took out two pouches that jingled like they contained silver or gold. Then Hunter placed a coil of relatively thick braided steel wire before him. It had metal rods for handles. "Know what that is?"

Flax shifted, his brows knit, "It's a garrote, isn't it?"

"It is. Know how to use one?"

Astonished he looked at the bounty hunter. The glacial eyes were frosty, unreadable. "In theory, yeah but..."

"No prisoners, remember."

"Yeah," he shrugged at a loss for words.

Hunter took up the garrote, deftly unwound it, gripped the handles. The way he held it made a circle of the wire then it crossed to the handles. "You come from behind, drop the loop over the head then tighten." Hunter demonstrated, pulling the handles apart. "It cuts off any cry and if you put enough strength behind it, it's quick. The wire slices the throat just as efficiently as a blade. If not, you've got to hold on for six maybe seven minutes. Better to cut the throat and be done with it. Clean it off on your kill's shirt or breeches before you slip it back in its sheath."

Flax nodded and hesitantly accepted the weapon. His worries must have showed.

"Flax," Hunter gripped his shoulder. When he met the frosty gaze the redhead went on, "Say I left those on the doors alive, drugged or bound. Or say you take a straggling acolyte in the hall alive, bind her and leave her behind. What if just one of them wakes or gets loose and manages to raise some kind of alarm?" A single red brow lifted. "What happens then?"

"All hell breaks loose," his voice was tight, almost a whisper.

"Damn straight. Any alarm before I intend for them to know we're there and we'll be hard pressed to save our own skins let alone any of their sacrifices. Got it?" The cool eyes searched his features.

Flax nodded, "I got it."

Hunter nodded, apparently satisfied, "With luck you won't have to use it."

"You... uh... Took this off of one of those bounty hunters." He looked at the wicked coil of wire in his hand.

"I did. Do you think she's going to be needing it?" Hunter's calloused fingers laced.

"No... The pouches..."

"I planned to share it with you." Hunter took them up and dumped them out. There was a decent quantity of silver, some copper and a few gold pieces. The redhead started dividing the coin into two equal piles. "By right it's mine. I took them. Their horses, their belongings are mine unless they've comrades to claim it. Mira didn't seem interested."

The trainer told me as much...even Lynia said the same thing. Not like they need it any longer...

"You deserve the pay, lad. I'll split Dextera's bounty with you if there happens to be one." Hunter gathered up the piles, put each one in a pouch.

"Thanks," he accepted the pouch, tucked it in his shirt. *What was it like? How'd it feel to fight them, kill them? You looked like... you were on fire afterwards.*

What'd you feel?.. "Where do I put this?" He held out the garrote.

"Good question." Red brows knit, Hunter considered. "I'll have to take a look at what dark clothes you've got. We'll find a place to put it if I have to make one. Now, I think I found you something you can use as a rufa."

He took a black ball of cloth from the little pack and shook it out. It was actually some eighteen inches wide, maybe four and a half feet long and it was made of some gauzy mesh like material. "Shall we find out if you can see through this?" Hunter moved around in front of him, offered it.

"Ya call this a rufa?" He took it, slung it around his shoulders then... wasn't sure what to do next.

"Not exactly," Hunter grinned when he met the glacial eyes. Kneeling before him, both hands resting on brawny thighs, the bounty hunter looked amused. "The rest of it was made into some revealing clothing for slaves. I bought this piece from a lady I know. She'll find the silver I left in her scrap bin."

Flax almost laughed, "You broke into a garment maker's shop?"

"Goddess no, lad, the door was open." Hunter managed to appear shocked that he'd suggest such a thing. "After I picked the locks of course." A broad mischievous grin flashed. "Still, I thought it would be very impolite to wake her in the wee hours of the morning just for something I could get myself."

After a moment he nodded, "Very impolite, I'm sure she'd thank you for lettin' her sleep."

Hunter sighed, "Don't have a clue what to do with it."

"Nope, sorry," he admitted.

Hunter shook his head, took the strip of cloth back, "Just watch close." The bounty hunter slung it around his own shoulders, then put the back up like a hood, "If I was just going to veil my features..." Deftly the cloth was slung across Hunter's face, draped across his features to the eyes and wrapped around his head. Then the bounty hunter undid it, "So if I want to veil my eyes too..." he seemed to think about it for a moment then dropped the back off his head. He wrapped the cloth so it veiled his eyes first then did the back like a hood, last he concealed his features, flipped what remained across his shoulders. "I can see, at least during the day." Hunter whipped it off, slung it around Flax's shoulders. Strong hands gripped the ends, "Wanna try or do you want me to do it first?"

"Lemme try," he took the ends, tried to visualize in his head what he was doing and mimic what Hunter had done at the same time. The redhead watched him thoughtfully. He could see through it, very well in fact.

"Well done. You can see okay?" Hunter adjusted it a bit about his shoulders.

"Yeah, great." Personally, he was rather amazed.

The bounty hunter nodded, "It shrouds you're features pretty well. At night you'll be unrecognizable. We'll just have to find out how well you see through it in the dark tonight." Hunter rose, stretched.

He undid the rufa... for lack of a better term, and left it hanging about his shoulders.

"I have to go back for the crossbow but I'll get it. We'll do a little practicing today. I want you to shoot and reload. You might think this is crazy but we should count together so we're in time tonight."

"Okay," Flax rose and his stomach rumbled.

"Hungry, lad?" Hunter offered him an amused smile, gathered up his black clothes and slipped his feet in the boots.

"How'd ya guess?" He vaulted down off the rock and the bounty hunter followed him.

"Just a hunch," the redhead started towards camp. "You eat, I'll feed our prisoner then go get your crossbow. It won't take long."

"You're not eatin'?"

Hunter shrugged, "I'll get something."

Five

Hunter wasn't gone long. For this trip into town he dressed in woodland leather breeches and the mottled brown boots. He wore the reddish brown harness from the trunk, then loosed his hair. He parted the center front, wound each side into a thick braid and bound them with leather strips. The back, he left loose and then he donned a headband with what looked like rykor tusks set above the brows, concealing the ties in his mane. Once he was dressed, the bounty hunter saddled his horse and rode into town.

Flax was outside, practicing the long-sword when he sensed he was being watched and whirled to see the bounty hunter leaning his rump against a boulder some thirty yards down the gully. A quiver hung at his left hip and there was a second strap crossing his broad chest.

Straightening, Hunter held up a rather heavy looking crossbow. "C'mere, lad, let's see if we can make this fit you."

He grinned, if it was close enough it wouldn't matter. "It'll be fine," he strode toward the bounty hunter as the redhead approached leading his horse. Flax noticed a bundle of burlap behind the saddle.

"Take a look at this," Hunter beckoned, turning the crossbow so the butt stock was toward him. Meeting the bounty hunter, he complied. The part of the buttstock that would touch his shoulder was a separate piece of wood. Two metal plates made a slender seam some two inches above the butt. The butt itself was covered with leather except for two metal eyes where two heavy screws or bolts were sunk even with the butt. "Watch," Hunter drew a short throwing knife and turned the bolts out alternating between them until the seam separated by nearly two inches. "Try it," Hunter offered him the weapon.

He accepted. The weight was a little light for him but... turning so he faced away from the bounty hunter, he raised the weapon to his shoulder. And damn if it didn't fit. The sights fell right into place and he aimed at a bush down the gully. "That's nice." He lowered it then snapped it to his shoulder. The sight was right there, and he settled into it naturally. "The length is perfect."

Hunter lightly tapped his bicep and he turned to meet the glacial gaze. "Give it to me," a strong calloused hand beckoned.

Placing the relatively heavy weapon in Hunter's hand, he watched as the bounty hunter removed the butt completely.

"Hold this," Hunter placed it in his hand, complete with bolts. Then the redhead removed the plate from the main stock revealing a neatly finished hole. "This too," Hunter passed the plate to him then sheathed his knife. Searching the quiver for a moment, the bounty hunter pulled out something cylindrical covered in leather. Hunter slid the cylinder into the hole, gently bumped it into place with the calloused heel of one hand. It didn't take Hunter long to put the crossbow back together. "Now try it," the redhead passed him the weapon again, sheathing the knife.

He accepted it and the weight was... He wasn't sure so he turned away, raised the weapon to his shoulder, sighted over the bow. "I'll be damned."

"The weight's better now?" he could hear amusement in the bounty hunter's voice.

Pointing the weapon at the ground, he turned to Hunter, "It's perfect." He was rather amazed that any crossbow could be so easily made to fit him. "What do I owe you for this?" Flax strove to sound matter-of-fact rather than nervous and hesitant.

The bounty hunter smiled, "For all practical purposes I'm your employer, Flax. It's my responsibility to provide you with what you need."

He searched Hunter's nearly unreadable features. All that met him was mild amusement and too blatant honesty. "Then you'll want this back?"

Hunter shook his head, "I already have a crossbow that suits me just fine."

Flax sighed, "You didn't have this made or anything?"

A broad grin flashed, "No. Kylonian ladies get tall and a good portion of them are strongly built. A lot of crossbows come that way," he gestured to the adjustable stock. "I did get the heaviest weight and I had the bower get me a pair of extra long bolts."

"Hunter," he started but he wasn't sure where to go. The redhead stopped him with a gesture anyways.

"Look, if it makes you more comfortable give me... say... Two silver pentas."

He nodded speculatively, "Take four?"

Hunter shook his head firmly, folded brawny arms. "Two."

Sighing quietly, he agreed, "Fine, two pentas, silver." He offered the bounty hunter his hand.

"Done," Hunter clasped his forearm in a warrior's shake. "You eat?"

"Yeah."

The bounty hunter released him, took up his rein and offered it to Flax. He accepted. "Good, so did I. Do me a favor and look after Copper for me while I go find us some stuffing for this target." It was almost a question. The bounty hunter took the burlap from behind the saddle.

"No problem." The blond giant shrugged, he really wanted to shoot it.

"Thanks, Flax." Hunter handed him the quiver too then started up the side of the gully, towards the grassland.

"Hey, one question?" he asked deftly slinging the quiver on the saddle. Hunter stopped, met his gaze and that single brow lifted. "Who are ya t'day? Or who were you when you went into town?"

"That's two questions." Hunter stated with a grin. Something shifted, changed and the bounty hunter took on a more friendly, less hard and cold air, then inclined his head, "I am Tymane, a mercenary and caravan guard. Friends call me Ty."

Tymane, the same name he wanted me to use if I had to go to that commander and tell her everything. "Well, hey, Tymane, pleased to meet ya."

Hunter laughed quietly then bounded out of the gully. He led Copper to the makeshift stable, took the gelding inside and removed the tack to brush him down.

Flax watched, listened as Hunter drew a map of the streets and alleyways surrounding the temple. Hunter was kneeling before the bunk, using it as a table. Flax sat on one hip at the bounty hunter's side. Dipping his quill, sliding that map aside, the redhead started on a second of the temple itself, outlining his plans, giving directions to the spiraling stairs downward. Flax listened, answered affirmatively when the bounty hunter asked if he understood. He only had a couple questions as the bounty hunter went on and they were answered concisely. The third map consisted of the galleries, the stairs leading up and down. Then Hunter drew the lowest floor and the altars, explaining where he thought the priestess' would be, where the sacrifices would be laid out.

The bounty hunter had also given Flax a grapple and cord just like his, albeit heavier. Hunter had him throw it a couple times, hook one thing or another to prove he was accurate with it. The bounty hunter asked him about his prowess with the three-pronged hook. He'd used one to sneak out of Lynia's house on occasions and had to be able to get back in just as quietly.

He'd practiced with the crossbow, wearing the black "rufa" veiling his eyes. He had no problem at all seeing through it. After running through all twenty-four bolts in his quiver twice, Hunter showed him how to reload and shoot quickly, keeping his eyes on the target. He practiced and the bounty hunter acted as trainer again. After shooting out his quiver three more times

Hunter told him he'd done well, very well. He happened to agree. All the bolts were consistently within the span of Hunter's hand at fifty yards.

Hunter had made sure the crossbow was in good working order, everything, from the limbs to the stock to the sights, was tight. The bounty hunter also checked over every bolt from the razor sharp broad head to the tip of the fletching and the all-important nock. When he was satisfied, he put the crossbow and quiver in the cave and took care of their prisoner. Dextera had finally realized that Hunter meant it when he told her to be quiet. He left the gag off her, allowed her to take care of certain business. He even took her to the creek to wash up. Once she was secured inside the cave again the bounty hunter asked him to spar. He did his best not to sound like he was jumping at the chance when he agreed.

As before it was more of a training session. The bounty hunter taught him things his mother's trainers never even touched on. Hunter was the most natural warrior/fighter/tracker that he'd ever met. It made the bounty hunter the only warrior Flax ever ran into that he'd hesitate to cross swords with.

The sparring session closed with the same slow quiet exercise that Hunter taught him the day before. It was starting to rain as they finished up but there was no thunder or lightening so they went to the creek to bathe anyways. Now, at just past the fifteenth hour it was raining steadily but none of it was leaking into the cave.

Before their planning session Hunter gagged and hooded their prisoner. The hood was different this time. It was snug leather and thick padding covered her ears and eyes. She wouldn't be able to hear them at all just in case her so called goddess could read her thoughts from a distance.

Finishing, the redhead met his gaze, "Any questions?"

Flax straightened his mustache, smoothed his beard, "You really think we can get out alive?"

A cool, feral, grin flashed, "Do what I tell you and we'll all get out alive."

He nodded, studied the maps the redhead had drawn thoughtfully. *I've got at least a hundred questions, none of which have much to do with this exactly...*

A strong hand gently touched his shoulder, "Second thoughts, lad?"

He shook his head, met the glacial eyes. They weren't cold or hard, in fact Hunter appeared far more understanding and sympathetic than he'd've thought possible. "No, I want to do it." He drew a deep breath, let it out, managed a crooked smile, "You can count on me to do my part."

"I know," Hunter squeezed his shoulder then released him to lace strong fingers on the bunk, turn his gaze to the maps. "But you don't have to do this. The Goddess knows you're too young." The red brows knit, jaw clenched. Hunter's beard had grown in already to the point where he'd trimmed it, shaved around it at the creek. It made him look older, more feral and hard.

When he gripped the bounty hunter's hard shoulder, his fingers brushed the scars. He managed to keep from looking at them, held the glacial gaze when Hunter turned to him. "I want to."

The bounty hunter nodded, offered him a smile, "Had to give you the chance to back out, Flax. Couldn't live with myself if I hadn't." The bounty hunter sat back, raked both hands through his spiraling red-gold mane, stretched. "Anything else? Anything at all? Questions, comments, objections, we should get it done now. In about two hours we won't have time to talk about anything."

"Except when we're waiting for them to all go inside," he pointed out.

"Yeah, but then we need to be quiet." Hunter rose, got their provisions from the hearth. "Hungry?"

He rubbed his stomach, "Yeah."

Nodding, the bounty hunter returned to his side, sat down, "I'm coming to the conclusion that you're always hungry." The provisions were placed between them.

Flax opened the bundle, found some dried meat, a hunk of cheese, some flat bread, dried fruit. "Not when I'm sleepin'."

Laughing quietly, Hunter caught his wrist, "Today, you have to share."

"I figured to," he offered the redhead a single piece of dried meat.

With a broad grin Hunter took the bundle from between them, "Sure that's all you want?"

He laughed as Hunter opened the bundle that was now in the redhead's lap. "That ain't all I want, gimme that." The bounty hunter blocked his attempt to grab it easily.

A single red brow lifted, "Here," Hunter placed a handful of dried apple slices in his hand. "That ought to do it."

"You bastard," he couldn't help laughing.

With a broad grin Hunter put the bundle between them, spread it open. "Eat as much as you want, lad. Though I suggest you keep it light."

He went about gathering a descent meal. "Oh, yeah? How come? Your belly feelin' deprived?" When he glanced up the bounty hunter looked serious.

"You're going into your first real battle." Hunter tore a piece of bread, shrugged, "Sometimes it can make a warrior... Physically ill."

He was tempted to believe the bounty hunter was teasing him but... he looked way too serious, "You mean that." It was a statement, no question to it at all.

Hunter nodded, "I've seen it happen. Don't worry, if it does.... I'll guard your back."

"That's comforting," he managed, *It is too, thank the Goddess no one'll get me cause I'm on my knees vomiting my guts out... Did it happen to you? Somehow I don't think you dropped to your knees and threw up at your first battle...* He considered the meal he'd gathered together. It was considerable but not really heavy for him... and he was hungry.

Hunter moved back to the wall opposite the bunk, leaned his back against it and stretched out strong legs. Holding out a hand for the water skin, the bounty hunter went on with his plans. "We'll get everything ready to go before we leave. It'll take maybe twenty minutes to reach the wagon, then, if the time is right, you climb inside and we'll go into town."

"Okay. Getting everything ready, that includes her?" He ate, took back the water-skin when it was offered.

"Yep," Hunter finished up his meal, wiped his hands on his black and gray leather breeches. "I'll get her ready and leave her with the horses."

"You gonna drug her?" he ventured.

"Aye, if only to keep her from trying something foolish."

He couldn't help glancing to Dextera, hooded, bound and gagged in the corner near the entrance. A pang of something akin to guilt passed through him and he forcefully pushed it away. There really wasn't a choice. *And she's a criminal, a murderess...*

"What else, lad?"

Tearing another piece of flat bread, he looked up to meet the bounty hunter's frosty eyes.

"You often look like you want to say something then never let it out. What is it?" Hunter elaborated, drawing a knife from his black and gray harness, checking its edge.

His half-smile cocked his mustache and he shrugged, dropped his gaze to the bread in his hands, "I have... probably a hundred questions..."

"We've got some time." Satisfied with the blade, the redhead replaced it then drew another.

He wet his lips, shifted to sit cross-legged as the bounty hunter replaced the second knife apparently satisfied with its edge. "Your first battle... did you..."

A cool grin flashed, "No, I didn't get sick. I did take a knife in the shoulder." The frosty gaze met his.

The bounty hunter smiled, cold, hard, and answered his unspoken question. "I killed her."

Hunter's willingness to answer him, talk, fueled his curiosity and made it easier to ask the next. "When you fought them, this morning... How'd you know I was there?"

"The same way you know when I'm there; you feel me watching or sense my presence. I could feel you watching. I heard you move to rise and wanted you to stay hidden." Hunter shrugged. He'd inspected three more knives replacing each of them after testing the edge.

"Okay... Then after..." Words failed him for the moment and his brows knit as he searched for how exactly to put it. The bounty hunter checked another knife, replaced it. "Afterwards you looked like you were on fire. You were so cold, but behind it..."

Hunter watched his thumb run along the edge of yet another knife, "What you saw in me, did it scare you?"

Flax's brows knit, "Not really. It did kinda... make me wary."

The redhead nodded, "When I told you that my blood burns when I kill I meant that. Bloodlust comes on me when I hunt, even if I'm just hunting game. It ... flickers when I'm sparing." A frosty smile spread across Hunter's features, the eyes went glacial, and that fire flickered behind the facade of ice. "Hell, just thinking about it fires me. I used to try to hide it but I can't so I don't bother any more." He drew a deep breath, the red brows knit and Hunter looked at the blade of the final knife he drew, "And it can be very intoxicating. I do my damnedest not to let it master me."

Flax swallowed hard but he wasn't afraid, not of Hunter. *Combat runs in my blood, fighting, sparing... I love it... need it. He said once that combat runs in his blood...* "You think it's in me?"

Hunter shrugged, "Your eyes blaze when we spar, lad. Weapons, combat, fire you. I know you want to go with me tonight. I know you won't balk and I'm pretty sure you won't be throwing up. All I can tell you is; master it. Do your damnedest and hold onto that honor of yours tonight despite how I'm trampling it." The bounty hunter sighed heavily, "I always try to do what's right, Flax, though I'm no one to look up to." Straightening, Hunter shifted to sit cross-legged; strong fingers combed the red gold mane.

Why not? If my sire had been like you... He looked at the floor. *I would never have been born... Or I'd be a product of rape... Yet, in a way, I'm that regardless. Does a slave ever have a choice. No... Yet no matter how smart, or strong or good lookin' I am because of him, no matter what I got from him... He's a slave... I'd trade this golden hair and my ororri night vision for a sire like this bastard of a bounty hunter in a heartbeat...* "I'm not sure about that."

Hunter laughed quietly, "You don't even know me, Flax." Drawing his short-sword, the redhead checked its edge. "Hardly fair for you, not knowing who you're going to be fighting beside." Replacing the short-sword, the redhead rose smoothly to his feet, drew the long-sword to inspect the blade.

Flax swallowed but his mouth was dry. He took up the water-skin, got a drink, shrugged, "I know enough." He felt the frosty gaze met glacial eyes.

"Do you?" a hard grin, more a bearing of the wolf's fangs, crossed the bounty hunter's features. Then it became a real smile, some of the ice thawed, "You're so curious." The glacial eyes went to the sword's razor edge, "About everything, aren't you? The scars that mark my back among a host of other things." The sword slid home and the redhead shed his harness. "When I was twenty-three..."

Flax stared, caught in the shock of realization for a heartbeat. *He's gonna tell me ...*

The bounty hunter laid the black and gray harness across the bunk. "I was inexperienced... more like young and reckless. I was hunting a troop of bandits, five sisters, operating in Cyrcania, Thyria and Tanlyra. Once they hit a caravan or some outlying estate they'd scatter. The highest bounty was on the leader, the eldest sister, so I went after her first." He donned his black and gray shirt, laced the sleeves around his forearms while he talked. "Well, I found her alone and I took her. Didn't realize she was meeting her sisters. They saw and followed. I was struck from behind..." The redhead tied the shirt then knelt to search through the box under the bunk. His brows knit as he considered a brown shirt then a red one. "They freed their sister and bound me." He choose a red tunic, donned it over the black shirt. "I was strung up against a tree, beaten with a Kylonian long-whip." Making sure the black shirt was completely concealed beneath the red one the bounty hunter closed up the box, slid it back under the bed. Sitting on the bunk, he unlaced the black boots to the ankles, turned down the tops so they looked like flares.

I've heard this tale... in a tavern in Bysenisa, only it was seven bandits... Flax couldn't help but stare, watch the bounty hunter's hard frozen features. Real empathy made his chest tighten and his throat thick.

"Then I was staked out on the ground." Frozen eyes met his, "I was raped, over and over... for hours." The bounty hunter stretched his hands into the red-brown bracers, fastened them over the red shirt's sleeves. "There is nothing worse than rape. It strips away dignity, tears at self-worth... shatters defenses like so much fragile crystal." The redhead put a pair of fingerless gloves; colliette claws, in the small black pack then attached it to the harness. From the pack the bounty hunter produced a thick black chain. It looked very much like a Kylonian style consortship chain. The redhead slung it around his own neck, fastened it. "I swore to myself I wouldn't let them collar me, brand me. I am no one's slave no matter what, even if I had to make them kill me or if I had to do it myself, they would never drag me to a block or lock a collar around my neck." Closing up the pack, he slipped the harness back on, fastened the rings. "When they finished with me, went to their furs and fell asleep, I got loose. They made the mistake of using rope. Knots in rope can work loose easier than knots in good leather." The red-gold mane was deftly woven into a single braid, secured with a wide brown leather tie laced up with darker brown. "I killed the four younger sisters, slit their throats. The eldest... I nearly beat her to death with my bare hands." He laced his fingers, studied them. "I stopped short of that and I didn't do to them what they'd done to me. I thank the Goddess I had the strength to keep from sinking to their level." Red brows knit and the bounty hunter's jaw tightened. "Sometimes I have nightmares. And sometimes... It still hurts me." The glacial eyes met his, "My name..." The bounty hunter smiled slightly, ruefully, "My real name is Tymiran. You may call me Ty if you like. If you've changed your mind about tonight you may stay behind or take your horse and go when I leave."

Suddenly confused, Flax shook his head, "I haven't... why would I?"

Tymiran shrugged, "My reputation is rather mixed. There are those who wouldn't fight at my side."

For a moment he was speechless then he shook it off, "I consider it an honor."

Hunter... Tymiran drew a deep breath, rose pushing it out. "I hope you see it that way when we're mounting our horses in a few hours. Get ready, I'll see to Dextera."

Flax rose, gripped the bounty hunter's hard shoulder, "Lemme buy you a tankard tomorrow evening?"

Giving him a solid smack on the bicep, Ty grinned, "Done. Now, we've got work to do."

It was dark as they neared the wagon concealed in a wide depression choked with brush. The rain had slackened to a drizzle. The sky was shrouded in clouds making the nightfall faster and darker than a clear night, even a moonless one. The depression was nearly a third of the way around the town from the stony gully and its campsite. Flax followed the bounty hunter, keeping low to the ground as they moved between the bushes. The bounty hunter took the feedbags and tethers off the horses, led them to the harnesses. Meanwhile Flax busied himself pulling down the mesh like netting draped over the wagon like a loose tent. He folded it up neatly as he'd been told then lowered the tailgate. There was a space in the center between the sacks of grain, a well concealed frame held some sacks up, completely covering the hiding place beneath and between. He pushed the folded netting in as far as he could then slid his crossbow in after it. Tymiran hitched up the horses quickly and efficiently then came around the back of the tarp-covered load of grain sacks. Shedding his harness, the bounty hunter bundled it up carefully then slid it in and to one side. His crossbow and quiver followed then a gesture indicated it was Flax's turn. He maneuvered into the somewhat crowded space. Knowing the bounty hunter would be without his harness made him kind of uneasy despite the fact that it was part of the plan. When he'd remarked that Tymiran would be unarmed a feral grin lit the hard features. Ty said he was never unarmed.

"Set?" the bounty hunter whispered barely audible.

"Yeah," he replied just as quietly.

With that Tymiran shut the wagon's low tailgate, strapped down the tarp. All Flax could see for the moment was deeply shadowed grain sacks and the rough frame holding the ones that hid him from view. At least the bounty hunter had thought to throw a thick stable blanket on the wagon bed so he wasn't lying on the bare boards. It wasn't wet either; the canvas tarp must have been treated with oil or wax because it seemed to be waterproof. It also made the sound of the rain on it louder but he could still hear the horses. At least he was dry; Tymiran would most likely end up soaked. Still, it was hardly comfortable, laying sort of half on his back half on his side with his legs bent.

He felt the wagon move; Tymiran was leading the horses out of the thicket. In a few heartbeats the wagon stopped then shifted as the bounty hunter climbed to the seat. The wagon lurched, moving forward at what he figured was a trot. He knew from their planning session that Tymiran would drive into town on the east road,

nearly opposite from the gully that held the campsite.
The cave that had been their campsite was all closed up,
covered over with brush. The horses were saddled in the
so-called stable, ready to go. Dextera too, was in the
stable but she was unconscious, drugged into a deep
sleep. Yet the bounty hunter had her bound and gagged
securely. Their packs were tied behind their saddles so
all they had left to do was throw Dextera over Flax's
cantle when they mounted.

Breathing the scent of grain and damp old burlap
Flax stifled a sneeze. His black rufa veiled his eyes,
features completely. The darkest pair of breeches he
owned garbed legs and loins in deep chocolate brown
leather. His dark brown boots were well padded so he
wore them with boot knives strapped in them both. A
hidden knife was also strapped in the right along the
inside of his calf. The garrote was hidden in the bracer
on his right wrist. Hunter... Tymiran had helped him hide
nearly a dozen blades in his clothes, there was even one
woven into his braid.

He stifled a groan when his left calf cramped.
Working his foot, stretching his toes got it to ease and
just about the time he was thinking of stretching a little
more, he heard someone call to the wagon driver.
Tymiran answered halting the horses and he heard a
pair of constables questioning the bounty hunter.
Tymiran climbed down at their order and came around to
the side of the wagon's bed. His hand curled around his
crossbow and very carefully he cocked it, silently
pointing it toward the muffled voices. The tarp was
loosened, folded back and he could see between the
grain sacks atop the carefully constructed frame. A tall,
strongly built lady was standing next to the wagon, next
to Tymiran but her attention was on the redhead. She
was asking why Tymiran's mistress didn't insist he

shave, at least wear only a mustache. With a shy smile the hard, cold bounty hunter managed to look embarrassed and suggestive at the same time. Tymiran inferred that he was shaved all over except for the beard and his long mane. The tarp was folded back into place, secured and Flax let out the breath he'd been holding albeit quietly. After an exchange he couldn't hear, the wagon shifted as Tymiran stepped back into the seat.

Flax said a sincere prayer of thanks to Rathitara for their entering the town safely then asked Her if the rest of the evening might go as smoothly. The sound of wagon wheels on wet stone paved streets reverberated though the wood beneath and around him and he gritted his teeth against a grunt. *This has to be the world's noisiest, most uncomfortable way to travel... If I even so much as suggest this to anyone else, ever, for any reason, I should be whipped...*

After what seemed an eternity, the horses slowed from a jog to a walk. He felt them making a series of turns then halting. His guts knotted with tension, anticipation... but they had been since they left the cave, since before even that. He'd been wound tight and ready... probably since the bounty hunter told him to get dressed for the evening's work. Stock still, Flax waited then realized he was holding his breath again. Blowing it out slowly, quietly, he concentrated on breathing normally and listening to the wagon's assorted creaks and groans. He felt the wagon shift as Tymiran swung down from his seat. Time stretched out, stood still, then the tailgate dropped quietly.

"C'mon." Tymiran's whisper was almost inaudible.

Carefully, he slid out of the wagon, crouched at it's back. They were in a narrow alley with run-down buildings flanking them. The one to his right was low, only a single story but the one to the left, his left, facing away from the wagon for the moment, was three or four stories with an ornate cornice at the roof's edge. The alley was dirty, dank. Refuse was piled near the building's back and Flax made out a tangle of three rats watching them with beady eyes. Doing his best not to smell the rotten stench around him he turned toward the wagon, looked beneath it and through the horses legs. He could see all the way to the alley's end where it intersected another.

The bounty hunter was already out of the red shirt and consortship chain. In moments Tymiran had his hair tucked down the back of his black and gray shirt. The hood went up, features were veiled and the black and gray harness fastened on. The bracers were traded for the colliette claws then the bounty hunter slid his crossbow out of the wagon along with both quivers, passing Flax his. He silently, carefully slung it over his shoulder across his chest so it hung at his right hip, opposite his quiver. Tymiran closed up the wagon, gripped his shoulder. When he met the frosty eyes the bounty hunter touched his own chest then pointed up, towards the roof. Another gesture indicated he should remain where he was for the moment and watch the bounty hunter's back. Flax nodded once.

Tymiran deftly removed the heavy grapple and cord from his small pack. Stepping away from the wagon a bit, he swung the grapple in a circle, let it fly toward the roof. Straining his ears, Flax listened for it to hit but try as he might he didn't hear it. Testing it's hold, the bounty hunter again gave him a nod then climbed the rope easily hand over hand. Within a few heartbeats Tymiran disappeared over the roof's edge. Flax watched as requested, up and down the narrow alley. There were no torches, no lamps at all here. He sensed/felt no one; he was alone with the wagon and horses... and the rats. There wasn't even any movement some thirty feet down at the alley's mouth. It didn't look like the other alley was lit much better than this one. Silently, he adjusted his crossbow's sling across his chest, holding the weapon at the ready. All the while he kept a watch up and down the alleyway, remaining crouched at the wagons rear. A quiet noise from above that could have been anything, a bat, a night-bird, a rat skittering along the building's cornice, drew his attention.

He glanced up, knowing it was the bounty hunter. The slight nod meant it was his turn and he settled his crossbow more to his back then moved to the foot of the rope. With a deep calming breath he straightened then climbed the cord. In moments he was crawling over the ornate cornice to the gently peaked slate roof and Hunter... Tymiran was winding up the cord. Crouching low, he scanned the roof, the neighboring buildings. According to the bounty hunter many of the shops and homes for a hundred yard radius had been abandoned. The exodus seemed to have started about three years previously. Imagine that coincidence. Tymiran thought perhaps the cult of Dehegra was forcing people out. At any rate much of the property now belonged to a couple prominent merchantess' with ties to the cult.

At a gesture from the bounty hunter, he followed Tymiran along the cornice, mindful of the drainage holes in the stone work. As they neared one of the many chimneys the bounty hunter paused, scanned the roofs adjacent to the building then all those visible. The bounty hunter climbed to the junction of chimney and roof while Flax stood just looking over the top. The temple square some two streets over was better lit than the surrounding streets and buildings. There wasn't a light to be seen in a window for better than a hundred yards all around.

Tymiran drew back, rose to his side. "You can see okay?" the bounty hunter whispered near his ear.

He nodded, not trusting himself to be able to keep his voice low enough.

"I'm going to the top, stay here, stay silent."

He nodded again then the bounty hunter was sliding to his belly on the rain-slicked slate, climbing to the peak. He scanned the rooftops around them, watched for anyone possibly watching them. There didn't appear to be anyone else on the roofs at all. He spared a glance in the bounty hunter's direction... And for a moment couldn't find him. Then a shadow rectified itself into Tymiran standing along side the central chimney. The bounty hunter was pressed tightly to the stone, almost melting into it in his black and gray clothing. Flax shook his head slightly in amazement. It seemed the bounty hunter could hide anywhere, anytime.

Drawing a slow deep breath, he concentrated back on watching the surrounding rooftops, the temple roof. He couldn't see the square before it's main doors but he'd wager Tymiran could from his place at the roof's peak. Time seemed to stand still except for the fact that he moved his gaze constantly from building to building. Drizzle soaked through his shirt at the shoulders, back. His breeches were dry and it was far from cold, in all honesty some of what was wetting his shirt was his own sweat. Though it was cooler than it had been it was still hot as far as he was concerned.

Finally, he sensed the bounty hunter's approach and spared a glance in that direction. Sure enough a darker shadow was sliding slowly down the roof toward him. Tension and anticipation sang in his veins, *Oh Goddess this is crazy, I can't wait...* In moments the bounty hunter arrived at his side, a gesture indicated it was time, another indicated they would drop down to the street instead of sticking to the roofs. When they were both on the ground again Tymiran led the way through the dank alleys toward the temple and around to it's rear. He watched their backs, staying close but not too close, watching and obeying the bounty hunter's signals to stop or get down, to stay back or move.

Then Tymiran crouched low, beckoned him to the bounty hunter's side. He moved silently forward until he was standing above Tymiran. At the bounty hunter's gesture he eased a look around the building's corner. The back of the temple was visible, some twenty paces from the end of a short alleyway. There were two ladies dressed from head to toe in red, leathers, cloaks, harnesses, thigh high boots. They were guarding a recessed door flanked by two oil-lamps. They both wore a sort of half mask covering their faces to cheekbones, flaring to flame like wings at the temples that swept back. Hoods depended from inside the wings, covering the hair. Each guard held a double bladed long axe. A light touch on his thigh brought him back from his discrete look.

Flax pressed his back to the wall, breathed deeply of the dank damp air. *We should face them, killing them unaware isn't... honorable... yet, we can't have them knowing we're here. Lives depend on what we do right now... and I agreed to do this his way...* Looking down he met the glacial blue eyes, read the fires blazing behind the frozen facade. Tymiran gestured for him to stay and he nodded once. The bounty hunter turned to glide back down the alley to another

intersection then he was gone. Drawing another calming
breath Flax carefully looked around the corner again.
The two sentries were still at their post, for the moment.
Noises of quiet conversation came to him, their meaning
drowned in the dripping of water from rain gutters and
roof drains, cornices and widow ledges. Then a deeper
shadow crossed the intervening space to the temple's
wall. Flax's heart skipped a beat, then he realized he
was holding his breath. Carefully, slowly he exhaled. He
could just see the dark shadow move toward them, then
one crumbled silently. The other stared in shock for just
a split second but it was long enough for Tymiran to grab
her from behind. There was an abrupt movement then
she too crumbled to a heap. Tymiran dropped to a
crouch, checked to make sure they were both dead
then... perhaps wiped a small throwing blade on one
sentry's shirt and replaced it. The hooded head lifted
and he felt the bounty hunter's gaze, saw the slight
beckoning motion. The bounty hunter moved into the
sheltered doorway, put out the lamps.

Checking behind him, he moved to the alley's
mouth then scanned the empty space between his
concealment and the doorway. In a heartbeat he
crossed it to slip into the shadows of the arched and
recessed door. Rising smoothly, Tymiran grasped the
harnesses of each lady and dragged them into the
darkest shadows. The glacial eyes met his for a moment
then Tymiran turned to the door. Crouching the bounty
hunter drew a slender... tool of some kind... A lock pick
... From the inside of his harness shoulder strap.

In less than a heartbeat a muffled click came to
him sounding way too loud in the near silence of the
damp night. Still crouched, Tymiran moved to one side
of the door, his back to the wall. At the bounty hunter's
glance, he did the same, holding his crossbow at the

ready. As quietly as possible, Tymiran worked the latch, pushed the door in, grasped a knife hilt. Light spilled out, onto the wet stoop. Meeting his gaze the bounty hunter lifted one finger from his hilt. Flax understood, he started a slow count to sixty. As he counted in his head he scanned the open space between the temple and the nearest buildings, the darker alleys. When he reached sixty, he met the bounty hunter's frosty eyes. Tymiran lightly tapped his own chest, indicating he was first. Flax was to count twenty, the bounty hunter signaled opening his hand four times, then follow. He answered with a nod then Tymiran practically dove though the open door. He counted twenty, scanned his surroundings, the ramshackle buildings, dank alleyways then he slipped inside, crossing the doorway as fast as possible.

Remaining on his feet, he pressed himself to the opposite wall feeling terribly exposed in the well-lighted hallway. Tymiran looked up from removing his garrote from the throat of another guard dressed like the first two.

Shit! Didn't even hear her or him killing her... Goddess, no one can be that quiet... His eyes met Tymiran's blazing glacial eyes and he'd wager the bounty hunter was grinning, that feral teeth bearing grin more like the threat of a predator. Slowly, Tymiran rose; silently moved to his side. A gesture indicated he should crouch so he did.

Strong fingers gripped his shoulder, the bounty hunter whispered near his ear. "Back outside. Start your count, three hundred just like we practiced, okay."

It wasn't quite a question. He really couldn't back out now and the only way to survive this, besides running, would be to follow the bounty hunter's plan. He absolutely didn't want to run.

He met the frosty eyes, "No problem."

Grasping the guard's harness, Tymiran hauled her body outside with them. He followed the bounty hunter out, took up a place flanking the door, watching the narrow courtyard, the alleyways. A strong hand gripped his shoulder, brought his gaze to those frosty eyes.

He'd wager that Tymiran was grinning behind his veil, "You can see well."

He nodded once.

"Remember you promised me a tankard tomorrow night. You have to be alive to buy me one."

He grinned, nodded and whispered as quietly as he could, "You remember you gotta be alive to drink it."

"One," Tymiran gave him a nod then disappeared slipping around the corner of the doorway.

Two... Three... He started the count, watching the broad space between the temple and the surrounding buildings. No matter how he tried he couldn't help but be aware of the dead bodies, mere inches away piled in the corner opposite him in the deepest shadows. With effort he concentrated on counting slowly, evenly, like they practiced together. It had taken him three times to learn to keep time with the bounty hunter. He'd started out too fast, always ending up seven or eight seconds ahead. Tension knotted in his gut but he didn't feel sick... wound tight, ready, maybe too ready.

It seemed an eternity to reach three hundred then he was there. Readying his crossbow, drawing a deep breath, he worked the latch as quietly as he could then leapt into the curving hallway. He scanned both branches of the passage, pointing his crossbow down one then the other. No one. He concentrated on listening, breathing slowly, silently, for a couple heartbeats, then started carefully down the left wing of the curving corridor. He hugged the inner wall, listening closely for anyone walking the corridor. He encountered no one and made his way to the archway on the central curving stairs. Up would take him to a bell tower and an upper altar room beneath an open skylight. Down led to the altar room Dehegra and her followers were using tonight. Despite the fact that the moon couldn't be seen the ceremony wouldn't be postponed, the blood moon came only one night a year.

Glancing upwards, he could tell they hadn't used that flight of steps for quite a while. Dust lay thick and undisturbed on the broad stairs. Looking down, he could read the passage of many feet, so many in fact that dust only lay in the corners of step and wall. Slowly, quietly, he started his descent. Hugging the outer wall, holding his crossbow at the ready, Flax made his way steadily downward. After a complete circle, he reached a place where the stairway leveled off. A series of arched latticed panels made up the inner wall. Halfway along this latticework was a cleverly concealed door. He spotted it only because Tymiran had told him what to look for. Even the hinges were concealed.

With a final glance back and forth along the corridor, he crossed to the door. Gently pressing the frame, he was rewarded with a quiet click and the door swung open. Flax glanced up and down the hall again then slipped inside.

Scanning the gallery, sweeping it with his crossbow, revealed it was empty as Tymiran told him it should be. It was some twenty feet long by a mere seven feet wide. Eight worn wooden benches were stacked four on either side of the door. Dropping stealthily to the floor on one hand and both knees, he carefully crawled to the latticed railing, cradling his crossbow in his free hand. Almost laying down behind the railing, he propped himself on an elbow and looked through the holes in the latticework. Dextera had been right, it looked very much like fifty people, mostly female, crowded in the open space below, before the altar. That was on a raised dais to his right at the edge of the circular chamber. In a way it looked like an eye. One large round room with the dais raised against the wall. The walls were painted in dark brown... rusty colored designs... *Oh Goddess, that's not paint, it's their blood...* Flax swallowed hard against the wrath rising in his throat. The altar itself was nearly against the curving wall. Five low platforms were arrayed before it. Their use was plain, the leather straps at each corner and at the center nearest the altar, the channels cut along the sides and in the center all running toward the altar, the bloodstains, clearly defined it even from his elevated position.

His lip curled and he stifled a low growl at the thought of what had obviously taken place upon those platforms. Two fire-pits full of kindling flanked the altar. The altar itself was mounted with a pair of large charred brass fire bowls nearly full of lamp oil. A horrid garland decorated it, the strung together scalps of some twenty-five or thirty sacrifices. Flax swallowed hard again. Dehegra had apparently been operating even longer than three years, perhaps killing her own sacrifices before she found this way to slake her terrible lusts. His mild revulsion at having to kill some of his enemies unaware faded away in the wrath the horrific sight instilled in him.

With effort, he concentrated on the plan. Looking across the altar room to the walls, he picked out the archway off the opposite staircase, it's corridor around the room that ran beneath his own. His gaze lifted to the gallery opposite and he searched the latticework for Tymiran. After a moment, he thought he saw a darker shadow amongst those of the unlighted gallery but he wasn't sure until the shadow rose above the railing just enough to reveal the slit between hood and veil, the frosty eyes. Even at this distance, Flax could meet that cold gaze and read the fires behind it, feel them like the heat of a forge. He knew immediately that Tymiran could see him though he doubted anyone else could. Flax nodded then heard a sound in the corridor behind and below him. He put his open hand to the lattice, the signal for possible trouble in the gallery, then rolled to face the door, crawl stealthily toward it on his belly. Approaching footsteps came to him and his guts tightened. The Goddess, the real Goddess, only knew why she was striding purposefully up the stairs. The real problem was; where exactly was she headed? If she was even just going to walk a parameter or check the upper halls she'd realize something was wrong when she didn't find the sentry that had been patrolling them.

I gotta make her come in here then take her out.

Only a heartbeat passed but the sounds of footfalls were fast approaching. He reached the benches, maneuvered to crouch low along them on the side of the door opposite the hinges. He could see a guard approaching now through the latticework. She didn't appear worried, more business like, and she was garbed like the guards on the door and in the upper hall had been. In a split second a decision was made. Flax laid his crossbow down very carefully yet allowing it to make some noise and she halted, cocked her head as if listening for something. Tension sang along his bones, muscles, tendons. Every nerve was alive and humming, anticipation tightened his guts.

Odds are she'll investigate because it's her job... At least I think she might... If I'm really shit out of luck she'll run for help... or holler for it... And if she does? Then I reach through the lattice and grab her... And just let everyone in the place know I'm here... Then we're both fucked... No, we're all fucked because Tymiran and I will be hard pressed to save our own skins... Getting the sacrifices out alive will be almost impossible.

Six

C'mon, lady, you wanna handle it yourself... To bask in Dehegra's approval... C'mon, c'mon... Flax reminded himself to breath, albeit slowly, quietly. His blood sang in his veins, burned like liquid fire in his flesh... *This is what he feels, what makes him look like a volcano is boiling behind those frozen eyes... Oh Goddess, he's right it's so intoxicating ...* She moved purposefully toward the latticed door, pressed the frame. The door opened inward and he could see her scan the room. Her right hand moved to her sword hilt and she stepped inside quietly, eyes searching the room as she pushed the door open to the benches stacked against the wall behind it. When she took another step, he rose silent as a striking snake. The garrote was in his hands quick as thought and he dropped it over her head. She stiffened, one hand flying to her throat, fingers digging frantically at the wire, the other reaching for a blade. No sound escaped her lips. Jerking the handles apart he felt her slump twitching against him.

Flax shuddered, trembled with the powerful sensations boiling inside him. Nevertheless, he quickly and quietly laid her on the floor then shut the door. Returning to the body, he crouched, unwinding the garrote sunk deeply in the flesh of her throat. *She's dead... I killed her... Goddess... forgive me... I don't feel anything but... Bloodlust...* Brows knitting, he stared at the body for a heartbeat then cleaned the garrote on her red cowl. Tucking the weapon back in its place, he took up his crossbow and crawled back to the latticed railing.

I had to... If I hadn't we'd never be able to make it out alive, let alone save them... Goddess, please help me master this... It feels... Good... Too good... It shouldn't feel like this to take a life, even an enemy's... Even someone like her, a mercenary protecting these murderesses... Or worse, a fanatic like them... Tymiran, would you help me master this? You have... What would you want from me to teach me how? What would you want, bounty hunter, to make me your apprentice? Can I afford it?..

Flax looked across the expanse of the chamber, met the glacial eyes through the lattice. A closed black-sheathed hand pressed the lattice, the bounty hunter asking him if all was well. *No, it's not... I've killed and Goddess help me... The bloodlust.... I am just like you.* Steeling himself, he put his own closed hand to the lattice. Yes, situation handled, no trouble. *But there is... I'm so high... Nothing but sex makes me nearly this high...* Tymiran signaled him to look below so he did.

Panels slid open behind and flanking the altar. Quite whispers of anticipation, then appreciation drifted through the on-lookers as the priestesses and their sacrifices entered. One priestess garbed in a blood red leather halter, tang and thigh high boots entered from each. Their features were concealed by a mask similar to the ones the guards had worn though more detailed and ornate. Fine gold stitched crimson cloth covered the hair. Each priestess was leading a naked young male. The priestess on his side of the room was tall, over six feet and powerfully built. She tugged the leash, turning to look back at her victim. Her sacrifice was probably six foot, strongly built but leaner, lighter than himself or Tymiran. Long blond hair fell in waves to his rump. He followed docilely, prodded along by a slave whip in the hand of an acolyte following.

The priestess on Tymiran's side was shorter, leaner yet garbed similarly. She too led a sacrifice but hers fought. For a Byrynthian male, he was short, no taller than five eight and stocky. His wrists and arms were bound tightly; leather cuffs secured his ankles close together. He could walk only by taking small careful steps but he wasn't walking at all. He braced his feet, pulled against the leash, struggled against the acolyte behind him, cursing his captress and her cohorts. The priestess struck him hard across the face and he stumbled, went to his knees. Tossing back long white blond hair, he spit in her face. Raising the slave whip, it's blades folded along the handle, the acolyte struck him a vicious blow to the base of his head. When he crumbled to the floor, the acolyte whipped him mercilessly until he stopped struggling. At the priestess' gesture the acolyte hooked her whip at her hip then gagged the young male. Together they lifted him, carried him, to the center platform before the altar. He struggled but was bound in place. Spread eagle on the platform, he lay chest heaving with his head toward Dehegra's altar. The first young male, the docile one, was led to a platform to be bound in place. He didn't fight at all and knowing he shouldn't be drugged, that fact kind of worried Flax. It was possible the young male had been driven over the edge of reality. *If he's crazy... Then what?..*

Two other priestesses emerged, their sacrifices followed, prodded along by the acolytes and their whips. The one across the chamber was tall, lean. She looked hard and sinewy, almost too thin for the lean muscle packed onto her frame. Her sacrifice was another short, blond male. He was well-built, probably just over five and half feet tall. Golden hair fell in bold waves nearly to his rump. He struggled a little but seemed overwhelmed and exhausted.

The priestess on his side of the chamber was... well, if Flax had to guess he'd say she was a merchantess. He figured her to be too soft for a warrior who practiced weapons every day. Still, she wasn't fat, just very curvy and soft. Her sacrifice had to be dragged to his platform. He was ororri, definitely short at around five and half feet tall. His golden brown skin was beaded by his struggles, marred by the whip. His hair was a very rich golden blond. It cascaded past his rump to mid thigh in a straight glossy curtain stirred by his struggles. Between the priestesses and their acolytes the sacrifices were bound in place.

A young female, evidently Dextera's acolyte until it was obvious that the priestess herself wouldn't show up, led in the fifth sacrifice. Her sacrifice was nearly six feet tall and strongly built. They were followed by a lady dressed as the guards in the upper corridors and on the doors had been. The guard pushed him forward by a fist knotted tightly in his nearly white blond mane of gently curling hair. He looked Byrynthian and he struggled, to no avail. As he was bound in place, he fought, slipped the guard's grip for a moment. She struck him a solid blow across the face that brought blood to his mouth visible even from the gallery. That ended his struggles and they finished binding him down in moments.

Flax swallowed hard, fighting the wrath and bloodlust boiling in his body. He forced himself to think only of the job at hand and choose a target. The acolyte turned priestess taking Dextera's place; she was first on his list. Then the other two, in order, across the room from him would follow. Then, if he had time, their acolytes and the guard assisting Dextera's stand in.

Tymiran would have the three under his gallery and the so-called goddess herself. The moment she appeared she would fall. He wasn't even supposed to be thinking about it.

Making a supreme effort, Flax cleared his mind, breathed regularly just watching the scene below. It was hard to stay focused though, as the priestesses removed their tangs to take their sacrifices. Turning his gaze to the crowd, he could sense their anticipation, read it written on half a hundred eager faces. It made his stomach turn, his blood burn, sear in his veins. Concentration and focus were elusive and yet he strove for them. Lives depended on him, on everything he did, and he'd be damned if he was going to allow them to win because he was so angry he couldn't think straight.

Pushing it away, he looked across the chamber at the gallery opposite, at the dark shadow behind the lattice that he knew to be the bounty hunter. He almost jumped when he met those cold eyes. Again the signal/inquiry, is all well? Drawing a deep breath, he put his closed hand to the lattice again, basically telling Tymiran he was okay. *I will do my part... We have to stop them, get the sacrifices out... no matter what... Werdeka give me strength; grant me focus and a swift blade.*

He strove not to watch as the sacrifices were mounted, brought somehow to readiness then taken. He strove not to listen to their protests, the grunts and groans, low growls of resistance. One of them was whimpering quietly and though it was so low one could barely hear it the sound seemed to fill the chamber. *He's right; there is nothing worse than rape...*

A ripple of whispers swept the room and Flax looked toward the altar. It seemed to be shimmering...

with heat waves. Glancing to the gallery opposite showed him the bounty hunter was ready; Flax could just make out the outline of Tymiran, aiming his crossbow through one of the holes in the latticed railing. He got ready as well. Maneuvering so he could sit unobserved and aim through the lattice, he set his sights on the priestess he'd chosen for his first target.

The air over the altar shimmered with heat waves, expanding to cover the bowls of oil and then the fire pits. Tinder erupted into flames and the fire pits were engulfed. The oil followed, bursting into bluish fire. He clenched his jaw, thought only of a wall in his head. Like a fortress, Tymiran had told him. Build it like it's a fortress around your mind. Don't think, just do it; see it there in front of your thoughts, between them and you.

Fire erupted upon the altar itself then a lady was standing in it's midst. She seemed to blaze with it, wrapping her limbs, lifting her hair. Her arms lifted in a widespread v, as if she was urging the fire to new heights. It seemed to obey, even the oil lamps flared higher as the fire pits roared and the oil bowls blazed with unnatural fury. Inside it, she was black as the darkest night... a negosi lady, he'd wager, if he could see her clearly but he only noticed absently. His concentration was on his internal fortress like Tymiran had told him. A sorceri could read thoughts and they didn't really know how powerful this one was or how well she knew her gift. Tymiran thought the chances were that she didn't, that was why she'd decided she was a goddess. Fire played over her body, glowed nearly white hot, then receded back to the fire pits and oil reservoirs nearly depleted now of their fuel.

Dehegra was tall, well over six feet probably close to six-six or eight. Her red hair settled about strong onyx skinned shoulders in a foamy mass of thick curls. Her lupine gaze swept her priestesses, their sacrifices. Obvious relish, cruel lust lit angular onyx features. Her ebony body, glistening with a sheen of perspiration was lean, hard.

Flax saw everything with detachment, from the corner of his perception. His eye was on his target, his concentration on his fortress. Distantly, he heard the quiet sound of a crossbow firing then he too fired. His target toppled and he shifted his gaze, his sights to his next target as he reloaded. From the corner of his eye he noted a crossbow bolt protruding from the so-called goddess' chest then another joined it. She swayed on the altar, grasping frantically at the fletching just barely protruding from her chest. Flax squeezed the trigger on his second target as a third bolt seemed to materialize in Dehegra's face, fletching sunk in the eye socket. Her black form toppled from the altar as his second target crumbled and his sights settled on his third. Confusion boiled in the chamber beneath them. A few rushed for the altar, others moved towards the steps but the vast majority where plainly just frozen in shock. His third target went down then he settled on his forth. Meanwhile two of the priestesses that were on his side of the chamber, Tymiran's second and third targets, were down. Then the bounty hunter's forth toppled. His fourth and fifth had fallen when he heard the pounding of approaching feet on the steps.

Rising smoothly, he reloaded without thinking about it. Crossing the chamber in two strides, he tore the door open, leapt into the hall. The first person to come into view fell with a crossbow bolt in her chest. Flax crossed the stairway to the wall. Tearing the closest oil lamp from its bracket, he smashed it on the steps behind him, against the fragile latticework. It burst into flames.

Shifting his crossbow more to his back, he drew his short sword, faced those coming at him from below. His blood was liquid fire in his veins, molten magma searing his muscle, sinew, bones to ash. Dehegra's followers hesitated for a moment staring at him with a mixture of wrath and fear. With eyes and features still concealed by the black rufa; he had no doubt he looked frightening. Taking advantage of their hesitation, he tore another lamp from its place and tossed it to the steps behind him. He heard the glass chimney shatter, the oil ignite as it spread across the stairs. Flames crackled behind him warming his back and the smell of burning oil and wood filled the air. Tymiran had been right though, the smoke drafted up the stairs, staying high along the ceiling. It would pour out the tower. With luck no one would notice the temple was burning. Flax grinned behind his rufa then started slowly down the stairs, drawing his assassin's blade.

Finally, Dehegra's followers surged forward and he met them. The first tumbled to the steps headless; the metallic scent of blood met his nostrils. Even through the rufa, above the smoke, he could smell it. The second fell in a knot of guts. Flax waded through them, sword and knife mere blurs of steel flinging blood. It splattered him in nearly scalding splashes to hands, forearms, chest. The scent filled him to overflowing, so thick he could taste it on his tongue, fanning the flames already burning through his veins. In what seemed heartbeats, he was alone on the stairs and he took the opportunity to clean and sheath his assassin's blade, reload his crossbow and tear down three more lamps. When he was finished, the gallery was blazing as heartily as the fire-pits had and the stairs were cut off from below.

Making his way through the litter of bodies and offal, he descended toward the din of confusion and battle below. He didn't pass ten steps when more of Dehegra's people charged up the stairs. He cut them down, parrying, blocking, slicing his way through, leaving carnage in his wake.

His blood sang in his ears, roared though his veins. The bloodlust swelled in him like a torrent, rushing and irresistible, drenching him. He arrived at the mouth of the stairway, reloaded his crossbow and pulled down a few lamps to block them before more enemies rushed him. A crossbow bolt slammed through the chest of the first lady, a deft swing of his sword took the second's head. He whirled, offering no stationary target, cutting a swath to the altar dais and Tymiran's side. The bounty hunter cut down the last of the acolytes and turned to face him momentarily.

He read the fires blazing in the frosty glacial eyes but it was more than fire. It was the same bloodlust coursing through his veins and yet the intensity he saw in the bounty hunter's eyes was double, even triple what he felt blazing in his own body. Flax would wager everything that he owned the bounty hunter was grinning, that feral frightening baring of the wolf's teeth. A toss of the bounty hunter's head warned him the moment he sensed a threat from behind. He whirled, blocked a long axe, pushed the blades and handle aside to sink his knife in his enemy's throat. She gurgled, reeled back, dropping her weapon. He kicked her in the chest, toppling her to the blood-spattered floor.

The bounty hunter took it upon himself to guard the dais and the sacrifices bound there. His speed boggled the mind. The curved eastern swords were a blur as he slashed, parried and struck. Graceful blades spun in deft hands reversing their grip as if they were a part of the bounty hunter rather than a weapon held in the hand. Any enemy coming within Tymiran's reach went down in a rain of blood or brains or offal.

Sensing another threat, he spun but a sword cut through his shirt, across his chest, severing the crossbow strap. He didn't take time to grab it as it fell. Instead, his sword sliced through the enemy's belly, spilling guts around her feet. The next saw her throat cut to the bone and she slumped dead on the stone. He shifted, countered, blocked and sliced, wading through those enemies left, driving them to the fire engulfed stairs. When the last one fell he whirled, scanning the chamber. All that met his gaze was death.

Bodies and blood were everywhere, only Tymiran remained standing, and those frosty eyes met his from just before the dais. Abruptly the bounty hunter whirled, faced the altar. A gore splattered onyx form rose up. Lips pealed back from bloody teeth, Dehegra screamed something at Tymiran. Flax couldn't understand negosi dialects but the intent was plain. She wanted them dead.

The bounty hunter didn't hesitate; he threw his long-sword with deadly accuracy. The blade split her face, buried itself to the hilt in shattered features. The so-called goddess toppled again. Quick as thought, Tymiran bounded to the altar then dropped behind it. Flax saw the gore-splattered blade of the bounty hunter's short-sword rise and fall. The sound that came to him could only be Dehegra's head being severed from her body. Tymiran threw back his head, raised both bloody swords and... roared the most chilling, feral battle cry Flax had ever heard in his life. It was... terrible... magnificent and he couldn't help but join in.

When the terrible cry died, he shut his eyes feeling the bloodlust soak into every limb; every inch of his skin tingled like he'd been sitting too close to a blazing fire. Muscles that should be fatigued only ached for more... *They died too quickly, too easily for what they've done, what they were going to do... I'm so high... No amount of wine or ale... Nothing else gives me this feeling... It's almost as good as great sex and that's crazy...* A shudder traveled through his large frame and he opened his eyes, scanned the gore splattered chamber. Tymiran was wading through the bodies, cutting throats to the bone, making sure every last one of them was dead.

Glacial eyes met his gaze across the chamber, a gore splattered hand raised to the veil, pulling it down, pushing the hood back from the feral features. A slight gesture indicated he could do the same if he wanted. Flax crouched to wipe his long sword on the shirt of one of the bodies then sheathed it. Tugging his rufa down to rest about his shoulders, he looked around for his crossbow and found it. It seemed relatively undamaged so he knotted the strap together and slung it over his shoulder, across his chest, settling it to his back. He rose, began checking the bodies closest to him to be sure those enemies were truly dead. Without thinking about it he too severed throats, it was the best way to make sure and he didn't want an enemy to jump on his back.

"Lad," Tymiran called quietly. The deep voice was rough, icy, dripping with menace.

"Aye," he looked up, met the bounty hunter's gaze. Flax found his own voice rough, hoarse.

"You are unhurt?" The question seemed oddly off hand then Tymiran gestured, indicating one of the fallen goddess' followers.

Flax answered as casually as he could considering the circumstances, the fires still burning in his blood, "I'm fine. You?" Puzzled, he watched her for a moment then saw the chest rise and fall shallowly. She was still alive and playing dead, waiting for one of them to come within reach.

"Unhurt," Tymiran was loading his crossbow silently.

Flax continued his... rounds, watching Tymiran take aim, squeeze the trigger. He winced when the bolt thudded solidly into her chest. She arched, uttered a strangled cry, then slumped back, dead, this time for real.

"Please?" a hoarse near whisper came from the altar. When Flax cast his gaze in that direction he met wide blue eyes. The nearest sacrifice, the first one bound in place and the only one gagged was straining against the leather strap across his throat to meet Flax's gaze. The last one bound in place was doing the same thing, only he wasn't gagged and he cleared his throat. "Please, will you... help us?" he implored, voice still hoarse, strained but stronger.

Flax glanced to Tymiran, considered an answer. *That's the plan but... How much should I reveal and should I even talk to them at all?..*

The frosty eyes met his gaze for the briefest moment then returned to the bodies, their enemies lying strewn across the floor. "Patience, lad. We'll get to you. Aryhen and I must make sure there are no more fanatics left to jump on our backs."

So, I'm Aryhen now am I?.. That's an ororri name... Implies that my mother was ororri and my sire arederi... How very interesting... Keeping his back to the five bound males, he offered Tymiran a crooked smile.

"Yes, sir," the captive lay back with a stifled sigh of relief. "Thank you, sir."

"Thank me when we're all safe." Tymiran growled low and cool.

He heard the male swallow hard; saw the nod when he glanced in that direction while continuing with the task at hand. It didn't take long; Tymiran was efficient, dispatching any left alive, even those who would obviously die in minutes with a quick slice of his short sword. The one who was gagged still watched him, fear and hope playing in an odd mix of emotions on guarded features.

Tymiran met Flax at the point furthest from the dais and the sacrifices. "Guard my back, Ary," a single red brow lifted pointedly.

Nodding his agreement, Flax kept his voice as low as he could, turned so his back was toward the altar, "The one to your right of center, he worries me."

"I noticed, lad. If I have to, I'll drug him." Tymiran gripped his bicep, "Let me do the talking, if you have to say anything keep it low and hoarse like it's a strain to speak. That'll disguise your voice as much as possible. Raise your rufa and hide your features but not your eyes, not yet. The ororri may be reassured if he knows he's not alone among half a dozen arederi."

He nodded, veiled his features as requested. Subtly, the bounty hunter indicated that it was time to approach the dais so he fell in step as Tymiran passed him. The one who was gagged watched them, blue eyes narrowing in suspicion, consternation, as they neared the dais. He met that frightened gaze, sympathy damping the blazing inferno that boiled in his blood.

"Your crossbow, is it loaded?" Tymiran asked sounding frozen.

The bounty hunter glanced to him and he shook his head, bringing the weapon around, fitting a bolt into place.

"Good, just keep an eye on those galleries and the stairwells. We'll be outta here in no time, lad." Crouching near one of the bodies, Tymiran cleaned his weapon, sheathed it in favor of his assassin's blade. Flax did as he was told. Turning his back on the dais and the altar, he held his crossbow at the ready, scanned the galleries and the fire engulfed steps. He listened to Tymiran mount the dais and move to the young male in the center, the one who was gagged.

"Easy, lad, try to be still."

A muffled grunt sounding vaguely affirmative answered the bounty hunter. Flax heard the sound of a knife cutting leather then the young male gasped, "Oh Goddess... they were gonna..." The gag was tossed away.

"What's your name?" Tymiran interrupted. More straps were cut. Flax heard what he thought was the captive pushing up. When he glanced to the platform the young male was sitting, staring at Tymiran, wide eyes confused. "Where you from?"

Shaking his head the youth watched as his ankles were freed. "Cal, I'm... Byrynthian."

"Cal, I'm Dyren, my… partner here is Ary." Tymiran told the stocky Byrynthian, helping him from the platform.

Gaze darting from the bounty hunter to him then back, Cal raked a shaking hand through his white blond hair.

He followed Tymiran to the next platform, "Let me help?" A quiet moment passed then the bounty hunter laid a knife hilt in Cal's hand.

The second captive was freed. His name was Merren and he was Thalusian. Cal had to help him to the edge of the dais near Flax. Merren was shaky, unsteady and he sank to sit almost curled into a ball on the dais's edge. The third, the one closest to the altar who'd asked them for help was also Byrynthian. His name was Vin and when Tymiran helped him to his feet he immediately sank to his knees before the bounty hunter.

Flax looked away, absorbed himself in watching the galleries. The gallery where he'd hidden was still burning, a blackened smoking wreak. By design, Tymiran had not lit fire to his gallery but to the stairwell below. The steps were ruined below the gallery but it was intact and clear as far as he could see. If the Goddess was with them no one would come down from above. Even the din of battle shouldn't have escaped the altar well of the supposedly empty temple. Besides the buildings were all but abandoned for nearly a hundred yards in all directions. Despite trying not to hear the exchange off to his left rear, he heard anyways.

"I… We owe you our lives, m'lord."

"On your feet, lad," Tymiran growled. "We'll talk about what you think you owe us later."

"Yes, sir," the sounds of someone... Vin, rising. "Thank you, sir."

"Name's Dyren, not sir. You wanna help, find some clothes for you and your brethren, here."

"Yes, sir... I mean... uh... Sure." Vin hesitantly, shakily, moved off the dais, toward the litter of bodies.

Hearing Tymiran or maybe Cal move across the dais behind him Flax turned his head just enough to glimpse the bounty hunter and his helper cutting the ororri loose.

Before he could say anything, the bounty hunter met his sidelong glance, shook his head slightly, "Just watch, Ary, guard our backs."

He nodded, scanning the galleries, the steps. They were still burning but it was dying down some, the oil basically used up. Still, the stairs were built of wood braced with stone; they were starting to burn in earnest. At that moment Vin returned to the dais, knelt before Merren. Flax heard the sharp intake of breath and spared them a glance. Vin had obviously touched Merren and startled him. The Thalusian looked terrified.

"Easy... It's Merren right?" the young Byrynthian asked. He'd evidently found a couple pair of breeches because he held one and was wearing a pair of dark reddish-brown leather. Merren's brows knit, he stared at Vin like he wasn't there. "I found you some breeches. Need help?" Very gently Vin slid a hand around Merren's ankle, lifted and slipped the breeches up his calf. After a shocked second, Merren took the leather and pulled it on. Vin moved off, searching amongst the bodies again for more breeches, maybe boots.

The ororri said something in his own lyrical tongue. It was no less shaky and hesitant. Tymiran replied, "Sorry, lad, I don't speak your language."

Flax heard him helped off the platform. "I'll not... be your slave." The remark dripped with apprehension.

"I don't take slaves. Neither does Aryhen."

He heard the ororri breathe a heavy sigh of relief, "I am... Durbar. There are... cloaks in the... the back room."

"Good, get 'em." Tymiran and Cal moved to the last sacrificial platform as he heard the ororri slide open one of the doors the priestess brought their captives through. "Easy, lad, look at me," the bounty hunter spoke quietly, gently as he could Flax would wager with the bloodlust still coursing through his veins. "C'mon, tell me your name."

"It's okay, he's come to get us outta here," that was Cal.

"Names matter not... I am Dehegra's, the goddess is to come for me." The voice was raw, ravaged.

Cal cursed under his breath. Vin returned, laid three more pairs of breeches across the center platform. Two pair of boots followed, then he sat down next to Merren and put on a pair of dark red boots.

"Dehegra is dead," Tymiran snarled behind him.

"A goddess cannot die..." it was a barely audible whisper.

"Well, Dehegra did. I killed her and she was human. That's it, look at me. You seein' me now, lad?

Dehegra is dead, she wasn't a goddess," Tymiran growled deliberately.

"Rathitara sent him, listen to him," Cal urged. "We have to get out, that's what the Goddess, the true Goddess intends but you gotta pull it together, okay?"

Damn, that's brilliant Cal, keep it up. He heard straps cut, the final captive freed and sitting up slowly.

"The priestess, she made him drink something in the anteroom," Cal nearly whispered.

At that moment Durbar returned with an armload of cloaks. He passed a couple to Vin, who slung one around Merren's shoulders. The Thalusian pulled it tighter about himself, shivered violently. Vin handed the ororri a pair of dark red breeches and Durbar shakily donned them. His hands fumbled at the rings for a moment. Vin caught his wrists making him flinch. The Byrynthian fastened the rings then drew Merren to his feet. Merren had a pair of boots on now and Durbar was in the act of closing the rings on the pair Vin gave him.

Tymiran snorted quietly, growled at the youth, "Look at me. That's better. Now listen. You are not to be sacrificed. The false goddess is dead. Say it."

"I am... not to be sacrificed. The false goddess is dead," the last young captive repeated obediently.

"Good, again." Tymiran ordered. Opening the small pack at his back the bounty hunter took out the heavy grapple and cord. "Ary, toss your line up to the gallery. Get the others moving. Cal and I will handle this."

He shifted his crossbow to his back, took the grapple and moved to stand beneath the gallery. *Hope he measured this right...* Swinging the grapple in a circle he threw it, hooked the railing. With a firm tug, he tested it. The rail snapped and dropped to the floor. *That went well... Okay, hook the floor. Means we have to climb over the railing but it'll hold better...* The second time he hooked the floor support just beneath the railing and it held. He'd go first for two very simple reasons. One; if it held him it'd hold everybody else. Two; he was armed. Flax hesitated, spared a glance for Tymiran, Cal and the last young male. *He looks dazed... or drugged and Cal said one of the ladies forced him to drink something... He is drugged... Probably with the same shit Dextera gave me... the stuff that opens you up to suggestion... She convinced him he's meant to be sacrificed, that's why he was so docile... Damn... I hope Ty can talk him out of it or he might just end up taking his own life...*

"...The false goddess is... dead..." abruptly the young male's eyes focused on Tymiran. "You killed her. You slew a goddess..." His eyes widened with the realization.

"A demoness," Cal interjected. "Not a goddess. The true Goddess sent them."

The lost youth searched Tymiran's features, obviously struggling to comprehend, "Rathitara sent you? To kill her?"

Ty exchanged a glance with Cal, "She did. I am her sword tonight, for the blood moon." The youth seemed to mull that over for a moment. Tymiran met his gaze, gave him a subtle signal to go ahead so he climbed. "So, lad, what's your name?" the bounty hunter asked.

"I am... Lorsek..."

As he climbed higher, he didn't hear the rest of the answer. The air grew warmer, smokey but it still

wasn't bad. The whole temple was acting as a chimney.
In heartbeats he was just beneath the railing, at the floor
supports. Since the rail snapped when he tugged on the
grapple, relying on it to hold his weight while he climbed
over it wasn't a good idea. He figured to pull it down, but
how to warn those below before he dropped it?

Getting a good hold on the floor support beams
with one arm, he reached up to grip the railing where it
fastened to the floor. Wrapping strong fingers around it,
Flax slid his hand as high as he could then gave it a
sharp tug. It snapped and he held onto the section that
came away in his hand. Looking down, he saw Vin
looking up. He didn't need to hear what Vin said; it was
a curse. The youth grasped Durbar's arm, drew the
ororri backwards with him and Merren. *Smart kid...
What am I thinkin'? He's prob'ly older than me...*

Flax's crooked smile flashed behind his rufa then
his gaze was arrested by the devastation he and Tymiran
wrought. The entire floor was smeared or splattered
with blood and darker fluids... at least the floor that
could be seen beneath the fallen bodies. The walls too,
had been repainted, the designs in blood completely
obscured by fresh gore. *That wasn't me... Goddess
forgive me, it was... Somehow, someway I'll master this
side of me; I have to... If I don't... I'll become someone
Tymiran has to hunt down...*

Clenching his jaw, he tossed the piece of railing
away, towards the far end of the room. It landed with a
crunch and a thud, falling onto some of the bodies.
Pulling down another piece, he tossed it too away as
Tymiran, Cal and Lorsek approached the cord. Taking a
deep breath, he climbed to the gallery, then lay on his
belly to make his grapple's hold on the floor support
even more secure. When he was sure it would hold
through six more climbs, he signaled Ty he was ready.

The bounty hunter nodded, sent Cal up next. In minutes the stocky young Byrynthian was clambering to the gallery with Flax's help.

Breathing deeply, Cal straightened, "Gimme a blade and I'll keep an eye on the steps." The young Byrynthian looked worn, haunted.

He considered for a moment then drew his short-sword, offered the hilt. For the significantly shorter Byrynthian youth it was more like a long-sword.

Cal accepted hesitantly, then moved toward the gallery door as Flax leaned over the edge, looking down the cord. Durbar was next. Within a few heartbeats the ororri gripped his hand and he hauled Durbar into the gallery.

Shaky golden fingers gripped his forearm lightly, briefly. The moment Flax met the dark feline eyes Durbar let go, almost like he'd burned his fingers. "He said... you will have to draw Merren up... he cannot climb."

Flax nodded. Hopefully, he looked more confident than he felt about the prospect. He'd never hauled a human being up thirty feet before. When he looked over the edge Tymiran was strapping Merren into a harness he'd scrounged. Tying the cord to the makeshift harness, Tymiran fastened his cord to the harness as well then gave him what was probably a signal meant as haul away.

Would have been nice if he'd let me get hold of the cord before he hooked Merren up to it. How the hell do I get started?.. After a moment's thought, he dropped to one knee then reached over the edge with one hand to grasp the cord. In one surprisingly smooth motion he rose, with the cord. Merren was relatively light, lighter than himself, or Tymiran for sure. Still, the ease with which he'd managed it surprised him a little. Carefully, he began to draw the cord upwards, hand under hand. Flax figured the youth to weigh no more than four or five sacks of grain. Many times he lifted grain to the loft in almost the same manner.

When Merren's hand gripped the edge of the gallery, Durbar was there to help him clamber up. Between him and the ororri they got the harness unfastened and off the frightened youth. The moment it was off, the shaking Thalusian youth looked up at him. Wide fearful eyes met his briefly, dropped to the floor. Then Durbar gripped Merren's arm, led him to lean against the wall. Quickly, deftly, he lowered the harness, stepping over the cord at the last minute so he could brace it behind his back. Next was Vin and he climbed fairly well. All Flax had to do was hold the cord steady. When Vin reached the edge of the platform, Flax drew him to the gallery. Lorsek was last and he had to be strapped into the harness and hauled up like so much grain.

Still, it wasn't long before the harness descended to Tymiran below. Unhooking his own grapple and cord, the redhead wrapped it up and stowed it in his pack with practiced efficiency. The bounty hunter removed the harness, cast it away, then looked up. A gesture indicated he'd be a few moments. Flax nodded to show he understood. Still, he hoped Tymiran would hurry. The sounds of the fire on the steps were increasing; the air was thicker, smokier.

Taking up a double bladed long ax, the bounty hunter glided through one of the doors behind the altar. Flax could hear lamps being smashed in the anteroom. When Tymiran emerged, the bounty hunter started smashing lamps in the altar well. Even though Flax knew it was part of the plan, he swallowed hard. If the fire spread too fast... If the bodies and oil and clothes burnt too quickly or with too much thick smoke... Damn, he really didn't want to think about it.

Instead, he glanced to the wall at his right. Merren and Lorsek were seated against it. Vin was with them, kneeling on the floor before Merren. Lorsek looked dazed, confused, tired. Merren appeared... like maybe he wasn't doing so well. Suddenly, he was more worried about Merren's state of mind than Lorsek's.   At least Vin was talking quietly, reassuringly to him. *Maybe a real good healer can help them... Goddess, I hope so...* Hearing someone approaching from behind he turned sidelong and met Durbar's feline eyes.

The ororri visibly squared his shoulders, swallowed, "The stair way... the fire... it's worse."

Do you always talk in fits and starts or is it part of the shock and fear?..

Durbar sort of shrugged, "Cal and I thought... maybe we should go..."

Remembering the bounty hunter's suggestion that he avoid speaking if at all possible, he shook his head, made a circular motion including all of them. Tymiran mentioned that they should all stay together at least until they got to the healers. To his relief, the ororri nodded then moved toward the door again. At that moment, he felt a tug on the cord. Looking over the edge, Flax met the bounty hunter's frosty gaze. Tymiran was standing in the only clear area of the room for the moment. Every lamp was smashed, the bodies burning, wood and wall hangings catching on fire, billowing smoke. Flax's nose wrinkled as the stench of burning flesh reached him then he tried to block it out. For all the destruction and the urgency of the situation Tymiran seemed unsettlingly calm and collected.

A red brow lifted, "ready?" the bounty hunter asked silently. He nodded and braced himself. The bounty hunter was by far the largest male yet to climb the cord... *Well, besides me...* He was also the fastest. With practiced ease Tymiran ascended the cord to climb to the gallery in heartbeats.

The bounty hunter immediately unhooked his grapple and rose to wind up the cord, "I'll lead, you take rear guard. Make sure they stay close."

Flax nodded then went to get Lorsek and Merren on their feet. While he was doing that the bounty hunter went to the doorway, secreting his grapple and cord in the pack at the small of his back.

"Vin, you take charge of Merren," Tymiran ordered. "Cal, look after Lorsek. Durbar, I need you to put the hood up on that cloak and keep it up and your eyes on the ground. We have a way to get you all out of town and to a healer but you have to trust us and do as I tell you." The frosty gaze passed over all of them and the bounty hunter received only nods of agreement. "Cal, Ary may need his short-sword."

Biting his lower lip, Cal hesitantly returned the weapon. Tymiran drew his boot knife, a fairly long and heavy blade and placed it in Cal's palm. "Thank you... warrior."

Tymiran shook is head, "When we're all safe." Again, he scanned them all and Flax caught the slight nod. Time to veil his eyes. Then the bounty hunter beckoned, easing into the stairwell, staying in a half crouch. "Stay low and quiet, follow me."

They did. Durbar was right on Ty's heels, Vin and Merren followed then Cal and Lorsek. Flax brought up the rear as ordered. He did his best to ignore the crackling of burning wood, the thickening smoke. A shudder shook the entire building accompanied by the cracking of timbers, then a terrible crash. The opposite set of stairs had collapsed from the gallery down. This one would be next. Tymiran ignored it, leading them steadily upwards. It wasn't a slow pace yet the bounty hunter was mindful that his charges were suffering the effects of days, maybe weeks of captivity.

When they reached the upper hallway, Tymiran paused, checking the ground floor hall for any enemies. Apparently there was none in sight because they filed silently into the curving passage and moved toward the back entrance. When they reached the doors the bounty hunter paused again. He beckoned and Flax moved up to his side. Gripping his harness strap, Tymiran pulled him down to whisper close to his ear, "I'm going out. Put these lamps out, count sixty then follow. Then have them come out, we'll take the same route back to our wagon."

Flax nodded then started to straighten. Red brows knit as the bounty hunter's gaze slid down his chest, over the rent in his shirt and the blood smeared on his exposed skin. The frosty gaze met his again. He shrugged, tossed his head slightly toward the door.

Tymiran nodded then slipped outside. Flax started his count, moving back down the hall, putting out lamps. When he reached fifty, he went back to the door. The five young males were waiting for him. Cal and Durbar were holding up the best. Vin seemed to be holding up as well, busying himself by keeping Merren from sinking into despair. Lorsek was steady on his feet if a bit dazed. It was Merren that worried him now.

Lorsek seemed to be coming out of the drug induced docility, albeit slowly. Merren was just... shattered was about the only word for it. He hit sixty, opened the door of the now darkened hall. It was pouring. Rain was literally coming down in sheets. That could be good, he wasn't sure.

The driving rain made the dark night even darker but he could still see well, surprisingly well. Searching the darkness of the alleyways and buildings across the small square, Flax spotted Tymiran almost immediately. The bounty hunter stepped from the alley's mouth, beckoned. Durbar went first, alone. Then Flax sent the other four across in pairs. All the while, he scanned the area constantly, kept his crossbow ready. Every time someone reached Tymiran's alley, he breathed a mental sigh of relief. When it was his turn, he held his crossbow ready and moved across the open space in smooth side steps, turning to face every way possible as he moved, guarding front, back, sides as efficiently as possible for one warrior. When he was safely in the alley Tymiran led off, back the way they'd come. They were all drenched to the skin in moments but the rain hitting the ground drowned all sounds of their hurried steps.

When he trotted up to the wagon, the bounty hunter was lowering grain sacks to the ground. He expanded the frame, covered it with the tarp securely except for the tailgate. Flax guarded their backs, watched diligently for any pursuit. The bounty hunter directed Vin, Merren, Lorsek and Durbar inside. Cal would ride with him in the seat. Obediently, the young Byrynthian male climbed to his place, took up the reins.

Removing the black and gray harness, Tymiran turned to him, "You keep that sword and crossbow ready. If any of the gate guards want to look under the tarp we'll have to kill 'em. Cal is unarmed except for a boot knife and I want him driving. If we have to fight on foot to give them time to get away we'll do it, Understand?"

He nodded, swallowed hard.

The bounty hunter stashed his harness with the crossbow, just behind the seat. Tymiran retrieved the red shirt, slipped it on. "Hopefully it's too nasty out for them to bother." Red-brown bracers were swapped for black colliette claws, rings fastened around the forearms with muffled snaps. Pulling his braid out of his shirt, Tymiran looped the consortship chain around his neck and fastened the fake lock. "I'll give Cal directions to a male healer I know. We'll meet up there with them if it's possible but I'll tell him not to worry about us. Okay?"

"Okay," Flax agreed in a very low whisper. The prospect didn't scare him and that was unsettling. Trying to fight the gate guards on foot, with the possibility of reinforcements coming to their aid... The possibility of being captured... it should all scare him and it didn't. *What's wrong with me?..*

"You be ready. The gate's gonna be the sticky part now. We make it through the gate and we're clear." Tymiran gripped his shoulder, squeezed reassuringly then indicated it was his turn to climb in the wagon.

Drawing a deep breath, Flax steeled himself for the noisy, cramped ride and climbed in. Positioning himself as before, he held his sword at his side, the crossbow across his chest. The space was cramped with all of them but manageable. Still, he'd wager by the time they passed the gates it would be close, stifling under the tarp. At least they were all alive and relatively intact. The tarp was secured then he felt Tymiran climbing into the wagon with Cal. He couldn't hear anything but the rain beating on the tarp. The wagon

lurched then rolled forward in earnest at what he
guessed was a slow trot. They'd be exiting by a different
gate, one on the opposite side of town from where they
entered.

Flax concentrated on listening and breathing slow
and evenly. Still it was claustrophobic, the press of five
bodies crammed into the space of a wagon bed too tight
for his taste. Vin was holding Merren in his arms tightly.
Occasionally he'd hear a low whimper or sob then Vin
whispering very quietly. Time stretched out, it had to be
a year before Tymiran's heel bumped the wagon box
three times; the signal that they were nearing the gate.
He must have told the others because suddenly they all
seemed to be holding their breath; even Merren was
silent. Flax said a mental prayer of thanks for that.
Personally he shifted his grip on the crossbow, adjusted
his hand on the hilt of his short-sword. Between the
driving rain on the tarp and the vibration of the wheels
on the cobblestone, street he couldn't hear anything
outside the wagon.

Abruptly, he felt the rattling diminish then halt
altogether. We've stopped... His guts clenched,
excitement wound through his veins reawakening the
bloodlust. Voices came to him only in murmurs, the
guards questioning Tymiran and Cal about their late trip,
their cargo. They didn't approach though, seemingly
content to stay in their guardhouse out of the rain. In a
few moments the wagon eased forward at a steady walk
for the horses. Flax started a slow count and got to one
hundred eighty before he felt them pick up the pace
again. It wouldn't be long before they were stopping
again. Then he and Tymiran would disembark and head
for the gully where their horses were stashed. Cal would
continue on toward the healer's so he and the bounty
hunter would have to catch up. *Nothing to it... Yeah,*

right. A hundred things could still go wrong but... So far so good... He felt warmth trickling around his ribs and glanced down just enough to see he was still bleeding but it had slowed. *Oh Shit... Hope I'm not leaving a blood trail. With all the rain it's probably being washed away as fast as it's dripping under the wagon. If it's dripping under the wagon... Does Ty know? Probably... Then again I didn't really let him take a good look at it... Maybe I should have let him bind it... Goddess grant the boards of this wagon bed are swollen with dampness and nothing's leaking through them... And if it is... Hopefully it's bein' washed way as fast as it's being laid down.... Unless they notice and get on it right away...*

Seven

Finally, after what seemed years to Flax in the cramped wagon bed, they halted again. He had to restrain himself from cutting his way through the tarp and frame to the outside air. He really didn't care if it was pouring. He just wanted out. The tarp was loosed, the tailgate dropped and he slid out as quickly as he could to meet the bounty hunter's amused gaze.

"If there's ever a next time, I'll ride in the back," Tymiran volunteered.

He looked away, striving not to laugh out loud.

Meanwhile, the others were climbing out. Tymiran directed them to dismantle the frame if they wanted and secure the tarp loosely so they could sit up beneath it and be more comfortable. Cal watched as the others readied the tarp. Durbar climbed up beside him as the others got situated in the back just behind the seat. Tymiran had his harness on, his braid hidden and his features veiled in no time. The bounty hunter retrieved his crossbow and quiver, slinging them on opposite shoulders.

Tymiran went to stand beside the wagon seat, "Think you can find Rayn's place?"

Cal nodded, "Yeah, no problem." The young male's gaze flicked from the bounty hunter to him, "We owe you... There are no words..."

Tymiran shook his head, "If we don't happen to show up don't worry. We'll either be around or we won't. Tell Rayn that Dyren sent you and will be around to pay his fees. Get moving." With that, he turned and walked away. Flax followed with a parting wave to Cal. He heard the wagon move off, turning north of east.

It didn't take them long to reach the gully and the makeshift stables. The center of the gully floor was now a stream from the run off of pouring rain. About thirty yards from the stable Tymiran gripped his arm. He paused, lowering his soaked rufa to meet the bounty hunter's gaze.

Tymiran likewise lowered the veil across his features, flashed him a cool grin, "Remember you're Ary or Aryhen. I may call you cousin every now and then, especially now when I think Dextera may be awake or half-conscious. Any other time I'll call you Flax..."

He couldn't help but chuckle, "That way she'll think we slipped up and she's found out who I "really" am."

Tymiran nodded, "She'll probably think we were in on it together from the start and that you're Hunter's partner and have been for some time. Just don't forget, within her hearing call me Hunter."

When they stepped into the stable itself, he took off the rufa and rang it out. "I'm fuckin' soaked," Flax grumbled to himself.

"I'll buy you new leathers, Ary." Tymiran went to his horse, checked the saddle girth. "Otherwise, are you okay?"

"I'm fine," he did the same with his saddle, slinging his quiver on the cantle and shortening up the strap. "Just wet." He spared a glance for their trussed up prisoner. She was lying very still and a little too stiffly to really be unconscious. Still, she was faking it well. He couldn't help it, his crooked smile cocked his mustache but he managed to keep from laughing.

"Put our package across your saddle and let's go then," the bounty hunter suggested. When he met the glacial eyes they reflected the mischievous grin he felt playing at his lips. Still, the fires of bloodlust burned in them. It was no longer a raging volcano, but it was there and he wondered if his eyes held the same hard gleam, blazing lust.

Taking the four binding straps that had been tied behind his saddle, he went over to pick up Dextera. He felt no guilt for her predicament at the moment. She was getting off easy, too easy, for her crimes in the last three years as far as he was concerned. He did as asked, picking Dextera up easily, laying her across the back of his saddle; the cantle, and strapping her in place like his pack. Not the most comfortable of positions. He'd wager she'd really be uncomfortable once she was soaked.

He and Tymiran led the horses out into the downpour. Mounting, Flax watched as the bounty hunter tugged his horse's reins, hid the stable entrance. Tymiran swung easily into the saddle then they started down the gully towards the creek. There was a trail out that way and they'd catch up with the wagon in no time.

Finally, he allowed himself to relax a bit. There was no sign of pursuit. There had been no alarm raised over the fire before they reached the gates or they would have had to fight their way out. The bounty hunter was sure there were no survivors beyond the seven of them. Personally, Flax agreed, there had been no other way out but to climb to the gallery as they had.

Flax stepped out onto the roofed veranda of the healer's home. Tymiran was leaning his back against one of the support posts and idly watching the horses. The rain had stopped and the temperature had gone down some. It now felt like a nice spring day as opposed to a sweltering summer day, for which he was truly grateful.

The bounty hunter turned his head just a little, "How are you, lad?"

He stifled a laugh, shook his head. He hadn't even taken a step and the bounty hunter knew it was him. "I'm whole. There isn't even a scar." Rayn had healed him up too after seeing to the others. Ty insisted.

"Oh?" Tymiran grunted, turning enough to meet his gaze as he strode to the bounty hunter's side. "Wager there's a nice one on your arm."

"Well, yeah, but that was already healing." He braced one arm against the post, scanned the yard before the healer's shop. It was dark, probably the second hour. He shrugged, "I'm not worried about it."

Ty nodded, turned his gaze on the yard, the trees, the stable.

"You didn't have to pay, not for me..." he started.

Tymiran shook his head, "It's my responsibility and it was no problem."

Definitely not going to get anywhere along that line... He sighed quietly, "Okay, what about you?"

The bounty hunter shrugged, "I took no real wounds. Rayn need to rest."

He considered. In all honesty the cuts along Ty's forearms, the couple across his thighs were superficial and would probably heal without leaving scars. "Rayn told me to ask you about the others, so, I'm asking."

Tymiran met his gaze then looked out into the darkness. "Cal, Durbar, Vin and Lorsek will heal. As long as they can learn to live with what happened to them and put it behind them, they'll be okay. Merren... Needs help. Rayn knows an empath that may be able to do something for him but he's... retreated so far inside himself he almost isn't here any longer. Maybe the empath can reach him, then again, maybe not."

He studied Ty's features. The bounty hunter appeared hard, cold. Still, Flax had a hunch that Merren's withdrawal affected the bounty hunter. Hell, it affected him. "They can't do it to anyone else and now they're answering to Rathitara for their actions," he offered.

Tymiran shrugged, "That's little comfort to Merren."

"What else can you or I do?" he meant it sincerely. If there were something else he'd do it. Still, he doubted the prospect.

"Nothing," the bounty hunter sighed heavily. "We can only kill them once. That's done."

The door behind him opened and they both turned. It was Vin. The young Byrynthian was wearing a pair of dark green gauze breeches. Damp white blond hair fell curling about bare shoulders. He'd obviously been to the bathhouse. Flax would wager they all had or would. He and Ty had washed up some at the pump and trough in the stable. Hesitantly, Vin met Flax's gaze then Tymiran's, "May I speak with you?" Tymiran had cautioned them all not to speak their names in front of the prisoner.

"Sure, lad." Tymiran straightened, turned. At the same time Flax took a step back dropping his arm from the post to sling his black makeshift rufa across his throat. He was supposed to be scarred and he wasn't so... he had to hide it. "What is it?"

Vin approached, gaze lowered, to within a pace of them. The pale blue eyes lifted to him briefly then shifted to the bounty hunter, "Please, may I speak with just you?"

A smile flashed across Ty's features, the glacial eyes met his, "Will you see that our horses and our package are ready to go?"

Flax nodded, stepped down off the Veranda and strode across the yard toward the stable and the hitching post. It was only some ten paces to his left of the house. Dextera was now standing next to his horse, leashed to his saddle. Her wrists were bound behind her back, the connecting clasp knotted in a strap around her belly. Her ankles were cuffed rather close together; she could stand but walking would pose difficult. The hood would make it more so. Tymiran even had Rayn check her over. She didn't have any broken ribs so the bounty hunter didn't have Rayn heal her. While Flax checked the saddle girths, their packs, he listened in on the conversation on the veranda. He couldn't help it; he was just too close not to hear.

"I... We owe you..." Vin started.

"Vin," Ty interjected firmly.

"Please, hear me out?"

Casting a brief glance at them, Flax saw Tymiran's shoulders lift and lower with the quiet sigh. "Fine, go ahead," the bounty hunter conceded.

Vin shifted, glanced his way and he busied himself tightening the tie-downs on the bounty hunter's pack. "You... both of you saved our lives." The young Byrynthian drew a deep breath, let it out slowly, "Cal, Durbar and I, we talked. Larsek is in no shape and Merren... I think he's lost." He could hear the tremor in Vin's voice. The young Byrynthian cleared his throat. "Anyway, we know what payment is your right... and you have every right to it, I'm not saying that you don't... Durbar said he'd fight you but Cal and I... We saw... None of us, not even all of us together could take you, either of you. I'm willing, so is Cal but if you'd be satisfied with only one of us, allow me to offer myself if it pleases you..."

"Vin..." Ty started.

"Please?" The young Byrynthian sounded nervous and a little desperate.

Flax stroked his mount's mane, looked over the horse's ears. Tymiran appeared guardedly amused and at the same time a little sad. Vin was looking at the boards of the veranda between his bare feet for the most part.

"Go ahead, lad." Tymiran leaned against the post, met his gaze for a moment and offered him a smile.

"I can cook and I can care for your animals. I can sew leather and clean it. I could care for your tack and I'd submit to your use, however you wanted me. I'd obey you and him and I can take a beating, if it pleases you... I know... I can't compare to... your young giant but..."

Ty laughed and Vin looked up at the bounty hunter plainly confused.

Flax could see the grin on Tymiran's face, "He is not my lover, Vin."

The young Byrynthian glanced to him and he shook his head. He strove to remain serious or at least composed but he couldn't hide the crooked smile playing at his lips.

The bounty hunter rested a hand on Vin's shoulder. The fair brows knit, confusion tripled on Vin's features as he met the bounty hunter's eyes.

"He's my son."

Flax closed his mouth the moment he realized he had it open. The bounty hunter's tone was so... sincere, so grave and honest that if he didn't know for a fact it was a blatant lie he'd believe it himself.

"And I don't take slaves," Tymiran added. "I think I mentioned that."

Vin studied the bounty hunter's features for a long moment then glanced at him looking very perplexed. "You're too young... He's..."

"He's sixteen, lad." Very gently, Ty brushed back curling strands of white blond hair drawing Vin's gaze. "My seed was taken against my will, before I was of age. The rest is none of your damn business." The bounty hunter's gaze shifted to the door just before it opened.

"I told you he wouldn't collar us," Cal stood in the doorway. He came outside.

Vin looked up at the bounty hunter, mixed emotions playing across his features; relief mingled with a touch of disappointment. "You want nothing from us? Any of us? You've done so much..."

"See that Merren gets to an empath," Ty shrugged, "and heal."

Vin dropped his gaze, nodded, "I'll probably never see you again, right?"

"It's possible we'll never cross paths again."

"How can I ever thank you?"

Ty stroked the curly white-blond hair, drawing the young Byrynthian's gaze, "You just did. You're welcome, Vin. If I'm not mistaken Rayn told you to get some rest."

Vin nodded, offered the bounty hunter his hand. Ty accepted, gripping his forearm. After a moment the younger male went inside, glancing back as he passed Cal.

Cal's gaze shifted from Ty to him then back, "Got a minute for me?"

"And what do you need to say to me or us?" Ty grinned but Flax saw weariness, he'd wager the bounty hunter really wanted to leave.

Cal closed the door, leaned his back again it. He was wearing black gauze breeches and a matching shirt cut Cyrcanian style. His brows knit and he studied Ty's features for a long moment. "Why... What brought you? I mean..." Cal broke off for a moment to draw a deep breath and push it out. "Did they try to do to you what they were gonna do to... us?"

Ty looked very much like he was considering, thinking about how much he should reveal, how far he could trust the young Byrynthian male before him. "They tried for my son. Cut his throat when they found their drugs weren't working on him. We're both lucky I'm good with a surgeon's needle or he'd be dead. As it is he can barely speak. It hurts him to talk and it probably always will. Rayn says there's nothing more he can do and I believe him. Let's say Dehegra and her cult owed us. We just collected on a debt."

Cal seemed to take it all in. He chewed his lower lip, swallowed hard, "They all look at me like... I dunno, like I'm in charge or some kind of leader..." His jaw tightened, brows knit and he blinked. Tears welled over. "Do you have to go?"

Tymiran gripped his shoulder, "We have a package to deliver. You don't need us any longer; you need Rayn and maybe the empath he contacts. There's nothing more we can do."

Cal looked away, struggled with his grief, "Yeah, I know..."

Sighing quietly, Tymiran drew Cal into his arms, held him. "They're all looking to you to comfort them and let them cry on your shoulder. You've no one left to turn to and you hurt."

"How do you know what I feel?" Cal clutched Tymiran's shirt, the back of the gray and black harness.

"I can read it on you, though you put up a good front. I can't stay and be your shoulder to cry on or your master, whatever it is you think you need from me... I can't give it to you. I can't make it go away, lad."

Cal nodded, clung to the bounty hunter and Flax looked at his saddle. "I'm not this strong..." Flax heard a quiet sob.

"Sure you are. You survived. Now, you have to go on living. That's revenge, Cal. You can beat them every single day for the rest of your life."

Flax made another circuit around the horses, checking the girths, the tie-downs. Removing the clasp between the cuffs on her ankles, he put Dextera up behind his saddle. Then he shackled her ankles together with a strap slung under his horse's belly and attached to his saddle. When he looked to the veranda again, Ty was holding Cal, comforting him, stroking his hair. The bounty hunter rested his chin atop Cal's head, met Flax's gaze for a moment, offering him a slight though weary smile. There was no sex to it, not an ounce of suggestiveness at all.

"She really... hurt me. I didn't want it but... I couldn't help it. My body betrayed me... That was horrible. She'd beat me, bind me... I hated her every minute of every day but I couldn't stop it..." Cal sobbed quietly, held on to the bounty hunter tightly.

Tymiran stroked the blond hair patiently, "It's over. She'll never touch you or any other again."

Cal nodded, slowly drew back, "I thank the Goddess for that. Thank you." He shoved his hair back, went to wipe his eyes, "You didn't have to..."

Tymiran did it for him, "Your welcome."

Cal sort of laughed, squared his shoulders, "Gotta go, huh?"

"Yeah, we do." The bounty hunter gripped his shoulder, "You're tougher than you think you are, Cal."

"Comin' from you that might just mean somethin'," a worn grin flashed. "Watch your backs and each other's," Cal met his gaze, waved.

He returned it, unhitched the horses and turned them around. Tymiran came down the three steps to take his reins, swing into his saddle. "Watch your back, lad."

"Oh, I will." Cal leaned against the post Tymiran had so recently vacated.

Urging his horse into a slow lope, the bounty hunter guided his mount from the yard into the surrounding hills. When they were about a mile away from Rayn's place the bounty hunter slowed his horse to a trot.

Flax guided his mount along side, "Where we headed?"

"Byruna, Commander Merissa is my best bet for a bounty," Tymiran answered easily.

"How long a ride we got?" he met the frosty eyes when Ty looked at him.

A red brow lifted, "We'll make camp in... say... four hours. After we get some rest we'll deliver our package. Why, you got some place else to be, Flax?"

He shook his head, "Naw, just curious."

Tymiran grunted a skeptical affirmative.

"You okay?" Flax met the glacial eyes pointedly.

The bounty hunter's gaze slid to Dextera and he caught the hint. Ty didn't want to talk in front of her, at least not when she could hear. "I'm fine, lad, really. Just tired."

He nodded, "Yeah, me too." *Later then, and by the Goddess I will ask those questions I've been struggling with... All of them, even if you holler at me...*

Flax followed Ty into the cave in the cliff. The horses were hidden in another cave nearby that had been set up similarly to the other makeshift stable. Dextera was housed with the horses. Her so-called goddess's death was sinking in, she was very quiet, unresisting now. The sun was rising; the sky lightening as they drew rein and it topped the horizon as they entered the cave that would serve as their camp.

It looked like it had just recently been expanded here and there maybe. He could see a little hearth and mantle over the bounty hunter's shoulder. The ceiling was just high enough that he could stand upright but the entrance was another story. Like the other camp, the entrance was tight and had been left natural. It had been covered with brush when they rode up and he pulled the brush in the opening after him.

He heard Ty's bedroll tossed on something, a bunk, he'd wager.

"Well, it looks like I finally get you to share my bed," the bounty hunter remarked off hand.

Couldn't possibly have heard that right... "What?" Before he got angry he stepped to Tymiran's side, gripped the iron hard bicep.

The bounty hunter met his gaze, mischief lit the glacial eyes, "I haven't built a bunk here yet, Flax. We both have to sleep on the floor. So, we will be sharing a bed, just not our furs." Ty laughed quietly.

"Very funny," he growled. Flax threw his furs down on the floor too. Stepping around his bedroll, he leaned his pack near the hearth and opened it.

A broad grin flashed, "I really wish you could see your face right now." Ty leaned his pack in the far corner near the entrance.

"You're just fuckin' hilarious when you're tired, ya know that?" Locating a pair of clean, dry, breeches he closed up his pack. Shedding his damp shirt, Flax dropped it to the floor right before the little fireplace. He crouched, spread his furs.

Tymiran stretched, pressed his hands to the ceiling, "Tell me a lady friend wouldn't tease you."

Flax sat down on the hearth, "She would," he conceded. *Though a lady teasin' me probably wouldn't put me off balance like that just did...* Opening the rings on his boots, he took them off.

He could just hear the bounty hunter unfastening his harness, "I apologize, I won't do it again."

Flax shrugged, his jaw tightened then he looked up. Ty was shedding his shirt; the glacial eyes met his. "No, listen... I'm sorry. I'm tired and I over-reacted. You treat me with more respect than most ladies do... Just threw me, that's all."

A slight smile tilted the red mustache, "I'd say. That look on your face..." Tymiran crouched to unlace his boots then seemed to reconsider, "Want me to go outside while you change?"

Flax chuckled, "Thought you said you weren't gonna tease me."

"I'm not, I'm serious. Do you want me to leave while you change?"

After a shocked heartbeat, he shook his head, "No... hell no."

"I don't want to make you uncomfortable, Flax. I'll go outside," Ty offered.

"I'm not Thyrian, I can handle bein' exposed to your... considerable charms," his crooked smile flashed.

Tymiran grinned, "You can tease me but I can't tease you. That's very unfair." He went back to taking off his boots.

"Who promised you life would be fair?" he rose, shed his damp breeches. It took a lot of will power and composure. He hated to admit it but he was mildly uncomfortable and very self-conscious. Because of that he was even more determined to appear at ease.

Tymiran, on the other hand looked completely, honestly relaxed. Then again he always seemed to be that way. The bounty hunter cursed quietly as he shoved the black and gray breeches down.

"Mine need cleaning too," he offered, drawing on clean breeches of soft light brown leather. A single ring fastened them at his left hip. He crawled onto his furs, found the sheet of linen, shook it out.

"I promised you I'd replace them, I will, tomorrow, or rather, later on today. I know a really good leather seamstress in Byruna." The bounty hunter kicked the knot of black leather to one side. Stretching a little, Ty rolled his shoulders, turned his head like he was trying to crack his neck. "After a few hours sleep we'll go into town. I'll see what Merissa and Judge Feavina will give us for our prisoner. Then we'll go see Leigha and get some new leathers." Pulling on leather breeches dyed in a green, leafy pattern, the bounty hunter tightened the laces.

He started to say "you don't have to do that" but he knew it wouldn't work. Ty would give him bullshit about it being his responsibility, about being his employer or something. *'Bout the only way I can keep him from getting me new leathers is to take off before he can... If I do that then I can't become his apprentice so... guess I'll have to go along with it...* "No problem," he shrugged when Ty met his gaze.

A single red brow lifted as the bounty hunter approached carrying the black and gray harness, "You're not going to argue that point with me?"

Flax shook his head, "What for? I'll just lose."

Tymiran chuckled, "Damn straight." Lowering himself to his furs, the bounty hunter laid his harness above where his head would be. Flax had his harness near his right hand. Ty had taken the left side of the cave floor, his left as he faced the hearth. Flax suspected that was because he was predominantly right handed and Ty was ambidextrous. It would give him more freedom to draw and use a weapon if the need arose. Rolling up a fur for a cushion, Tymiran then loosed his braid, shook it out. The bounty hunter lay down nearly on his stomach, his body wrapped around the fur. Ty drew his strip of linen across his back, hips, shoulders.

Flax reclined on his back, drew his linen over him. He put his hands behind his head and tried to relax but his questions nagged at him.

"What is it, lad?" Tymiran asked almost making him jump.

I was just wondering... "Nothing, really."

"Flax..."

"It'll keep."

"Not if it keeps us both awake. You can tell me anything, Flax."

Goddess, he sounds tired, so am I but... he bit his lower lip, "Yeah, I know..."

Sensing movement, he looked at the bounty hunter as a strong hand lightly gripped his arm. Glacial blue eyes met his and they weren't frosted over, icy cold. They were sympathetic, far more understanding than he'd once presumed this bounty hunter could be, "It's not my place but... I'm proud of you, Flax. You fought well, very well. Did what you had to and kept your head. You did better than many warriors twice your age could have and I am honored to have fought at your side."

He swallowed hard, touched deeply, "As I am to have fought at yours, warrior." It was all he could come up with.

Tymiran smiled, released him to wrap his arms around his makeshift cushion. "What's on your mind, lad?"

About a hundred things that aren't really any of my business... and a few that might be... "I uh... Will you help me master... it? My bloodlust... I mean... you have and you're doing something with it... Something that doesn't have bounty hunters tracking you..." He paused, drew a deep breath, staring at the ceiling in the dim light of the cave. It was slowly growing light outside.

Tymiran pushed up on a forearm, "Go on."

He nodded slightly, swallowed hard, "What would it take for you to accept me as your apprentice?" Tymiran's brows knit, he saw it out of the corner of his eye because he was keeping his gaze on the ceiling. "I'd give you all the silver I have... My horse if you want her... Name your price, I'll get it..."

"Flax, I wouldn't want payment of any kind." Clenching his jaw, he looked at Tymiran. The bounty hunter appeared thoughtful. "When will you be eighteen?"

His gut tightened at the question. He immediately felt guilty for what he assumed was the reason behind it. "Five months and about three weeks. Why?"

The bounty hunter lay down, "I was going to ask you if you'd like to stick with me until then. That way I can guard your back; keep 'em off you until the bounty expires. When you're eighteen your mother no longer has any claim on you so she can't offer the bounty on you past your eighteenth birthday."

He rolled to his side, propped his head in his hand, searching the bounty hunter's features. He couldn't find any words before Tymiran went on.

"If you think you'd like to learn to be a bounty hunter, we'll take a few contracts, go on a few hunts. At any rate I'll teach you all I can, or all you're interested in learning from me, until then."

"After I'm eighteen, then what?" he had to ask.

"Then, if you're sure you want to pursue it we'll draw up a formal apprenticeship agreement. If you're not sure... then we can keep it loose or you go on your way." Tymiran sort of shrugged, snuggled into his furs. "I have to tell you, Flax, I don't think you have this in you. Not that I don't think you're capable, I just don't think it's for you."

"Why not? I'm good at hunting. I can track and stalk well. I'm... fairly smart..."

Tymiran laughed quietly, flashed a grin, "You're very smart. That's not it."

"Then what?" He lay down again, got comfortable. *That was a hell of a lot easier than I thought it would be...*

Tymiran sighed, "I noticed you feeling a little guilt, a little sympathy for our prisoner off and on. Even though she planned to rape and murder you, even though she tried to kill you, you still felt for her. That could be very dangerous."

He considered. Ty was right but... "I can learn."

"Maybe. I've never tried to teach anyone how to be ruthless and cold. I'm not sure it can be taught." A tired smile crossed the bounty hunter's features, "It's more likely that being cold and ruthless is a character flaw I have and you don't."

Flax's crooked grin cocked his mustache, "I can learn to think like you do, to be cautious and... practical."

Tymiran grunted; it was vaguely affirmative. "Honestly, lad, can you drag a prisoner into a garrison knowing she'll be sentenced to death or to the mines for the rest of her life? What about a young male, a thief or maybe a bandit? Can you drag him to a garrison commander knowing he'll be sentenced to the collar and iron?"

Flax considered, "You do it." Truthfully, he wasn't quite as sure now. Young males being sentenced to slavery... he hadn't thought about that aspect of it. Still, he wanted to try.

"I figure they've earned it, whatever the sentence is unless they're not guilty but I can tell. You can too. I'll wager I can teach you to read people; you already do pretty well on your own." The bounty hunter's eyes opened, "We'll give it a try. Change your mind, talk to me, let me know."

"Thanks, Ty." He got comfortable, drawing the linen more tightly around him, snuggling into his furs.

"Don't thank me yet, you haven't heard my ground rules." Tymiran offered him a grin when he opened his eyes.

"Ground rules?"

The bounty hunter nodded, "There's just a few. One, I'm always in charge of a hunt and we do things my way. I'll entertain alternatives if and only if there's time and we're safe. Otherwise, you can fight with me later, if we're still alive. Understand?"

"Yeah, I kinda figured," Flax agreed.

"Two, until I say otherwise, you plan on warming some lady's furs, she's got to talk to me first, understand?"

Astonished down to his toes, he pushed up on a forearm, "No. Why?"

Tymiran laughed, "Because, she may be a bounty hunter or a slaver. I take prisoners that way, and until I'm satisfied you can tell the difference, she's gotta talk to me."

Amused and mildly embarrassed, Flax looked across the chamber, "What am I supposed to tell 'em?"

"Tell 'em I'm your brother or your sire or your manager, I don't care what tale you spin. Ought to let me in on it ahead of time though, so it works."

He sighed; as much as he disliked clearing bed partners through Tymiran it was actually a practical precaution. That didn't make him like it any more but that really didn't matter. Dextera tried for him and he couldn't see past her lust. "Okay. Am I gonna like the next one?"

"We'll see." The bounty hunter met his gaze with one half closed eye, "Three, bed partners don't travel with us and they don't belong in camp. It's not secure enough and they may learn things I'd rather they didn't. Understand?"

"Yeah." That was reasonable.

Tymiran drew a deep breath, let it out slowly, squeezing his cushion, "Four; when we're at tavern, an inn or a rooming house we get adjoining rooms and the connecting door stays unlocked. If it happens that someone does try for you, then I can help. If for some reason you suspect trouble you can retreat to my room and we deal with it together. If we can't get adjoining rooms with a connecting door then we get one big room and I take the floor. Understand?"

He nodded, "Makes sense. After I'm eighteen, then what?"

"Word has to get around that the bounty on you has expired. By say... next Summer Solstice you should be safe." A single red brow lifted, "We stick by rule number two until I say otherwise. As for the other three, they stand. Agreed?"

He raked a hand through his hair, "Agreed."

"Just one more thing," Tymiran smiled slightly when he looked at the bounty hunter.

"What?" he dreaded the answer, he really did.

"You need to talk or come into my room, knock unless you're very sure you don't mind witnessing whatever I'm doing with my bed partner."

"Goddess…"

"I'm serious, Flax. Of course, emergencies are a different matter."

"I'll knock first, I swear, on Sheposha's Bow."

Tymiran laughed quietly, "I promise not to tease you or go out of my way to embarrass you if you do the same for me. Fair enough?"

"Yeah, fair enough." He agreed, getting comfortable, rolling to his back again.

"What else?" the bounty hunter asked.

He sort of shrugged, shook his head, "I'm not sure it's any of my business."

Tymiran laughed quietly, "Look, lad, you can ask me anything. I just won't guarantee you an answer. If I don't want to talk about it, I won't."

Drawing a deep breath he pushed it out, nodded, considering how to word it so it wouldn't sound accusatory. "You said… swore you'd never raped anyone." He felt the bounty hunter's gaze, met it. "Does that include slaves?" Flax fully expected to be told to go to Hell or worse. What he got was a smile.

"I don't rape slaves, I don't have to. I make sure he's willing and not just because the owner says he is. I talk to him, look in his eyes, make sure he wants to serve me before I take him to my bed."

He looked at the cave ceiling a little embarrassed, asked. "Why do you answer my questions so… easily?"

"Why does it matter?" Ty countered.

Flax chuckled, "Hell, I dunno."

"I answer because I want you to trust me," Tymiran added evenly, honestly.

"I don't understand..." he started, bit his lip, brows knitting.

"How one male finds another sexually attractive?" Tymiran provided.

"Yeah... I mean... I just don't get it." He thanked the Goddess for the relative darkness of the cave, because heat rose up his neck, face. He'd wager he was red with embarrassment.

"I'm not sure I can explain that to you." Ty rolled to his back, rested a hand on his chest, slipped the other behind his head. "I can't understand how you can only see ladies that way."

"Like, when you were walking toward the table I was sittin' at in the tavern with Dextera. I could see how ladies might want you but... it doesn't make me want you." He hoped he didn't sound as uncomfortable as he was.

"We're just different, lad." The bounty hunter sighed quietly, "I don't wanna bed every good lookin' male I see just like I'm sure you don't wanna go to bed with every good looking lady you run into. I have boundaries just like you do. You're a damn good-looking kid but I don't see you that way. I never did." When he glanced at Ty, the bounty hunter offered him a slight smile, "Don't be offended or anything."

He laughed, "I'm not."

"I like it with ladies too, Flax." A grin flashed across Tymiran's features, "Maybe I'm just greedy."

When his mirth passed he sighed heavily, "Okay, I guess I'll never understand it."

"Don't feel bad, I don't get it either," Tymiran added.

"How 'bout this, why'd you tell Vin I'm your son? Why tell 'em anything?"

"Tell a few things that seem personal then they think they know something about us. Maybe a year from now if you run into Cal and he calls you Ary you can effectively prove you're not. You're not scarred, and you're voice isn't hoarse like it's a struggle to speak. It was dark, other things were on his mind and he'll convince himself he was mistaken." Ty shrugged, "I said I was your sire because it was the easiest lie to tell convincingly. The whole story gives them a reason to believe we just wanted revenge. Telling it in front of Dextera adds a little more confusion to your identity and mine." The bounty hunter paused, a heartbeat passed in silence, "Besides, that's just about how I think of you."

I feel that way too, Tymiran, Goddess, I wish you were my sire... You would never have allowed Lynia to put a bounty out on me... You'd never let her barter me to some noble lady... He couldn't say it, not right now... Flax swallowed hard, "My sire is a slave. My mother bought him to make beautiful children. He was taken at twelve. I met him once. That was enough," it all came out with a growl, his deep voice rumbled with an undercurrent of anger.

"That's rough," Ty rolled to his side, pushed to an arm to meet his feline eyes. "I know my sire, he's my mother's consort. He's also a fine carpenter, a real artisan though he denies it. I like him, now that I'm grown he's one of my closest friends."

He nodded once, *must be nice...* "Sometimes, I hate him."

The bounty hunter shook his head, "Don't. You don't know him..."

His jaw tightened, "I don't care. Lynia told me more than once I was meant for the collar, with my ororri eyes and golden hair. That if he hadn't begged for my freedom she'd of... I'd trade it, my looks, my pretty hair and eyes..." he snorted, "Lynia's nearly noble blood, in a heartbeat..." he met the glacial eyes, searched hard features, "for a sire like you." *If only you were my sire...* He felt the tears well and he didn't fight it. *Goddess it feels good to let some of it go, to just tell someone who might at least try to understand...*

Tymiran dropped his gaze, red brows knit. "Flax, if you knew me, really knew me, you wouldn't say that. My bloodlust is like a drug. I'm addicted and I don't care, at least most of the time I don't. I do what I do for the rush it gives me and the gold it brings me, not out of any high morals or sense of honor."

He shook his head, "That's not true, at least not entirely. You could have left them to die; you could have left me to fend for myself. You didn't. If you didn't have any honor you'd be a criminal, an assassin."

Shrugging, the bounty hunter met his gaze, "There are things I won't do, even for gold. Still, I'm no-one to look up to."

"I think you are," he asserted firmly.

That got him a wry smile, "I appreciate the compliment, Flax." Ty's features sobered and the bounty hunter looked toward the entrance. "Goddess grant I do nothing to change that in the coming weeks. If you do happen to change your mind..." Glacial eyes met his but they weren't hard and cold, "Feel free to tell me or to keep it from me."

He started to say it wasn't possible, that his opinion wouldn't change but he held it back. "I doubt anything'll change."

That single red brow lifted, the wry smile returned, "But it's possible if not probable, ay, lad?"

"I honestly don't know, so I can't say it's not, right?" his own crooked smile cocked his mustache.

The bounty hunter seemed to consider for a moment, "Right." After another moment Tymiran reclined to his side, wrapped his body around the fur he'd rolled up. "There anything else you want to talk to me about right now?"

Flax thought about it for a moment, "No."

"You sure?"

"Yeah, I'm sure."

"I'll teach you all I can, all you wish to learn from me. I can't promise you anything beyond that, Flax. Understand?"

You can't promise you'll change or hide what you are... You can't promise me you won't take males to your furs or scare the shit out of someone if you see the need... I get it... I won't hide who I am either... "I understand. Perfectly."

"Good. Get some rest. We both need it," with that the bounty hunter snuggled into his furs comfortably.

"I'm fuckin' whupped," he rolled to his side facing the cave wall, getting comfortable.

"Me too, lad. Rest well."

*   *   *

"He gave me half of Dextera's bounty, fifty gold pentas," Flax ran a hand over the braided front of his mane. Then his fingers found the slender braid that started at his temple, ran along its length. *Never did put the beads back in... he was right; they did make a lotta noise...*

"So, what made you decide against becoming a bounty hunter?" Via's slim brown fingers gripped his left forearm just above the consortship chain twined around his wrist. Her green eyes sparkled with warmth and a measure of mischief.

"What can I say?" Flax's crooked smile tilted his mustache of brushed gold. At twenty-seven he was now full grown and seven foot four. His rich golden mane cascaded down his back to his hips at the shortest. At it's longest his hair fell to mid-thigh. His mustache and beard were trimmed short and neat. A scar bisected his right brow and eye socket. It slanted backwards to end between the rise of his cheekbone and the corner of his jaw. The consortship chain caught the light as he lifted his mug, took a long drink. They were seated in the rear of the otherwise unoccupied dining room of the Green Door Inn. The same tavern he and Ty had patronized off and on back then. He and Via could see the entryway and part of the barroom from their seats. "He was right.

I'm not hard hearted enough to drag males to the collar, not for thieving anyways." With a shrug, he looked into his ale.

Slender fingers tightened on his arm, "You still look upon him as a sire?" she asked gently.

"Ty..." Flax glanced out to the entrance as a lady entered the tavern, hurried into the barroom. He watched without really appearing to do so. She looked familiar, lean and strong, blond shoulder length hair falling about her shoulders. In fact she looked rather like Commander Merissa but she wasn't wearing the garrison commander's insignia. "Was my sire in all but blood. He taught me a lot and he listened."

Sensing his distraction, however slight, Via touched his mind, <<What is it, lover?>>

<<Not sure. I think that's Commander Merissa.>> Flax sensed her concentration, her arts working though there was no outward sign.

<<She's High Judge of Byruna jurisdiction now and she's upset.>> Via's brow arched as she enlightened him.

Judge Merissa was rousing a patron from a barstool. The lady patron in question looked to be some fifty or sixty years though it was hard to tell for sure. Short cropped white hair stuck up all over like down on a round head. The rest of her was round too and she wasn't happy.

"Leave me alone!" she snarled, shoving the judge away.

"By the Goddess, Ashira, if Ty dies because you're a drunken sot..." Merissa growled back, grasping the lady's thick arm, tugging her determinedly toward the door.

Ty?! Can't be...What if it is? His alias here is Tymane... Folks call him Ty... <<Via...>>

<<I heard.>> She rose and moved toward the entryway as if she intended to intercept the two ladies. Flax followed, he didn't think Merissa would recognize him but then again, he wasn't exactly inconspicuous or commonplace.

Merissa was making some progress toward the doors when Ashira jerked away. For a moment she tottered on the edge of balance then drew herself up to her full height of merely five and a half feet.

Muddy brown eyes fixed on the judge with an indignant glare, "A healer should be treated with some respect."

The judge drew a deep breath, let it out slowly, "Please, Healer, come with me and save my Hunter."

Ashira nodded, her ego appeared to be appeased, "That's better. All you had to..." as she took a step she fell on her face, passed out cold.

"Oh, shit," Merissa stared down at the healer for a heartbeat. "Fetch me a cold bucket of water," she demanded with a glare to the barkeep. By the look on that lady's face, she didn't think one bucket would suffice.

"Perhaps I can help," Via ventured gently.

Worried blue eyes turned to the sorceress, "You wouldn't by chance be a healer would you?" Merissa sounded desperate.

"I am," she offered the judge a comforting smile.

"One of my Hunters is gravely injured…" Merissa's gaze flicked to him then back to Via, then turned back on him. Her brows knit as if she was concentrating, studying him and trying to recall where she'd seen him before.

Ordinarily it wouldn't matter. As far as he knew, Merissa knew Tymiran so it shouldn't matter if she recognized him. On the other hand he had no idea what had happened and what was going on and it wasn't like he could ask Ty what the bounty hunter wanted him to do. When he was with Tymiran he went by Errenbar or Erren for short, an ororri name. That's how Merissa knew him. As it turned out he didn't need to come up with an answer.

Understanding, caution flashed across the Judge's features. "Forgive me, you strongly resemble a warrior who passed through town some years back. His hair was darker and his eyes green, I think, but his stature was similar. Pardon my error."

"Absolutely, lady." He was thankful for her cover but now he couldn't reveal himself as Errenbar while with Via. *Damn, this shit could get complex…*

Her gaze shifted back to the sorceress, "If you would come with me?"

"Of course," Via agreed.

As the sorceress crossed the street with the judge, he unhitched the rykors, followed. The judge indicated the rojoi warrior seated on the garrison lock-up steps. The young warrior had come to fetch a healer for Tymane.

The rojoi had his face buried in his hands; thick dark hair fell forward concealing his features. No harness, no shirt but the medium red-brown skin was striped with welts.

When Via rested her hand on the coppery shoulder the rojoi looked up, stricken dark brown eyes met her gaze. "I understand your friend is gravely injured. I can help. Take us to him."

"Yeah... sure," the rojoi rose unsteadily.

Flax tracked the weltering down the well-made chest and stomach. Lines of bruising disappeared into snug black leather breeches.

Via raised a single dark brow, "You're not feeling too well, yourself. And you've been beaten."

Abruptly, Flax saw the look in the dark brown eyes, the relief as all discomfort was washed away. In moments the red-brown skin was unmarked.

"Better?" the sorceress asked.

"Thanks... Ty's... I think he's dyin', please?"

"Show us the way," she turned, accepted her rein from him and swung gracefully into her saddle.

He mounted Night, his huge female rykor as the rojoi and Merissa mounted their horses.

They followed the rojoi northward out of town to a game trail he felt was familiar. Cold certainty chilled his blood as they moved along it. It had been years, yet the feeling of familiarity grew. When he saw the lightening blasted stump of a big maple tree he was positive. The rojoi was leading them to the hidden camp he'd stayed at with the bounty hunter off and on during the time he spent as Ty's apprentice. It seemed to take forever, the trail seemed miles longer than he remembered, then the cliff rose above the trees. Another few moments and they drew rein at its base. He picked out the brush-covered entrance; drawing his axe, he dropped to the ground. Striding to the entrance, he pulled the brush from it then started to maneuver inside.

Via caught his arm, drawing his gaze. "You just stay out here, lover. There's nothing inside you need to fight."

But I want to see him... Pushing it back, he nodded, moved aside sheathing his axe, accepting the reins.

Via disappeared inside then the rojoi followed. The moment she entered the cave she touched his mind, showing him... At that moment the rojoi paused, looked up, met his gaze. He fought to keep what he was seeing through Via's eyes off his face but it was terrible. The bounty hunter was lying on his back in a pile of furs before the hearth. Embers from a dying fire threw highlights across deathly pale features, gore matted hair. The color was impossible to tell any more, it was tangled with clots of blood and darker things. Gore showed thickly on the powerful left arm. Ty's beard... was gone. *Why?..*

He concentrated forcefully on the rojoi before him. *He's young... not a whole lot younger than me though... Looks worn, near exhaustion. He's washed but there's still blood on his arms, hasn't shaved lately either... What happened?.. What have you been through?.. How'd Ty come to this... the bastard is invincible, indomitable...* Instead of asking any of it, he offered the rojoi a crooked smile, "Don't worry, if anyone can save your friend, she can."

"Thanks," the rojoi managed, entering the cave followed by Merissa.

He waited with the animals wanting to go inside and see for himself and not wanting to at the same time. Via had crossed the room to Tymiran's side, seated herself before the fireplace. She threw back the furs and he swallowed hard. The broad sweep of Ty's powerful chest was... Torn to shreds. The skin almost stripped away completely. *A long whip, they beat him with a long whip... Goddess.* The bounty hunter's chest rose, fell shallowly. *The rojoi's right! He's dying...*

<<Easy, lover. He's not lost yet.>> Via admonished him.

Someone had sewn up a gash along Ty's ribs, two arrow wounds in the stomach and one in the thigh. *Had to be the rojoi, that's not his work, it's not neat enough...*

<<There's another crossbow bolt wound in his shoulder. The belly wounds are the problem. They go all the way through him, Flax. His intestines are perforated. He's feverish but I believe I can save him.>>

Their link stretched, thinned down to just a whisper in his mind as Via laid her hands on Ty's chest and forehead. Exhaling, Flax looked down at the reins in his hand, loosened his grip. He'd been holding them so tightly his nails had dug into his calloused palm. Swallowing hard, he scanned the forest, tried to clear his mind. He could feel the connection to Via but it was now like a half heard whisper through a wall. She wasn't sparing him much of her attention and that was perfectly all right with him. He wanted her to concentrate on her arts, on healing Ty. Moments passed while he revisited his memories of the year he spent as an apprentice bounty hunter. The hunts, for game as well as criminals, the sparing sessions, Ty had taught him so much. *How'd he get here?.. Is this a Hunt gone wrong?.. He's not on the wrong side of the law; Merissa called him her*

Hunter... Who's the rojoi?.. Well, I have an idea but... Besides the obvious... The lad looks like he's been through it too, been beaten and in a battle probably in that order... Abruptly, the link with Via tightened and he could see the inside of the cave again, like a veil of silk over or behind what really lay before him. The bounty hunter looked... alive. <<Is he?>>

<<He's whole, Flax.>>

<<He didn't wake?>> He knew as much about healing as Via could explain to him. It was always better if the injured party woke. That meant there was still energy, strength to draw on left.

<<He's exhausted. Although he'd come to the resolution that he'd die he still fought it every step of the way. His will to live is the only reason for him still being alive when we arrived.>> She gestured, cleansing all the blood, dried gore from Tymiran's body, hair, even the furs. When she looked at the rojoi Flax could see the relief written blatantly on the coppery features. "If you get his feet we can get him off the floor." Together they lifted Tymiran to the bunk. The rojoi sat at the bounty hunter's feet, covered him with furs.

<<Via, Ty... Tymiran always wears some kinda beard even when he's using an alias. If Merissa's calling him Ty he's got to be using Tymane and Tymane wears a beard trimmed neat...>> he gave her the best mental picture he could from his memories.

"Thanks," the rojoi sounded rather dazed as he adjusted the furs covering the bounty hunter. "Thanks so much."

"You're welcome. I'm glad I could help." Seating herself on the edge of the bunk, she considered the bounty hunter. "I'd wager my rykor this warrior wears at least a mustache."

"He had a beard," the rojoi provided, a shudder assaulted him. "When they chained him, Lemala used hot beeswax to yank it out."

"Easy, It's over," Merissa comforted the rojoi but Via heard her indignation on the bounty hunter's part.

Via nodded, her fingertips brushed along the bounty hunter's jaw and Ty's red beard grew in just as he remembered it. She rose, turned toward the rojoi.

"He's goin' ta live. He's really goin' ta live." Coppery features revealed deep relief, gratitude; dark brown eyes stared at the bounty hunter with amazing devotion, admiration.

Via lightly rested a hand on the coppery shoulder drawing the dark eyes, "Yes. Still, you have a job to do. Make sure he eats, start with soups and stews. Keep him warm and make him rest. He'll recover but he'll be weak at first." She gestured, cleaning up the rojoi as she had the bounty hunter.

After declining payment Via told Merissa she'd wait outside so the judge could guide them back to town. As the sorceress maneuvered from the cave her link with him loosened. Emerging, Via offered him a smile.

<<Thank you,>> his own crooked smile tilted his mustache.

<<No thanks are necessary, lover.>> Via accepted her reins from him.

He nodded, shrugged, <<Thanks anyways. Who's the rojoi?>>

<<As far as I can tell he's a very worried companion, maybe a lover. He feels a lot of grief and guilt. For some reason he holds himself responsible, though not directly.>> Now she shrugged, <<I can't tell more without being intrusive.>>

<<That's plenty.>> He turned thoughtful, *How do I contact Tymiran without endangering either of us? Be nice if I knew what the fuck was happening...*

<<If you'd like to go in...>> she started to suggest.

He was already shaking his head, <<Not without knowing what's going on. The rojoi may not even know who he is... though I doubt that, it's possible. I'll leave a letter with Merissa and sign it with the alias he gave me. He'll know who I am, if it's okay I'll tell him who you are and where he can contact us.>>

<<Fine with me, Flax.>> Via smiled warmly at him then turned to the judge as she emerged from the cave. Gently, she severed their link.

Again Merissa offered them payment, which they refused, then lodgings and food. They agreed to stay at Merissa's house and partake of her hospitality overnight. Flax just thanked the Goddess the frosty bastard of a bounty hunter was still alive. The first line of his letter read; "I have yet to change my opinion."

The Price of Justice

Bounty Hunter/ Early Years #2

A.M. Helmuth

*Dedicated to my husband, Daniel J. who passed away
November 12 2018.*

One

Flax woke as someone approached the door of his room at the Green Door Inn. Whoever it was, she was stealthy, furtive. *Definitely not someone passing my room to go to their own...* The latch was tested quietly as he slid from beneath the furs, drew his short-sword from his harness hanging next to the bed.

As much as he favored the heft and length of his long-sword, he had to admit the bounty hunter was right. Length and sweep and a room in the dark weren't good combinations.

His deep blue feline eyes searched the darkened room thoroughly. Even in the dimness of a moonless night, he could see well. Ororri had excellent night vision and he'd inherited it from his sire. He'd also gotten his golden hair from his ororri blood. It fell to his hips at it's longest in a shining cascade of white gold with deeper brushed tones underneath. Two slender braids at his temples bound in wide leather ties laced with red fell well down his chest. Still, Flax wasn't pure ororri. His sire had been his mother's slave. He was half Byrynthian. His mother; High General Lynia of the Protectress' Elite Guard, hadn't been pleased when he'd disappeared shortly after his weapons training had been officially concluded. She promised him to a noble-lady's daughter and put a bounty out on him for his safe return. For now, it was a private contract, the garrisons had not been notified, soldiers weren't hunting him. He thought it was unlikely Lynia would resort to that. And yet, only the Goddess knew, at the moment, if it was a bounty hunter on the other side of his door.

Ordinarily, it wouldn't be particularly difficult to hide a blond-haired-blue-eyed Byrynthian in Byrynthia yet Flax was far from ordinary looking with his ororri eyes and hair. Still, there was a bigger problem than his feline eyes. As Ty once pointed out, the number of half ororri youths over seven feet tall was relatively few. Right now he knew of one, himself, and he really stood out in a crowd at seven foot three.

Built powerfully muscular, he was well trained in weapons, thanks to his mother, and he was gaining skills by leaps and bounds as the apprentice of a bounty hunter who'd taken his side in this tangled hunt. Flax had come to thank the Goddess every day that Tymiran was on his side because if the ruthless bastard had been hunting him, he'd have been dragged home in chains already.

Tymiran was spoken of as one of the best bounty hunters in the northern provinces. From what Flax had seen personally, he'd wager Ty was the best. To anyone else the bounty hunter was tall; six-four, and broad, powerfully built, yet lithe and dangerously graceful. Tymiran was from the northern regions of Byrynthia. Red-gold hair fell to his waist, curling, spiraling and thick. His beard, brows were redder than his hair and glacial blue eyes reflected the bounty hunter's nature; hard, cold, ruthless. And yet, the bounty hunter had helped him out of a jam. Ty had taken Flax's side and offered his protection against a powerful High General, Flax's mother. He'd risked his life to save five helpless prisoners meant to become sacrifices to a false goddess. That had been some six and a half weeks ago. Flax was learning a lot from the bounty hunter; weapons skills, woodcraft, concentration and focus.

He heard Ty grip the handle on the other side of the door of their adjoining rooms as a lock-pick went to work on his main door. He moved toward the adjoining door as it silently eased open. It swung either way and was equipped to lock on either side. Ty opened it into his own room, slipped through.

The bounty hunter was armed with the conventional short-sword he carried when posing as Tymane, his mercenary guise. Woodland leathers sheathed the bounty hunter's loins and legs. Unless Flax missed his guess they were gray, green and brown, perfect for autumn. Flax wore only a tong, its single ring clasp nestled against his lions just beneath his right hipbone.

Ty beckoned subtly, glided silently to one side of the door. He took the other just as the lock clicked.

A quiet exhalation of air came to him from the other side of the door. Flax met the bounty hunter's glacial blue eyes in the darkened chamber. Bloodlust burned behind the frozen surface. He felt it too, not as intense as was written on Tymiran's features yet his blood burned in his veins with it.

Very slowly, the door started to open a crack, an inch, two. Ty flattened himself to the wall, the slightest gesture, nod and a pointed glance to the door handle told him to pull it open. He made a slight gesture, a question; *fast?* Another nod was the answer. The door had eased open another two inches. Stealthily, with a light touch, he wrapped his hand around the handle, met

Ty's eyes again. The slightest nod answered his unspoken question and he jerked the door open. A dark figure stumbled inward with a curse. Before the figure could regain her balance, Ty caught an arm, spun whoever it was around, dumped her to the floor with a deft foot. The tip of the bounty hunter's blade nestled beneath the intruder's jaw.

She gasped, it was definitely a female. Flax noted her shape despite the dark clothing, the hood of her short cloak hiding her features.

A gesture from the bounty hunter and he closed the door, lit the nearest lamp.

"All right, thief, give me reason not to slit your throat and drag your carcass before the judge," Tymiran growled. His voice was as frozen as his glacial eyes.

"I'm not a thief," she whispered breathlessly.

The bounty hunter flicked the hood back from her face and returned the blade to its threatening position. Flax recognized the fifteen-year-old daughter of the Inn's owner's sister. She'd been working the dining room earlier. In fact she'd drawn their ale if Flax recalled correctly.

"Deirha, what are you doing here?" Ty's voice lost none of its frostiness despite the recognition.

She chewed her lip nervously, glanced from the bounty hunter to him. Tymiran, Tymane as he was known in Byruna, lifted the blade beneath her jaw slightly getting her attention. "I... You won't tell? Please Tymane... I didn't mean any harm..."

"Answer," Ty growled, low and threatening, it brooked no argument.

Dierha swallowed hard, "I just wanted to look at him."

Tymiran/Tymane glanced to him. He met the glacial gaze, puzzled to his toes. Tymiran appeared amused, so amused he was fighting a grin.

"You broke in here so you could look at Erren' while he's asleep," it wasn't precisely a question. Errenbar, Erren' for short, was Flax's alias here in Byruna. It was an ororri name and implied that his mother had been ororri rather than his sire.

She gulped, started to shift nervously but with the blade against her throat thought better of it. "Well... Um... He's really beautiful... the most beautiful male I ever saw..."

Ty nodded thoughtfully, still his blade hadn't lowered, "How long have you been breaking into handsome patrons' rooms just to admire them in their sleep?"

Eyes widening, she glanced to him again. Flax did his best to appear angry and cold. *I'm not gonna help her, no way...*

The bounty hunter lifted his sword slightly.

Deirha gasped, "A few weeks..."

"You've been peeping in on your aunt's handsome patrons for weeks, have you?" The bounty hunter rested his sword point on the floor. "On your feet."

She scrambled up, "I'm sorry, truly I am. I didn't mean you any harm..." she stepped toward Flax, imploring him to accept her apology.

He put his sword up, holding her back. "Keep the hell away from me," Flax growled indignantly. *Well, I hope I sound indignant, angry, maybe even threatening...*

Ty caught her by the shirt, "Do you realize I could have slit your throat for this? And what happens to your aunt's business if it gets around that her hirelings sneak into patrons' rooms? Never thought of that, did you?

Deirha looked at the floor, "No... I didn't think anyone would catch me... Or anything."

"You just didn't think." Tymiran/Tymane pointed out. "Listen to me, lass," he gave her a shake with his fist in her shirt. "You go creeping around again at night and I'll catch you at it and drag you to your aunt. Even if I'm not here, I'll find out so it stops now. Understand me, Deirha?" By the bounty hunter's tone it was barely a question, closer to a command.

She nodded and Flax thought he heard a snuffle. When she glanced up he could see she was fighting tears.

"Go on, then. Back to your own room." Tymiran/Tymane stepped aside. Flax opened the door and she fled.

Drawing a deep breath, he let it out, shut his door and locked it. "She could have been killed... damn." He raked his free hand through his long golden hair.

Tymiran shrugged, "Personally, I'm insulted."

Flax gave the bounty hunter a perplexed look, "Insulted?" He crossed the room to slide his own sword home.

Ty nodded, locking the door. "She said you're the most beautiful male in the world..."

"Oh no, now wait, she didn't say that."

"What did she say then?" a single red brow lifted, amusement laced the hunter's hard features.

Flax sighed, raked a hand through his hair, "So, she thinks I'm... good lookin'."

"I believe the exact words were, the most beautiful male she's ever seen," Ty provided.

He offered the bounty hunter a glare.

"Whatever," Ty shrugged. "At any rate, what does that make me?"

Flax stared speechless for a moment then threw up his hands, "By the Goddess."

Ty laughed, "Better get some more rest, lad."

"Right," Flax seated himself on his bed, raked strong hands through his hair. "Like I can sleep now."

"You can sleep. It's barely the second hour." In a few long strides the bounty hunter pushed through their adjoining door. "Night, lad."

He rose, stretched, "Night." Under his breath, he grumbled, "Coulda put the damn lamp out," as he moved to do just that. He snuffed out the lamp, stretched. His feline eyes adjusted instantly and he clearly saw the adjoining door open into Ty's room just enough to admit the bounty hunter.

Caught in mid stretch, Flax's brows knit in puzzlement but before he could say anything an abrupt gesture silenced him. Tymiran remained pressed to the wall for a moment then glided silently to the window. A couple terse gestures were as eloquent as any spoken orders. *Act naturally, get into bed.* Still perplexed down to his toes, he complied.

Flax moved to the bed as if nothing at all was amiss. Climbing upon it, reclining, elicited the loud creaks that always accompanied the bed taking his entire weight. Crouching, Ty moved past and beneath the window then rose to look out for long tense heartbeats. Flattening himself to the wall, the hunter indicated he should lay down. Flax did, drawing a single fur over himself, snuggling down comfortably. At least he hoped he looked like he was snuggling in comfortably. Narrowing his eyes to slits, he watched Ty closely. Pressed tightly to the wall, the bounty hunter met his gaze, glanced significantly to the window then met his eyes again.

Someone's watching! Shit!.. Clenching his jaw, he swallowed hard, stifled the urge to roll out of the furs and draw his sword. After long tense minutes, the bounty hunter slid down the wall, stealthily moved next to the bed, so low and close that Flax couldn't see him.

"Flax, slide off the other side. Pile up furs to look like you're in there as you go. Silently, now. Stay low, don't talk, meet you at the foot," the bounty hunter ordered in his nearly inaudible whisper.

Stealthily, slowly and smoothly, Flax did as he was told, then crouched next to the bed. Shifting to all fours, he crawled to the foot. When he looked along the foot-board, Tymiran met his gaze, crouched behind the opposite corner post. The bounty hunter beckoned subtly. He moved to crouch at Ty's side under cover of the bed's big foot-board. Flax was surprised to see the bounty hunter had his swords. He hadn't heard them drawn from his sheaths.

Ty leaned close, whispered near his ear, "Stay low as you can, go through the door to my room."

He nodded, accepted his short-sword from Ty and slipped to his stomach. Quietly and stealthily as he could, Flax crossed the open space to their connecting door, slowly he got to a crouch then sidled through. Ty's room was darker; the drapes were drawn. Still, he could see well. Even though he felt he was alone in the room, he crouched, back to the wall flanking the door, sword ready. Tense heartbeats later, Tymiran crept through the door then rose, baring Flax's naked long-sword. The bounty hunter gripped the hilt so the blade nestled almost hidden along the muscular arm until it jutted up from behind the powerful shoulder. At the hunter's gesture, he rose too, staying against the wall. The click of the lock seemed unnaturally loud in the leaden silence. Gliding noiselessly across the room to the window, Ty flanked it, carefully peered out between the frame and draperies. Flax waited, scanned the dark room, strained his senses for any sound. Momentarily, Ty turned to the fur strewn bed. The bounty hunter beckoned, laid the long-sword across the nightstand. As Flax complied Ty separated two blankets from the covers.

"Someone was watchin'," he whispered, nearly as low as Ty's almost inaudible whisper. He was getting better at that, still, his deep rumbling bass voice just didn't drop that low without practice.

The bounty hunter nodded then climbed on the bed. Folding the blankets into triangles, he hung them from the wrought iron canopy frame like slings above the head of the bed, then climbed down. "Deirha only told us part of the truth." The bounty hunter explained softly. "Someone put her up to it tonight, perhaps challenged her somehow, with a wager or a dare."

"To test me or us," his blood ran cold.

"Aye," Ty agreed, settling Flax's long-sword in one blanket sling. "How's that?"

He shrugged, "For what?"

Glacial eyes met his, bloodlust burned in the bounty hunter. "Makeshift sheath. I left your harness. Someone tries for you they might notice the harness missing and be alerted. With the sheathes in place, bed curtains hanging over it, the swords missing aren't so noticeable."

Flax nodded thoughtfully, "Think they'll try anything now?"

Ty shook his head, selecting a few cushions, a few furs. The hunter dropped them to the floor, "Doubt it, but I can't be sure. I'll wager it'll be tomorrow after we've ridden out or after we've made camp. Still, can't be too careful." When the bounty hunter held out a calloused hand, he laid his short-sword hilt in it. Ty settled it in the second blanket/sling/sheath.

"So, I'm staying in here tonight," he concluded.

"Yeah." The bounty hunter took down his reddish brown harness from its place next to the bed. It was the harness he wore when he was passing as Tymane. Crouching, Ty spread two of the furs, arranged the cushions laying the harness under the edge of the bed. "Try to get some rest, lad. Wager you're going to need it come tomorrow." With that the bounty hunter stretched out on the makeshift bed, drew the last fur over him.

Flax was just a little perplexed, mildly uncomfortable, "I... Don't wanna put ya outta your bed..."

"Think I mentioned that when we share a room I take the floor." Tymiran rolled to his side, one cushion wrapped in powerful arms.

"Yeah... But..." *It just doesn't seem right... I'm the apprentice here... And if I wasn't... Whatever it is that I am, we could share the bed. Not that I don't trust him... but the thought does make me uncomfortable... Prejudiced bastard, that's what I am... Damn.*

Glacial eyes met his through the spiraling red-gold curtain of the bounty hunter's mane, "Look, lad, I appreciate your concern but I could still use some more sleep, so climb in already and relax."

He sighed, "Yeah, right," Flax muttered under his breath. Still, he climbed gently into the big bed, almost as large as the one in his room, and got comfortable. Experimentally, he reached up and gripped the hilt of his long-sword then the short-sword. They were right where he needed them to be.

"You can reach 'em okay?" Ty asked.

He jumped, *How'd he know I even reached up and touched them?..* "Yeah, they're perfect, thanks."

"No problem." The bounty hunter sounded relaxed, nearly asleep.

"So, um... Where's your fur warmer?"

"Sent him back to the kitchens." Ty sounded rather like he was stifling laughter.

"In case of something like this?" Rolling to his back, he slipped both hands under his head, stared at the strips of red gauze draped over the canopy's iron frame.

"Just in case."

So I'm not uncomfortable with a slave around, you sent him away... So damn careful of my... sensitivities... Before he could voice it Tymiran elaborated.

"A slave is no good in the middle of a fight, lad. I'd hate for him to get hurt or killed because someone came for one of us in the night."

Hadn't thought of that, "Oh."

"I'd have to pay for the healer or reimburse the owner for the slave. It just makes sense to get him out of the way." The bounty hunter sounded serious, matter of fact but...

Unless I miss my guess... "Ain't just the coin?"

"No," Ty shifted in the furs, "it's the mess too."

Flax rolled to look over the edge of the bed, down at the bounty hunter.

Lying on his back, hands beneath his head, Ty grinned up at him.

"You bastard..." he couldn't help but return the grin.

The bounty hunter laughed quietly. Flax pushed up to a forearm, striving not to bust out laughing too. In a moment Ty's mirth wound down, "Seriously, I just try to prepare."

"You think of everything," he shook his head with amazement.

"Nobody can think of everything but I try." Ty sort of shrugged, "Can we get some rest now?"

Flax yawned, nodded, then got comfortable in the furs.

*   *   *

Flax sensed movement in the room. Immediately he was awake, rolling out of the bed, snatching his short-sword, lightening quick... Despite the fact he already knew it was Ty. If asked how he knew he couldn't have explained it to anyone's satisfaction. The presence, the movement just felt like Ty. Fast as he was, and he was damn fast, the bounty hunter was poised for a fight, swords bare in his hands.

The hunter flashed him a cool smile, bloodlust flickered behind the ice in the glacial eyes. "Well done, lad."

"My ass," Flax snarled good naturedly, "coulda killed me."

Ty shrugged, returned his blades to the sheathes in the red-brown conventional harness. The hunter was dressed in woodland leathers, the gray and brown streaked breeches, a wrap around Cyrcanian style long sleeved shirt that matched in color and tied at the left. The red-brown harness hugged Ty's strong chest. The bounty hunter stretched callused hands into red-brown bracers that just covered his hands, not the fingers or thumb. Tightening the laces around his forearms, Ty trapped his shirtsleeves. The right bracer sported five extending blades. Three throwing knives rode the left. One was six inches, the second seven. The last knife was eight inches. Stepping into brown flared boots, Ty sat on the bed to tighten the laces.

"You're quick, lad," the bounty hunter remarked.

"Yeah, but you're still quicker." Setting his sword back in the makeshift sheath, Flax watched the hunter tie his boots. "So, where are you off to already?" He had a feeling he knew the answer but he asked anyways.

"I want to look around outside before anyone else is up. Hand me my pick," Ty indicated the ivory hair pick on the bedside stand.

He complied then watched as the hunter deftly combed out the thick curling red-gold mane. Flax wanted to go along but he figured he already knew the answer to that one too. Before he even had a chance to frame the question Ty answered it.

Rising, the bounty hunter gripped his bicep, "Sorry, lad. I can't make a lesson out of this. Tymane and Erren' are caravan guards not bounty hunters. I have to be inconspicuous."

Nodding, he considered, "S'okay, besides, you'll make it up to me."

"How?" Ty looked amused, mildly suspicious as he put his pick in his pack.

"Something special for breakfast?" Flax grinned.

"That's it?" the bounty hunter laughed quietly. "I'll wager I can do better than that but order whatever you want. I'll take care of it."

"You sure?" Flax's crooked smile flashed, "Ya know how I can eat."

Tymiran nodded, "I know. Still, order whatever you want." The bounty hunter rose, "Anyone wants to join you, decline. I'll be there as soon as I can." Hard features grew cool, almost unreadable. "Get dressed, get your pack together. You might want a warm shirt when we ride out. Go out through your room."

"Protecting my reputation?" Flax teased.

A single red brow lifted, the slightest hint of a smile cocked the red mustache, "Folks will think what they want of us, lad. I just don't want our watchers to know we saw them."

"You saw 'em, I didn't." He considered, "What about your pack?"

"It's ready. I'll fetch it when I come back in. Anyone asks, I went to see that the horses would be ready."

"Okay," Flax agreed. The reminder that someone had been watching them... him sobered his mood. "You think they were after me?" It was about half question, half statement. Tymiran had enemies but Tymane didn't, not really and Flax was the one with the bounty on his hide.

Ty shrugged, "They weren't interested in me. Stay on your toes this morning. Something doesn't feel right."

Golden brows knit and Flax stifled the urge to rake a hand through his hair, "Watch your back."

A cool smile flashed across the hunter's features but it was more a bearing of the wolf's teeth. "I will, lad. Doubt they'll try anything now but you never know. Lock the door after me." With that the bounty hunter left the room.

Flax locked the door as Ty said. Then he picked up the furs and cushions off the floor. He took down the makeshift sheathes and mixed the blankets in with the rest of the bedcovers.

He looked around the room searching for anything out of place, anything that said he'd slept in here rather than his own room. There were a few long blond hairs in the bed so he plucked them up and took them with him back to his own room. Messing up the furs on his bed, he left the vagrant strands of his mane in there. It didn't take long to get his pack together, clean his teeth and wash up with the basin and pitcher. Brushing out his mane, Flax bound it all in a Byrynthian braid, took up his pack then went to the dining room to wait. He chose a table in the corner where he could watch the kitchen doors, the front windows and the entrance through the wide dining room archway. He ordered a pot of black tea, two mugs and a hearty breakfast for the two of them.

*   *   *

Tymiran offered Flax a wave as he passed the wide dining room archway on the way to pick up his pack. *Have to remember to tell him he chose a good place to sit...* He checked the room thoroughly. The lad was smart, he'd removed any evidence that he'd slept in this room. Taking up his pack, Tymiran went to the dining room, slid into the bench across from Flax at a table leaden with food. The young giant's woolen shirt was shoved through the straps of his pack, as his was on his pack. Meeting the blue feline eyes, he lifted a red brow. The lad was busy chewing.

Flax swallowed, cracked that crooked smile, "I'm hungry."

"Really? I would have never guessed." He laughed quietly. Filling a plate from the many dishes before him, Tymiran dug into his own meal.

"Tea?" Flax lifted the pot.

"Aye, lad. Thanks." Tymiran watched the steaming black liquid fill the mug. Keeping his head down, like he was concentrating on eating, so no one watching could tell what he was saying, or even if he was talking at all, he spoke quietly. "There were three of them outside your window last night. Thought I saw 'em all but..." He took a forkful of eggs baked with sausage and cheese, chewed. "Better to read the tracks, know for sure. Still, doesn't mean there aren't more with 'em. The two ladies in the opposite corner have been pointedly avoiding looking this way at all. Ever see 'em before?"

Flax's feline gaze met his then glanced discretely to the ladies mentioned. "Nope. You?"

He grunted a negative. Flax's breakfast choices were delicious. At a regular conversational tone he remarked, "Horses will be outside waitin' for us by the time we're done."

"'S great," Flax answered casually.

He could read the tension in the powerful shoulders, feline eyes, but Tymiran would wager no one else could. Despite the bloodlust flickering through his veins, he felt a familiar rush of paternal pride. *Things I've no right to feel... And if he really looked at me... Really saw... I wouldn't read such admiration in those ororri eyes...* "Figure we'll head north. Caribou will be migrating from the highlands soon. The moose will be rutting. How would you feel about some hunting?"

Flax's features lit up with genuine anticipation. "You mean it?"

He nodded, "Next deer we get I'll make a moose call. See if I can't call you in a big one, if you're game."

"Oh, yeah," the lad's enthusiasm was evident. Flax turned thoughtful, bit his lip, "What do we do for coin?"

Flax knew they were well off but Tymane and Errenbar would be suspect if they didn't even discuss it.

Tymiran shrugged, "We can make some silver off the extra meat. If the pelts and antlers are nice it could mean gold."

"Excellent," that crooked grin flashed.

Tymiran returned it, dropped his voice low again as he tore a piece of fresh bread. "Merissa just walked in."

Flax met his gaze, glanced surreptitiously toward the archway. "Looks like she's pissed."

"That's an understatement." Tymiran sighed quietly. *Wager she just received orders to fetch High General Lynia's vagrant son back to her in the capitol. Didn't think she'd resort to that but time is running short... Damn... If we'd left yesterday...*

Merissa was the garrison commander and she was wearing her uniform. A well fitting mail shirt sheathed her shapely upper body. The sleeves fell just past her elbows in loose angular folds. Black leather bracers with mail ornamentation graced her forearms. Breeches of black leather sheathed strong legs snugly. Three narrow stripes running down the outside of her right leg marked her rank. The uniform alone would have told him the reason she was looking for him would be official business.

At six foot she was just a hand under his height. Her golden blond hair was cut short, in graduated lengths falling over her forehead, framing her face. She was strong and fit as the best of her soldiers. If the uniform hadn't been enough to tell Tymiran her errand was serious, the expression on her comely features gave him the distinct impression he was in deep shit with her. He flashed his apprentice a broad mischievous grin as

Merissa approached. In a heartbeat the garrison commander was standing at their table.

"Hey, Merissa," Ty greeted her genially, "tea?"

She exhaled quietly, like she was striving to calm herself, "We need to talk."

"Have you breakfasted, lady?" Flax/Errenbar put in.

Her jaw tightened and she gave Flax a frosty glare. "Ty first, then... then we'll talk."

"What the Hell'd you do, lad? Hang her breeches from the weather-vane?" Tymiran/Tymane spoke casually then he lowered his voice, spoke through his teeth, "Can we keep this just between the three of us?"

"I been good, I swear." While he was being subtle Flax shrugged in response to his playful question.

Merissa folded her arms, sighed, "Fine. For the moment." She kept her voice low enough that those at the next table couldn't overhear.

"Sit, okay?" Tymiran/ Tymane offered, making room on the bench for her. "Have some tea at least."

A curt shake of her head, "Let's you and I go outside."

Tymiran glanced at Flax. The ororri eyes met his gaze and he read growing apprehension. He gestured slightly, *It's okay, relax.* He shrugged, "I'm not quite done here." Lowering his voice again, he picked up his mug, made as if he was sipping, "How many soldiers are waiting for me outside, Merissa?"

With yet another sigh, she slipped onto the bench next to him, her arm settled around his shoulders and she leaned into him so she could whisper in his ear.

"Today, I can almost understand this need of yours for secrecy so I'll play along..." her lips brushed his ear, "just for now. There's no-one waiting outside for us. Not today. Don't push me, you've a lot of explaining to do, Ty, a hell of a lot of explaining."

A sly smile, lit Tymiran's features, sexy suggestion laced his expression. Turning toward her a bit, he rested his left hand on her knee, drew circles with his fingertips. By looking at him one would have been sure she was whispering intimate suggestions, proposals, propositions. Deftly, he caught her mouth in a kiss. Merissa's strong fingers knotted in the hair at the nape of his neck. She kissed him back, hard and demanding. Tymiran grunted, responded, mildly surprised. He hadn't really expected her to accept his attention so readily. He'd rather expected a hard right to the jaw. Warmth spread through his limbs, her mouth took his, caressed, devoured. It felt genuine, very genuine... pleasantly so. *Surprise, surprise...* long moments passed then slowly, almost reluctantly she disengaged. Merissa met his gaze, she looked... a little surprised, a little disconcerted, just a little, then it was gone.

"Outside," she suggested.

Tymiran nodded, "Certainly, lady."

She rose and he followed. Taking his pouch from his harness, he tossed it on table, meeting Flax's slightly apprehensive gaze. "The horses should be ready by now. Pay for our meal from my pouch, lad, meet me at the livery. As soon as the commander is through with me, we'll leave." He gestured discretely, keeping it hidden from Merissa. *Stay ready.* "Give me ten, fifteen minutes?"

"Sure," Flax/ Errenbar flashed him a knowing, crooked grin, "That's pretty damn quick, Ty. Sure she'll be satisfied with that?" The apprehension had dissolved, trust and stubborn determination replaced it.

Tymiran flashed an answering grin, "I'll do my damnedest." He turned, following Commander Merissa, she was beyond doubt, all soldier, all business again. He sighed quietly, preparing himself for the dance he was about to do. It was never easy to lie to Merissa, and he was going to have to lie, a lot.

He followed her from the inn, down the broad steps. She paused, perhaps waiting for him to come even with her. Tymiran took advantage of it without missing a step. He took the steps at an angle, heading towards the livery stable. Sure enough their horses were saddled, standing at the hitching post. He heard Merissa curse quietly as she lengthened her stride to catch up to him. There weren't that many folks about yet. It was coming on the seventh hour, shopkeepers were just opening front shutters, unlocking doors. He strode towards the livery, past it and their horses then turned down a wide alley running along it towards the paddock in the back. As he turned the corner, he slowed his pace to a stroll.

"So, what was it you needed to talk to me about, Merissa?" Tymiran met her gaze side long.

"Don't pretend you don't know," she practically growled at him.

"Perhaps I don't," he shrugged. They were about half way to the paddock fence.

"Ty, the bounty has been set on him for months. You know, you have to." Merissa strolled casually at his side but she was ready, tense, as if she expected a fight.

"Ah," he nodded as if she'd confirmed his suspicions, "You're referring to Lynia's errant son." He stopped, leaned back against the barn with his hands at the small of his back, willingly adopting just about the most non-threatening stance he could manage. Tymiran chuckled quietly, "The High General has finally decided to send orders to garrisons to detain her son," he concluded.

Merissa folded her arms, surveying him up and down with cool impatience. Her guard didn't lower one bit.

Looks like she's not going to believe I'm innocent and non-threatening... Oh, well, it was worth a try... "You think what she's doing is right?"

Merissia sighed, "What I think doesn't matter. He has to go back. I have orders..."

"He's not who you think he is," Tymiran stated flatly. This was, in a way, from a certain point of view, true. Merissa would definitely call it a lie. The look she gave him spoke volumes. "You want the whole story?"

"That would be nice for a change." She flashed him a bright smile, as insincere as it was sunny. "You could even tell me the truth."

He returned the smile, going for genuine. "I met with Lynia, I didn't care for what she wanted me to do and why. I let her think what she wanted but I wasn't about to take her contract. Some weeks after meeting with her I ran into Errenbar in a tavern. The lad was in a spot and I took his side of it, thinking, just as you do, that he's Flaxon. Three ladies thought they could take him. Apparently he'd been having a lot of trouble with bounty hunters..."

"Imagine that," Merissa growled. There was a distinct note of skepticism in her voice.

"He swore he wasn't who they were looking for and he swore to it emphatically. In fact, he was so emphatic that I suggested we go see an empath. He agreed. He was telling the truth. The lad's name is Errenbar, he's Kylonian and ororri, and he's a big son of a bitch..."

"Over seven feet I'd say."

"Definitely over seven feet," Tymiran agreed. "He fell in with me because I took his side in that latest attempt to collect Lynia's bounty. I offered to help guard his back. I sort of put the word out that Flaxon was caught and on his way home. As long as Lynia kept the contract private we had no real trouble, now... Things get more complicated with you and every other garrison on the lookout for someone so similar in appearance to Erren' it's damned inconvenient."

"Inconvenient, there's an understatement," her cool gaze searched his, studied, then she looked down the alley toward the paddock. It was very clear to him that she was thinking hard, considering everything he'd said and the implications. "The empath..."

"Located in Kylonia and unwilling to get mixed up further in Byrynthian politics," Tymiran volunteered.

Merissa nodded, "Of course."

"Just for the sake of argument, what do you think?"

Her cool, considering gaze met his, narrowed almost suspiciously.

Tymiran lifted a brow inquisitively, "Think it's okay to give your first born away in exchange for political alliance, without his consent?" He read what she was going to do in the tension in her frame and decided, in a fraction of a heartbeat, to let her do it.

Strong hands seized his shirt and harness straps fiercely. Merissa tugged him closer, face to face, eye to eye. She glared into his eyes, lip curling in a snarl...

He spoke before she could in a nearly inaudible whisper, "Would you do that to your son, Merrissa? Your first born, albeit male, would you just give him to some noble lady's daughter?"

"I don't have children, Ty." She let him go, pushing him against the wall just a bit roughly.

"If you did," he shrugged casually, put a foot against the wall, keeping his open hands pressed against the planks behind him,

She glared at him like she wanted to grab him and slam him against the wall once or twice for good measure. Yet, he could read her answer on her comely features and offered her a wry smile, "I didn't think so."

Merissa drew a long breath, let it out slowly, as if she was getting a handle on her temper. He knew it for what it was, pretense. She was far too calculating and controlled for him to have rattled her nerve so easily. "That's quite a tale you've spun for me, Ty."

"Would you like me to swear to it?" he offered.

She gave him a knowing look, "I don't think that's necessary."

"If you say so."

"Siding with him could make Byrynthia... too hot for you."

"Siding with a half blood ororri lad?" Tymiran mused, "A lad who has nothing to do with any Byrynthian general or noble lady? How could that make Byrynthia hot for me?"

"Right," Merissa nodded speculatively. She cocked her head, her gaze ran over him, head to toe then back again to study his features. There was a distinct light of lust in her eyes. "That order..."

"Has nothing to do with Erren'," Tymiran supplied.

Merissa made a slightly dismissing gesture, "That order, it could still be unopened, sitting atop the pile of reports on my desk."

"Really?" He asked casually. *She can't be suggesting what I think she is...* "The courier..."

"All she wanted was a meal and a bed." Merissa shrugged, "She said nothing of its importance or urgency. The seal wasn't unusual in any way; there was no real reason to open it immediately."

He nodded his agreement. *Wonder where this is going.* "So... you didn't even cut the seal when she brought it?"

Merissa shook her head, "Not as far as anyone else knows."

"That would be... opportune. So..." He lifted a single brow inquiringly, "how does this come to pass?"

Merissa seemed to consider. "This," her gesture took in his stance, "seems a bit submissive for you."

"I can be submissive if the situation warrants it, Merissa."

"How submissive?" her voice dropped lower, took on a husky hint of suggestion.

He shrugged, "That depends."

Deftly, she reached out, caught the knot in his shirt, stepped closer. He dropped the foot against the wall to the ground, walked his feet apart a bit so they were eye to eye.

"What if I opened the rings on your harness?"

"What if you did?" he offered her an inviting smile.

Merissa tugged open the left ringclasp on the bottom set of straps, the tertiaries. The left ring on his secondary straps followed then the primaries. Pointedly looking him in the eyes, she tugged open the ring on his left shoulder strap. Tymiran straightened a little, shrugged and let the harness drop off his left shoulder. He settled back against the wall. Stepping closer yet, she deftly untied the knot in his shirt, parted it, let it fall open. Merissa took a little step back, her gaze ran over his exposed chest and belly. The light in her eyes was unmistakable.

"What do you want, Merissa," it came out low and husky.

"What do I want?" The backs of her slender fingers lightly stirred the red hair on his stomach. Merissa stepped close, almost against him. "I want you, Ty." Her hand pressed against his belly, slid around to his side then up to the rise of his strong chest. "I want you in my furs."

Tymiran's brows knit, he wet his lips, "Terms? Conditions?"

"One week, I have you all to myself."

"I don't have a week to give you right now. Erren' and I have to leave." He subtly offered her his mouth.

"I know." She kissed him, hard and devouring.

Tymiran didn't bother suppressing the quiet sounds of pleasure, need, the kiss elicited. Her hands ran along his ribs, exploring and setting his skin alight. As she devoured him, sounds of pleasure escaped her. The kiss was long, hungry, as if she was trying to taste every subtle nuance of him. As she drew back, her gaze met his, slender fingers slid up his chest over the shoulder unburdened with the harness and pushed his shirt off it. She caressed the muscle, bared his bicep, tricep to the elbow. They were both breathing deeply, her breasts pushed against her mailshirt enticing him to cup them in his hands. Her hips, loins, thighs, sheathed in snug black leather, tempted him to wrap his hands around her ass... He resisted the urge.

Flax needs my help, I've responsibilities to that lad... 'course this may be one of them. If this is what it takes to get us out of town unscathed I can easily give her a week... Unless... she wants a down payment right now... Damn, do I have that kind of time? Doubt it, seriously doubt it...

He touched his tongue to his teeth, upper lip.

"By the Goddess, you are fine male, Ty," Merissa's gaze ran down his chest and belly, following her touch.

Tymiran pushed his shoulders against the wall, arched into her caress, moaned softly.

A quiet gasp answered him. Her hands attempted to encircle his waist then slid up his rippled stomach, over the rise of his chest. One hand gripped the hair there, the other slid along his ribs. Tymiran grunted, closed his eyes and writhed for her, pushed into her rough caress. The hint of pain ignited fires in his loins he hadn't indulged lately.

"So, how submissive can you be?" She whispered, her arm slipped around the small of his back, she pressed against him. Merissa kissed him. This time it was quick and left him wanting more.

Tymiran met her gaze, "I won't be bound and I won't be beaten." He offered her a sexy smile, lifted a brow, "Beyond that, we can negotiate, experiment."

"Let me leash you?" She tiled her head, her lips, tongue, teeth teased his neck.

He chuckled low and husky, "No locks."

"No locks," she agreed, lips moving against his skin.

"We can give it a try," he breathed barely audibly.

She pressed the length of her body against him, kissed him long and hard again. Tymiran let himself get lost in it for the moment. Heat and need burned in his blood, lit every fiber on fire. He pushed his iron hard shaft trapped behind the leather of his breeches against Merissa's loins. Slowly, reluctantly, she drew back, met his gaze.

"Want me here? Now?" Tymiran offered. *Want her... So bad I ache... But Flax and I have to get out of here... I have to wrap this up...*

Shaking her head, Merissa parted from him, stepped back. It was a slow, reluctant process, but all too quickly she was a pace away. "I'm already wrapped up in a mess with you, if I get caught by one of my own soldiers having you in this alleyway... Nothing we can say will change the charges." Looking away, she ran a hand over her hair, straightened her harness and shirt. When she looked at him again her brows knit.

Tymiran was leaning against the wall behind him, hands behind his back, harness and shirt open, knees slightly bent, feet apart. He offered her a grin leaden with suggestion, ran his tongue along his teeth and upper lip, shifted his hips.

"Goddess..." Merissa looked away. "Straighten up, Ty..." Her gesture hinted that he should get dressed.

He obliged, standing up away from the wall, straightening, tying his shirt, refastening his harness. "After Lynia's bounty is revoked, it'll take a couple months for the word to get around. I want to be sure Erren' is safe before we come back here, before I give you an uninterrupted week of my time."

Merissa nodded in agreement, "Of course."

"Around Solstice I head north for a while," he cautioned.

"I know," she seemed to consider, "Flaxon won't be eighteen until the spring equinox. The bounty has to expire then, she won't have any further claim on him. As for our orders..." Merissa shrugged.

He nodded; there was really no telling when Lynia would rescind them, if at all. She could have Flax detained for the hell of it then release him when she chose just to mete out a little punishment.

"We'll be back around... say summer Solstice," Tymiran ventured. "Things should have settled down by then."

She nodded, "I'll have to send out a couple patrols after you. Later, like after noon, when I get through the pile of reports and dispatches on my desk."

"I would expect no less. Don't worry, we won't get caught." He flashed her a mischievous grin.

"I would expect no less, Ty." Merissa bit her lower lip, "I look forward to seeing you around the summer Solstice."

Deft and swift, he caught her wrist, pulled her close and turned. Locking a powerful arm around her, he pressed her against the wall, covering her mouth with his, stifling any outcry. He kissed her hard and long, devouring, exploring. He pressed his powerful body against hers, taking full advantage of his height, making it clear he was bigger, stronger, pushing his loins against hers. She didn't fight him, at all. That was a bit of a surprise. In fact, her loins pushed against his, slender hands gripped his shoulders. He moaned, heat and need blazed in his blood. He drew back nearly breathless, she was too.

He searched her gaze, "We'll have a whole week, you sure you want to keep me leashed all that time? There are so many avenues to explore."

"Yes, well, I'll have to think on it," Merissa grinned, sultry and suggestive, "Until summer Solstice, Ty."